THE
GUILTY
SISTER

BOOKS BY ARIANNE RICHMONDE

The Newlyweds
The Wife's House

ARIANNE RICHMONDE

THE
GUILTY
SISTER

Bookouture

Published by Bookouture in 2021

An imprint of Storyfire Ltd.
Carmelite House
50 Victoria Embankment
London EC4Y 0DZ

www.bookouture.com

ISBN: 978-1-80019-863-0
eBook ISBN: 978-1-80019-862-3

Again, for Betty Kramer, for offering me your heart and home and family, and for opening up a beautiful new world to me in Manhattan and Central Park, and of course for sharing Nancy. And to all the brave and special, special-needs souls in the world, especially the dogs.

Be yourself; everyone else is already taken.

Oscar Wilde

CHAPTER ONE

Sara

Now

The detective handed me a coffee. I was expecting it to be in a Styrofoam cup like you see on TV, but it was paper. I took it and counted to ten trying to calm my nerves, my hands trembling slightly, wondering whether I should keep my mouth shut or come clean. I realized, too late, they now had my fingerprints all over the cup. A ruse to trap me, no doubt, their friendliness masquerading as a kind gesture in offering me a drink. Would they sample my saliva from the cup for DNA? Probably. I'd seen this box-of-a-room at least a hundred times on cop shows, but as an onlooker, an observer, cozy and safe on my couch, snuggled up to Poppy, sipping a glass of wine. Right now, I was in it. I was the antagonist. Square in the middle of it all. And it was real life, not fiction. I closed my eyes, willing it all to go away. The mess I'd started. I only had myself to blame.

When I finally looked up, the detective was waiting for me to speak, rapping her fingers on the table, her eye contact unbroken. But what could I say? I challenged her with my gaze, challenged her to throw the ball in my court. I didn't want her to see how nervous I was. Perhaps she was too smart for that? I sipped the coffee tentatively to bide my time. It burned my tongue. So I curled my fingers around the cup, allowing the heat to comfort me a little. The air con was up high. Was this on purpose to make me uncomfortable?

They had told me plainly that I was "not under arrest," yet I knew that did not let me off the hook. They had dressed it up in such a friendly manner. They called this "an appointment." As if I'd called ahead asking to come in for a chat myself.

The walls of the interview room felt like they were caving in on me. There was nothing but this desk in the middle of the room and three office chairs, not quite as uncomfortable as usually depicted on TV; the officers' seats on rollers, mine on straight legs, so they could move in on me, but I was trapped. Nothing on the bleak bare walls, just the glare of the bright, neon lights above. Cruel and invasive, showing up every pore of your skin. No clock. I guessed they didn't want suspects (or perpetrators, which did they think I was?) to know for how long they were being interviewed, or rather, interrogated.

Let the masterful game of cat and mouse begin, I thought, wondering if I had the skills to outsmart them.

I supposed they were all gaping in on us from a one-way mirrored window: the other detectives. I was being videoed—they had alerted me to that fact—and anything I said would be recorded, used in evidence against me, matching up any lies I told so they could lock me into my story. They had their wily ways. They'd be measuring the weight of my guilt, looking for me to slip up, confess. It was soundproofed, the room. My ears felt muffled, but I knew they could hear every single word I said. I hadn't asked for a lawyer. Not yet. I assumed that would make things look worse. And if they did decide to arrest me mid-interview, they could only detain me for so long, legally speaking. Another thing I'd learned from cop shows.

I knew my rights.

The door swung open and the other detective strolled into the room. This one was the nice guy, I assumed. The good cop.

Because he smiled at me. I returned the gesture briefly back, wondering if that made me look guiltier.

I knew what I was being accused of.

Murder.

Murdering my twin. Although they hadn't mentioned her yet.

"Coffee okay?" the good cop asked. Detective Elba, his name was. He had a dangerously affable, easy air about him, instantly likeable… he reminded me of Will Smith.

I shook my head. "It could be better."

"Honesty. I like that," he said, his lips tipping up into a broad grin. His friendly eyes held mine. Probably about five foot ten? Not tall. He had a hint of a Bronx accent.

The other detective who'd been eyeballing me—the woman, Detective Pearce—was a petite blonde: a tough cookie with an attitude. I admired her bravery for joining the force. What kind of person would do this job? Risk their lives every single day in New York City? It really was commendable. I had no qualms about paying my taxes, knowing my money was helping to keep our city safe from criminals. But now that *I* was their target criminal, I resented the NYPD's fastidiousness. Here I was: their sitting duck.

I considered requesting an attorney, as was my legal right. Have one with me while I answered their questions, but my tongue was stuck to the roof of my mouth and I seemed unable to speak. Plus, there was no way I could tell the truth. I was screwed.

I wondered how long before they found out what I'd done.

I guessed it was a matter of days before my world came crashing down on me.

If I hadn't met Bradley, I wouldn't be here now.

CHAPTER TWO

Bradley

Four months earlier

It was a warm April morning, early—it must have been around seven a.m.—when Bradley first laid his discerning eyes on Sara.

He was on his usual daily journey to work, hurriedly striding along the sidewalk of Fifth Avenue, wearing a three-piece suit and polished, handmade shoes. He cut into Central Park, his briefcase moving in time with his clippity-clip pace, his earbuds in place, in case he needed to make or receive an important call. He would always walk through the park, a small detour but worth it, down to 59th and then across to catch the Lexington Avenue 4 train—in the spring and summer especially. In winter, he'd usually forgo the walking—it was too cold—he'd just ride the subway the whole way.

But today, heading to work—he always arrived an hour earlier than he had to—Bradley decided, because it was such a beautiful day, to take a stroll, head in the opposite direction for a change, so he did a one-eighty and veered north.

After fifteen minutes or so, he found himself by the little boat pond, officially known as Conservatory Water, breathing in the scent of cherry blossom and watching mothers with their small kids, and joggers and dog walkers, and all manner of Manhattanites going about their eventful park business.

He noticed the dog first. A black and brown mutt that gave no clue to what breed it was. Medium in size with big pointy, caricature ears. Maybe a mixture of terrier and German Shepherd, with a little Labrador thrown in? It was zipping along, its sturdy front legs trailing a pair of wheels behind it: a contraption that helped it walk. A kind of dog wheelchair, although the dog seemed to have mastery over the apparatus and not vice versa. Bradley discerned the dog's back legs, held up by stirrups, like legs belonging to a rag doll, yet active, moving helplessly (without thigh muscles to support it) but making all the normal movements any dog would make, were it in good shape. Muscle memory, he supposed. Its two front legs pattered along at a pretty fast pace and the wheels followed smoothly behind on the path. It was a brilliant but simple contraption. He had imagined how many people must have advocated putting the dog down to "save its misery" to "not let it suffer," but the creature was supremely happy. Thrilled with itself and its surroundings. Wagging its tail as the wheels spun along behind, the dog even let out little yips of delight. It lifted Bradley's heart to see such determination and joy juxtaposed against so much adversity. If only all of us, he thought, could be as valiant and upbeat as this little dog.

Its walker, a woman, who looked in her late twenties, kept up a brisk pace herself, a small smile tipping up her pretty lips, her long dark hair blowing faintly in the morning breeze. No makeup, no airs or graces, just a regular-looking girl in sneakers and jeans. Another dog sped across the path, not on a leash. The woman and the disabled dog paused while the other dog, a white standard poodle sporting a fancy pompom, sniffed the handicapped dog's behind. The woman and the poodle's owner laughed and chatted briefly, and then the cute woman and her wheelchair mutt moved along.

Bradley didn't have time to study her closer, so he overtook, circling back around the pond, and carried on his brisk journey, wondering what it would be like to date her. Pretty, but not too pretty. Not intimidating. Not unapproachable. She had a lovely, soft look about her. A little dreamy maybe. But thinking about dating made him nervous. He didn't want his heart broken into tiny pieces again. When Cassandra died, his whole world had folded in on itself, and he asked himself if he'd ever be able to love again.

He had vowed to himself to never get too involved, to just have fun without giving too much of himself. Sex without love: that was the way to go. Choosing women for short-term commitments had been working pretty well, or so he had thought at first. His plan was to shoal up as much money as he could while he could, and when it came to settling down—because he did want a family—he wanted someone to love him for who he was. But he'd been going about things the wrong way; at thirty-nine, he was aware that things needed to change.

When he found the right woman, he'd take it slowly. He would not rush in.

Lately, in the last few months, he'd had that creeping realization that he wasn't getting any younger and he was missing out on what mattered in life. His friends back home had settled down, yet Bradley's lonely heart was meandering, roaming without purpose, wasting time. The "fun" he'd promised himself had turned out to be the opposite of what he'd imagined: a string of vacuous affairs that left him feeling empty, even worthless. Who were these women he had nothing in common with, who saw him only for his veneer of wealth? He'd been choosing so badly. Invariably things went pear-shaped within a month or two, sometimes within weeks, or even days. Either they wanted to move in with him yesterday, or they had addiction issues. Or partied with abandon.

No, Bradley had been there done that. His old friend and confidante, Delilah, was right. He needed to regroup, reevaluate his situation. His work was just a means to his true pathway in life. He needed to milk his situation while he could, buy as many stocks and shares as possible, date the right girl, and buy his dream home in Hawaii. Bradley was just a regular guy from a pretty simple, suburban background. Nothing fancy, nothing unusual, but he'd always had drive, and that inner drive had made him push himself to make the most out of life. He was an opportunist, in a way, knowing a good thing when he saw it, snapping it up without hesitation. He'd worked hard to get where he was, and although he wanted to pat himself on the back for what he'd achieved so far, he couldn't deny he felt that razor-sharp edge of insecurity running along his spine. So he made up for it with a smattering of bravado and his confident smile. At work, he'd bring his colleagues donuts and coffee (he learned that tip from *Dexter*, his favorite show). He liked being the nice guy, the one they could depend on, the one they trusted.

He knew his parents were less than impressed with his life, though, as things stood now. The partying, the glitzy show of worldly goods he pocketed like shiny marbles. He couldn't throw off that materialistic pull, that need to prove himself, that deep feeling in his gut that he was nothing without his beautiful apartment, the closet of hand-tailored suits, his sleek dress watch. Where had this come from? For a Minnesota boy from a humble family, with parents who wanted nothing more than for their son to do an honest day's work, he had no idea how he had become so covetous for material cornucopia, the outward trappings of success. A bandage for his wounds? Possible.

He felt like Bud Fox, sometimes, Bud from the movie, *Wall Street*. It had been a revelation when he saw that film. He was only a little boy when it came out, but he'd seen it on TV recently and the story had moved him profoundly, so much so, he had vowed he'd make changes to his lifestyle. Like Bud, he had sold his soul in a way. Sold it for *things*. Exchanged it for a way of life that was alien to everything he'd been taught by his parents and the values they held strong. His dad would be watching a game of football on TV now, drinking a beer, his mom shopping at the local mall, comparing prices, picking the generic brand, his old school friends maybe playing pool in the local bar or, in summer, cooking up a barbeque in their backyard, kids running around excitedly. But Bradley had wanted more than just a nice, stable, two-point-two-kids life. Always searching for something to make him feel whole. He knew money wasn't the answer. So, what was? What was the magic ingredient if money wasn't the answer? So he'd gone to the other extreme in his pursuit: he'd tried to get spiritual with Ashtanga yoga, but he found out that a lot of those yoga people were covertly ambitious. It was quite a paradox: their competitive ego spirits clawing to be fed: proving how open their hips were, how flexible their hamstrings, and how lean their muscles. Forget Ujjayi breathing, it was the six-pack they were all after. He'd gotten willingly sucked in to the spirituality of it, but Bradley knew better; it had turned into a competition.

Yearning to prove how adequate he was, all he felt was inadequate. This, he knew, was the antithesis of what yoga was supposed to be, but, inexplicably, he'd ended up in a class full of alphas. Ambitious, master-of-the-universe hardcore yogis (despite the class being mostly female), their strong jaws and challeng-ing eyes masked by serene, "spiritual" smiles as they performed the perfect *asanas*. It catapulted Bradley to a place that actually felt even more false than the state-of-the-art stove that lorded in his kitchen, in his multi-million-dollar apartment, unused, shining—never-made-a-meal-in-its-life perfection. Like some piece of artwork that was not there to be enjoyed, but only as part of the seamless package. Yes, his apartment on Fifth Avenue had cost him. He felt like he had made a pact with the devil for that apartment, with its view of Central Park, because none of it was true. He was denying his real self—whatever that even was—in favor of a lie.

And what was it all for?

He needed to make changes in his life, and he would start with the right partner.

He spotted the pretty woman again—the disabled dog's mother—two weeks later, this time, by the bronze *Alice in Wonderland* statue. This time, in the afternoon, on a weekend. The truth was, Bradley was actively… not stalking her exactly, no, but doing everything he could to bump into her.

She was hovering about with a coffee in her hand, talking to a group of dog owners, while a couple of kids scrambled atop the giant mushroom worn smooth by so much use, the White Rabbit looking on, checking his pocket watch. Bradley, too, glanced at his watch: a Patek Philippe. He did so love this exquisite watch. A cut above the more obvious Rolex.

Minneapolis seemed centuries away.

He tried to imagine what the woman's life story might be. Cherry blossom drifted across the park in pink and white. Little snowflake petals rested on her dark, Italianate hair (was she foreign?) and her skin seemed to glow, incandescent in the April light. It occurred to Bradley that she might be a dog walker, a nanny to this particular dog-on-wheels. She seemed to have so much time on her hands, didn't appear to have regular work hours. She was unhurried. Un-hassled. Not your typical New Yorker. Now she was laughing: a cute, girlish laugh, and then she put her hand over her mouth as if bashful to be showing such emotion. As if happiness had not come easily to her and she was surprising herself with her own joy. Completely charmed, she was, by a man with a silver-gray Weimaraner.

Suddenly, and overwhelmingly, Bradley wanted to be in that man's shoes.

These dog people were like that: they gave the easy impression of belonging to a private club in Central Park. They'd often meet, Bradley noticed, the same time of day, and chat while their dogs played. A kind of Doggygarten. Bradley had heard snippets of conversation. They would discuss their "kids." Their meals and sleeping habits, the health of their stool, even. He'd heard one talking about "projectile diarrhea." Some of the animals wore little tartan jackets or even bobby pins to clip the hair off their faces. All shapes and sizes. All sorts of breeds. There was one man who pushed his dog about in a baby stroller: a Yorkshire terrier that wore a pink bow on its bangs. A girl, he supposed. Bradley often felt envious that he didn't have a park social life. He simply used the park to pass through, hardly even having time to appreciate the place. These people and their dogs *were* the park, just as much as the squirrels, or the reservoir, or Sheep Meadow, or the Belvedere Castle, or the trees. These people and their dogs were the soul of Central Park.

He felt like an onlooker.

A voyeur.

Bradley slowed by the Alice statue and glanced at the brunette. She met his eye for just a second: a brief half-smile catching her lips before she quickly turned away. Her dog zipped around as if it didn't have wheels at all, as if it were perfectly fit. It was a joy to watch, and he wondered how the creature had become disabled in the first place.

Bradley yearned to strike up a conversation. He took a breath, wishing to call over her way about her dog. *Cute dog*, he'd say. No, that sounded sarcastic, considering. *Nice weather*. No, how lame was that?

Just as he took two steps forward, she headed off the other way, calling "Poppy, come on girl. What a good girl! Who's a pretty girl! Come on, Popps. You ready for din-dins?"

It was the way she gazed at that helpless animal with so much love in her eyes, telling Poppy how pretty she was—when the mutt dog really wasn't—that made Bradley fall for this brunette. She was a kind person, that was obvious. Wasn't it time for him to open his heart up to a little kindness? Kindness was undervalued in this world.

Really. No kidding, he thought. *That warm-hearted girl-next-door could be the one for me.*

CHAPTER THREE

Sara

I loved Central Park. I never understood how anyone could think Greenwich Village or SoHo cooler than my neighborhood uptown. They were really missing out. Ironically, rents down there had eclipsed those up here, yet those people lived, in my opinion, in a concrete metropolis because they didn't have Central Park's 843 acres within walking distance.

I counted my blessings every day to have a job where I worked from home. To be able to come here anytime, come rain, howling wind, or snow, exercise Poppy and exercise my mind. There's something about walking that puts your brain into gear, unlocks part of the subconscious that can solve problems that have been plaguing you for weeks. Central Park was an extension of my office, in a way. I'd come up with design ideas for book covers I was working on. I found inspiration all around me. Nowhere, probably in the world, could match Central Park for people-watching, for idea-spinning.

I looked up at the spring green of the foliage, the blue backdrop of the sky bringing everything into crisp relief. Squirrels scrambled along the branches of the stately elm trees; trees that had strangely survived disease here in New York yet had succumbed in other parts of the country, their arcing graceful boughs like gothic cathedrals, protecting us from rain and sun, and in the backdrop, the most incredible skyline in the world: the skyscrapers of

Manhattan peeping through the trees. And pink cherry blossom floating like wedding confetti.

I love New York, I thought, counting my blessings, grateful for all I had and pushing away any wistful thoughts, any nostalgia about what I'd lost.

As well as my unofficial office, Central Park was my social hub. I didn't like going out: dinner parties, clubs… no, that wasn't for me: I was pretty shy. I'd get my daily fix here, chatting to other dog owners, watching them watch with vicarious pleasure as their dogs chased each other's tails and woofed; some wildly bumptious, others like old dowagers with droopy ears, or gentlemen dogs in little tartan coats that trotted neatly by their owners' sides, nose high, tail quirked up, ignoring the mayhem around them.

The people here seemed to be infused with a serene, gently pulsing sort of energy, different than the frantic, rapid-fire energy on the streets or subway. Like they were leaving fierce thoughts amidst the traffic and sidewalks when they marched through one of the park entrances, stepping into another world, a new milieu, and in an instant their faces would soften, their strides relax. Each season had its own pace, too. In winter, dogs and children might look like a Lowry painting: white, snowy background, splashes of red or blue scarves, stick figures from a distance. Or when Wollman Rink was frozen, people would go ice skating below the forever evolving skyline; skyscrapers looming above like the open hand of a protective mother.

Central Park always looked to me like a piece of art. Movement and energy and emotion and people splashed into one great big canvas, the crisp architectural skyline always in the background, never letting anyone down. However you felt, New York would hold you up. Make you survive. Infuse you with energy.

I love New York. I felt the city in the marrow of my bones. I dreamed with her at night as I slept and as she lay awake with her glimmering grasping lights. My heart beat along with the rhythm of her pulse, mending a little more each day.

Today was sunny but with an icy edge to the air. Spring could be like that in New York City. You never knew which way it could go.

My old camera slung around my neck, I snapped away: an old lady doubled over pushing a shopping cart full of stuffed plastic bags, muttering to herself as she shuffled along. A jogger in box-fresh sneakers, his neon-green feet pounding the paths, hardly breaking a sweat, while at his side, a woman (his girlfriend, his sister, his client?) puffing along, her lungs wheezing miserably, her thighs wobbling as she dragged each foot, one in front of the other, wishing she were anywhere else but here. A man, earbuds in place, yelling into the void, his phone tucked into a pocket nearby. A child having a meltdown, rolling on the ground, screaming at his mother while she stood there helpless in high heels, as a Filipino nanny rushed forward to save the day, scooping the kid up and showering him with kisses and, just like that, the waterworks stopped and the boy laughed. As I swung my gaze around, a city slicker in a two-thousand-dollar suit, chin stately raised, his mind far, far away, breezed past them, not noticing anything except maybe the birds tweeting in the trees or the sharp blue of the sky. But then, as if he could feel my eyes on his handsome, slightly arrogant gait, he caught my gaze, tipped me a flash of a smile and continued briskly on his way.

Each person had their story, their past, their shame, and above all, their secrets. Secrets they kept tightly under wraps.

I was no different.

My secret owned me.

CHAPTER FOUR

Bradley

Of course Bradley knew he was crazy to be romanticizing about the girl in the park and putting her on some kind of lofty pedestal. But when, that night, he found himself in the midst of a screaming match with his latest hookup, on the roof terrace of his penthouse, and she threatened to jump—strung out after four double gin and tonics and hell knows what prescription meds she was on—Bradley remembered the warm sheen of the park-girl's hair, her makeup-free face, her sweet smile as she sipped her coffee and chatted to her dog friends—and he knew he had to stop getting involved with narcissists.

His interest in the wheelie-dog girl was teetering on obsession. He couldn't imagine her doing drugs, or screaming like a banshee, or hurling curses at him, accusing him of being a sociopath, like some of the other women.

Tomorrow he would approach her. He'd hang out at the park all day if need be and start a conversation.

CHAPTER FIVE

Sara

Poppy was my savior. Rescue dogs, as far as I was concerned, meant only one thing: they had been invented to rescue humans. And I was definitely someone who had needed rescuing. I tried so hard not to think about the thing that had broken me, splintered me into tiny little fragments. Every day was a new start, and Poppy kept me grounded. I had learned this: to treasure all the good in the world. The luck I had simply by being alive, and how I would never take anything for granted again, because you never know when—or if—devastation is lurking around the corner, waiting to smite you when you aren't even looking, saying "boo" to you from behind a door. So every little good thing I held to my breast and proverbially kissed it with appreciation. A child's smile. The winter sun throwing down its warming rays on my face, the kindness of a stranger opening a door for me, the chirp of a bird, and not least, my adorable dog.

I lay on the floor, facing the ceiling, while Poppy scrambled all over me, both of us lapping up the love, giving each other a new lease of life. No, she couldn't replace what I'd lost, but she was my tonic, my medicine. And there is nothing better than caring for another to take you out of yourself. When someone has less than you, it makes you aware of how blessed you are and that there's always a little more to give, even when you have lost so much.

Poppy and I were level and she loved this game. She wore a soft pink covering attached at her waist so she didn't get carpet burns for the times she was without wheels in the apartment. Cheek to cheek as we were, her long tongue licked my face, her little white paws trampled on my chest. I laughed and laughed to the point where I felt the muscles in my stomach ache. Who needed the gym? My midsection got a workout from all my laughter and racing about with Poppy in the park as she barreled along. It appeared like she was wearing cute little socks, or booties, and no matter how dirty those paws might become on a rainy day, it wasn't long before they were the brightest white again. Poppy looked after herself like the true little lady she was.

When she wagged her tail, her behind followed, her little tush gaining back more muscle each day, while her weak legs tried to keep up. This is what I could give another and I was glad to do so, knowing that what I had lost I would never get back. I could give unconditional love to a little soul who had less than I did. And my gift was my gain. Because things were on the up and up. Lying on the floor, I gathered her in my arms, drawing her on top of my chest and we touched noses, her pointy ears up and alert. She wiggled, she squirmed, she voiced her pleasure with delight—hence her name, Poppy Delight—a kind of whinnying, wolfy, growly groan. She smiled as she spoke. Dogs can smile, they really can. Nothing made me happier than seeing Poppy happy. It took me out of my old world, away from the pain, away from the trauma of what had happened.

Yes, this dog had saved my life.

As she scrambled of top of me, I whispered sweet nothings in her soft pointy ears. "I love you," I said. "Thank you for being my rescue dog. I love you with all my heart."

CHAPTER SIX

Bradley

It was a week later, when Bradley was in the middle of the park at Le Pain Quotidien (the narcissist girlfriend issue still unresolved—she'd thrown a plate at him last night and he was nursing a cut lip) that someone nudged his elbow. And some strange dog was sniffing his legs as he sat at the café table, peacefully reading the paper. He wasn't in the mood; he wanted to be left alone.

"Excuse me. Excuse me, sir, could I ask you a huge favor?"

He looked up. Two blue eyes gazed at him expectantly. Dark hair with natural highlights of chestnut tumbled over the shoulders of a girl in a baby-blue, cable-knit sweater. It took him a beat to realize it was *her*. The woman with the disabled dog-on-wheels.

"Would you mind holding my dog's leash while I whip in and grab a lemonade?"

He stared at her, his lips not moving.

"They don't allow dogs inside," she explained, "unless they're assistance dogs. I've tried to argue my case but… two minutes, tops, I won't be long."

"Sure," he said. "No problem, take your time."

She handed him the leash and he took it, the pooch waiting patiently while her owner fled inside to join the line. Minutes later, she was out, holding her lemonade.

"Thank you. Thanks so much." Her smile was that smile of kindness he had noticed before.

"You're welcome. And you too, Poppy," he added before he could stop himself.

The woman's eyes rounded in surprise. "How do you know my dog's name?"

He was tempted to say, *Just a guess*, but he thought that would freak her out. "I saw you by the *Alice in Wonderland* statue, a week or so ago. Calling your dog."

"Oh, right." She smiled nervously but didn't look convinced. "Actually, her full name is Poppy Delight."

"Delight, huh? That's cute. I guess it must be challenging looking after a handicapped animal."

She frowned. "Handi-capable, you mean?"

He wanted to kick himself. What a negative thing for him to say. The worst chat-up line ever! "She's very cute," he said again, digging himself out of his hole.

The girl was prettier up close than from a distance. Up close, she had beautiful translucent skin sprinkled with a few light freckles. Her eyes were Wedgwood blue.

"She *is* cute, and what's more, she saved my life," the woman said about her dog.

"Not the other way round?" Again, he'd spouted out the wrong thing.

"We saved each other. Her sweetness and sense of fun make me smile every day," she said. "Caring for her is the most rewarding thing in the world. Poppy's the best thing that has ever happened to me. Nice meeting you, and thanks again." Sipping her lemonade, she moved off, the dog's wheels spinning behind as the duo whirled away.

Well that went down well, he thought. Bradley, who had already paid for his breakfast, leaped up and followed them. "Wait up!" he cried after her.

But the woman didn't seem to hear, or if she did, she was ignoring him.

"Hello! Beautiful brunette with the special-needs dog, wait up!"
She turned around and grinned.

They started out talking about the dog and how the wheelchair
worked. Bradley thought that was the quickest way to gain the
woman's trust. Show interest in her dog. And he *was* interested.
Fascinated, in fact. The sheer amount of work and painstaking
trouble involved looking after the animal must be monumental.
Maybe she was getting paid to do it... was it her professional
job? Dog walkers actually made great money in New York City.
Sometimes they inherited not only the dog after an owner's death,
but hundreds of thousands of dollars, even whole apartments.
New York was certainly a place where crazy things happened.

"So how does this canine cart work?" he asked.

"The wheelchair?"

"They call it a wheelchair even though there's no chair?"

She laughed and gave him a demonstration. "Well, the arms
of the wheelchair clip into this harness," she explained, pointing
to two metal bars that went either side of the dog's body. "Then
Poppy's hind legs go into the holes that are protected by foam-
covered straps, and then each strap is held together with neoprene
to form a kind of cradle that supports her back end. These stirrups
are designed to both support her legs, so they don't drag, but also
so she can use her legs, keep her muscles moving, even though
she can't support herself on her own yet."

"She can go to the bathroom okay?"

"Sure. The straps don't get in the way."

"Well she certainly looks happy."

"She is," she said. "She adores her walks."

It turned out the woman did have a job. She, Sara, worked
from home. She was a graphic designer, primarily working on
book covers.

"It's fun," she told him. "Very creative, and part of my job is
to read a lot of books. Some book designers don't read the books

they'll be working on, but I think it's important. And I'm a real bookworm anyway. Plus, I get to work in my pajamas. And stay home with Poppy. I hate leaving her alone."

"What if someone invites you out for dinner?" he said, wondering if he had a chance with a date.

"I have that covered. My neighbor looks after her. A lady in my apartment building. Mrs. Scott's in a wheelchair, too, so she and Poppy have a whole lot in common. She loves it when Poppy comes over. Has a whole set of blankets and bedding for her. A spare water and food bowl. They watch soaps together, or romcoms."

Bradley nodded and shot her a wry smile. "Cool." He was wondering what would be an appropriate first date. The theatre? The ballet? Dinner and a movie? Or just dinner? Maybe just dinner. He could get to know her better.

"You pay Mrs. Scott? Like a babysitter?" he asked, trotting alongside the duo.

"No. I offered, but she won't hear of it. I painted her a little oil. A portrait of her son, to say thank you."

"You're an artist? I mean, you—"

"All art's connected. Painting doesn't pay the bills. I create e-book covers, paperback covers, hardbacks, with or without dust jackets, audiobook covers. And anything else the client asks for. Logo designs, promotional stuff for marketing, for Facebook and Instagram ads." And then she added with enthusiasm, "I love what I do."

"Anything I've seen? Like in bookstores?"

"Sure. I've done covers for quite a few *New York Times* bestsellers."

Bradley grinned. "Impressive, I'd love to see your work."

"Sure."

"You on Instagram? Facebook? I'll friend you." He pulled out his phone.

She paused for a long time before shaking her head and answering, "Nope. Too much of a time suck."

"That's great. That's so great you're not on social media. Not even Twitter?"

"Tweeting should be left to the birds."

He laughed. "Website?"

"I'll tell you only if you promise to not check it out till you're home. You need to look at my website on a bigger screen to appreciate it. Not a phone."

Bradley nodded. His questions were spilling from him uncontrollably. "So, you get a lot of work doing these covers?"

"Work's been pretty full-on lately."

"What are you working on now?"

"My latest is a commission for a murder mystery series. So far, I've done books one and two, and now I'm waiting for the design brief to come in from the publisher for book three, and, with any luck, if the series takes off, there'll be more."

"Interesting," Bradley said. And it was interesting. He had never thought about book covers before. He didn't read novels, in general. He'd read a Tom Clancy once, but preferred books about history. World wars. Or how-to books. "Is the process complicated?"

She nodded. "It can be. Sometimes I use up to five or even six different photos to get the effect I want. I take my own pictures and also use stock photos too, or buy images from other photographers. I use filters, tricks to blend and shade, to distort."

Bradley felt triumphant that he'd been able to engage Sara for so long in conversation. He said, "Sounds like a very cool job. Pretty arty too."

"It is. I also love doing dog memoirs, too. So far I haven't come across a book about a special-needs dog like Poppy. I thought about writing my own memoir, but then decided against it." She looked at him shyly, but he held her gaze.

"Why?" he asked.

Her eyes flicked away from him uneasily. "I don't like drawing attention to myself." And then she added—and this Bradley thought was really telling—"I think I was put on this earth to make others shine."

They stopped at a water fountain, one that also had a lower part especially for dogs.

Bradley digested what Sara had said about not drawing attention to herself. Most people didn't admit to being a wallflower. This woman fascinated him. He hadn't met anyone so passionate about their work for a long time. It was refreshing. All the working women he knew were powered by ambition. Sara's motivation, it seemed, was creation in its own right. He was intrigued.

They carried on walking. Every once in a while, she stopped again and fussed over Poppy, chatting to her like she was a child, asking her if she was tired or ready to go home. But the energetic animal wanted to keep on going. Unlike a lot of dogs who sniffed and stopped at every corner, every tree, this one trotted along with a mission.

"So how did you and Poppy meet?" Bradley inquired, keen to keep their encounter going as long as he could. By now, he felt he was tagging along. He was aware he was asking her way too many questions and didn't want to spook Sara, but surely any questions about her beloved dog would be well received?

She kept up her pace—now heading toward the 79th Street exit. "That's a long and gruesome story," she responded, wrinkling her nose.

"Oh, I'm sorry. Abusive history? She came from a shelter?"

"No. I found her here, in the park. I'd seen her running. You know, around the main loop? Round and round she'd go. I think her old owner must've been an athlete or something. Nobody could catch her, not even the park police. Then one morning I found her by the 72nd Street entrance, on Fifth. She'd been run over. A hit-and-run. She was bleeding badly, guts spilled out. It was horrific. At first I thought she was dead."

"Shit, I'm so sorry. How nasty."

"Outside one of the apartment buildings there was a driver sitting in his limousine, reading a newspaper, waiting for his client. I managed to persuade him to drive me and Poppy to an emergency vet because none of the cab drivers would stop when they saw me with Poppy in my arms. I'll never be able to thank him enough. I was covered in blood. We were both covered in blood and still, he took us to the vet."

"That's a beautiful story. Gives you faith in humanity."

"It does, doesn't it? A mobility problem does not need to be an end-of-life decision for an animal. I wish more people knew there are options out there. You know they make these wheels for all kinds of animals? Horses, goats, pigs? Even geese. Poppy's wheels are not forever, you know. Little by little we're hoping she'll build up strength in her back legs and be able to use them again."

"We?" It occurred to Bradley that of course, trust his luck, Sara was bound to be married. Why hadn't he thought of that before? He looked down at her left hand. No ring.

"Me and the vet," she clarified. "And Bernard, the driver who helped me save her. Poppy had a couple of operations. We sometimes pass by and say hi. I keep him updated, we're still friends. I'm so grateful to be able to work from home so I can be there for her—I've been getting tons of jobs lately. Thank God. It's taken a whole year to clear my credit card debt for Poppy's vet bills, so I welcome any freelance work coming my way."

Bradley, nodding, smiled, still striding along by her side, but preparing the question that had been on his mind since he'd first spotted Sara a few weeks back, said, "Are you single, Sara?" He winced at himself. "Sorry, that's a pretty intrusive question."

"For now."

Her answer: "for now" was clear, Bradley thought. *If you want to go out with me, make your move.* So he did. "Would you like to have dinner with me sometime?" he asked.

She shrugged, keeping up the pace, now out of the park, her pink sneakers pounding across 79th. He wondered where she lived.

She gave him a quick smile. "That's a sweet offer. But… well, I'm kind of busy."

"Okay. Then how about a coffee? In the park? I mean, if you're here anyway."

"Sure. Coffee would be nice."

He wasn't convinced. He needed to pin down a time. A date. "Same place tomorrow? At Le Pain Quotidien? Early morning, as soon as it opens? Like seven? Is that too early?"

She nodded. "That could work."

"Cool." He dug a hand into his jacket pocket. "Here's my card. If you can't make it for whatever reason, call me. And, well… even if you can make it, you can call me anyway."

But the next day Sara didn't show up. And she didn't call either. It made him more intrigued than ever.

Who *was* this woman exactly?

He *had* to know more.

CHAPTER SEVEN

Sara

The park had always felt like my sacred, private space. Sure I had my park friends and we'd chat about this and that—nothing very deep, mostly about our dogs, but I was wary of some handsome, charismatic guy (who probably had a string of women on speed-dial) pursuing me. Bradley was suddenly here there and everywhere. A too-good-looking man with expensive shoes and immaculate three-piece suits. Tailored, it looked like. If not tailored, designer. Who wears a three-piece suit these days? His ties were definitely made of the finest silk, and each time I saw him it would be a different pattern or color. It was like he was some kind of throwback to Cary Grant's era. Yes, I was tempted. But no. I was way too vulnerable to let myself fall for a man like Bradley.

My familiar pattern of my walks in the park with my dog was now broken. I couldn't help but feel watched. Not unsafe but just… self-conscious. Shy. Unprepared for his attention. Because he was so apparently into me. Questions, questions, questions! I wasn't sure if I should be flattered and charmed, or freaked out. What did this man want? I wasn't the prettiest of women, I wasn't rich, or glamorous, or hip.

I googled the place where he worked: he'd given me his card. Bradley Daniels, Junior: *Wall Street*, it said simply, and rather chicly, I thought, in an understated, un-brash way. And I guessed he was for real, because I caught a flash of his Patek Philippe dress watch and polished silver cufflinks: three-dimensional dice. They were beautiful. Stylish. But a reverence for material status wasn't my thing, and I was not personally impressed by his affluence. I came from a humble background, and even now with my well-paid job I had tons of bills to pay and didn't really relate to a moneyed man like Bradley. I was brought up with a certain set of values, and ostentatious wealth of any kind was frowned upon by my parents. I brushed his invitation for coffee off. I didn't show for our first "date." Didn't call. A little rude, but I did not want to get my heart battered and bruised by some swashbuckling guy with a charming smile. Finally my heart was mending.

It really was easier just to go day to day, taking one step at a time. And a love affair of any kind was not in the cards for me. At least, not in the near future. It wasn't just Poppy who needed to learn how to walk again. It was me.

I would have loved it if I was able to have a little passion on the side, but I had to be careful, because when you're vulnerable it's easy to get hoodwinked and trust the wrong person. Passion and lust can be confused for true love for those of us with open hearts, and sadly there are people who take advantage. And what you perceive is real love sometimes just isn't. Being on my guard and avoiding intimate relationships wasn't me being cold, but just street-smart. Perhaps I was being a coward, but it was wiser for me to concentrate on work, and Poppy, and living a full life without some gorgeous-looking man getting in the middle of it all and screwing with my head.

Men were an enigma to me anyway. I never understood how their minds worked. I knew there must be great ones out there, but trust my luck I would either cherry-pick a psycho, or some guy I'd fall in love with too hard who'd end up shunning me and breaking my heart. I wasn't about to open myself up again to being hurt. The harder you love, the harder you fall.

So I forced myself to forget all about the Wall Street guy, as I came to think of him in my mind. Or at least, I willed him away from my daydreams.

No, I did not dare tempt fate.

But three days later, there he was again. Standing under a giant black umbrella in the spitting rain. He loomed large and stately, brandishing this perfect umbrella like he was in *Mary Poppins* or something, making magic happen. The shower had come from nowhere, yet Bradley was prepared, unlike most of us seasoned dog walkers taken unawares. Just as I had decided to embrace the soak, he rushed over, catching me as I made a beeline from the pond—Conservatory Water—to the shelter of a large elm tree, Poppy's wheels spinning splashes of water as she and I dashed for refuge.

"Beautiful brunette with Poppy Delight!" he yelled across the park, turning a few curious heads my way to see what he was shouting about.

I couldn't help but burst out laughing, despite myself, and Poppy let out a woof as if to say, *I know you!*

Bradley promenaded over at a clip, his polished shoes slapping through puddles, and immediately sheltered me with the great black hood of his brolly.

Linking his arm through mine, he said, "Can I walk you home?"

What could I say? I was so grateful for the roomy umbrella, big enough for all three of us, and of course I was flattered by his courteous attention and secretly pleased he hadn't given up on me. So he walked us through the park, across Fifth, and Madison, and Park, under the protection of his grand and manly, oversized umbrella, until we reached Lexington. I let him walk me to Butterfield Market, where they always allow me to enter with Poppy by the side door and look after her while I grab a few things from the deli counter, or a coffee-to-go.

He waited, standing there under the deluge, Poppy with him as I hastened in and bought fresh asparagus and things for dinner, half fearing he might dognap Poppy—how crazy was that? But when you've had the best part of your life stolen from you in one fell swoop, it's something you never get over. I whipped about the store, grabbing this and grabbing that and found Bradley patiently waiting outside, chit-chatting to Poppy. Not scrolling on his phone, nor looking bored as might be expected, but genuinely animated by my little girl. In that moment Bradley stole a tiny sliver of my heart and slipped it into his buttonhole.

Still, I needed to be prudent, my voice of reason told me. Just because he was handsome and gallant did not make him immune to being a psycho. He now knew where my local grocery store was, my neighborhood. Pretending I had somewhere else to go, so he wouldn't see where I lived, he insisted on lending me his umbrella. I felt terrible as I watched him walk away in his two-thousand-dollar, Merino wool suit (I'm guessing), soaked to the skin. Poppy and I zipped around the block in the opposite direction from my apartment, then surreptitiously made our way to my building on 79th and Lexington, sight unseen.

Secretly though, I hoped to see him again.

CHAPTER EIGHT

Sara

Two weeks later

"So you hardly know this guy?" Cece asked.

Every evening my sister and I would talk. I wanted to wean myself from her, to gain my independence, to not always second-guess what she'd think or say. But that's not how it works with twins, especially identical ones. Our evening phone conversations sometimes ended in tears and then I'd promise to push her out of my life, but then I'd be needing her again, longing for her voice of wisdom. Hankering for any scraps she'd pass my way. She had a power over me I could not explain, and even though I hadn't seen her in the flesh for so long, she controlled me in a way I could never understand, nor fully accept.

"We've been hanging out a lot in Central Park," I told her. "Me and Bradley and Poppy. I have to admit, I really like him. He's unusual, different."

"You told me he was handsome. Like, sexy handsome or nerd handsome?"

"He's not your type, Cece."

"Don't get sensitive, I'm just curious."

"Lucky you won't be meeting him."

There was a long, long silence. Then she came up with, "That was a cruel thing to say, Sara. Really punishing."

The atmosphere buzzed cold. I felt a chill run down my spine followed by a menacing sense of guilt for feeling anything less than pure love for my identical twin. What she did had made me unforgiving. What she did had ruined my life. Years had gone by and still I couldn't get over it. And by not forgiving her, the layers of guilt just piled on top of me, over and over, like heavy wet blankets that I couldn't shrug off, no matter how many times I told myself to move forward. Sometimes I could hardly breathe.

I picked up the phone and flipped over to Instagram. Scrolled through my twin's verified account: @sea_celia, the little blue tick making it all so real, so professional. I felt proud, in a strange way. She had 950,000 followers. Was following only thirteen accounts herself. Thirteen was her lucky number. It wasn't my lucky number. Like her handle suggested, nearly all her pictures had to do with the sea. Golden beaches with turquoise waters, mostly in Thailand. Always in a sexy bikini, her butt firm and round, the bikini bottom always hoisted high up, resting on her hip bones so you could appreciate the extent of her long, tan legs. There were lots of selfies, too, gazing into the lens, the eyes in these pictures looking so much bluer than mine.

She was what they call "an influencer."

It seemed strange to me what people were into. How much time everyone wasted caring about stuff that just wasn't, in my view, important. The world was on the brink of a climate change disaster, wars, famines, and health pandemics, and here were 950,000 people focusing on her ass. Talk about distraction. I was as guilty as the next person. The hours I had spent thinking about my sister was shocking.

I had been to Thailand. In reality it really was as beautiful as these photos, and that's where I had last said goodbye to my twin. Anyone might think that my life in New York was lonely and pathetic in comparison to Cece's dreamy fantasy. My Thailand visit was just before I saved Poppy, when I had been living alone and ak from my lonesome city life, when I did nothing But with Poppy now in the picture, traveling was not g I hankered after. Did I want to be a social media star? 1 ⟋as happy with my lot. I was.

And that's the truth.

But still, I couldn't look away.

Life is about what you can give it, and glamorous bikini shots didn't seem like something I should get flustered over. And I knew her pictures gave hard-overworking people hope; a dream to cling onto. Maybe it got them through a long cold winter at the office, or looking after a brood of demanding kids. Maybe it was offering something good to the world, although secretly I did worry about the big carbon footprint of her followers. Did they actually hop on a plane and go to Thailand? I doubted it. In my sister's last post she had hinted that she might come back to the States. *Florida has some great beaches. Any recommendations for the best beach? To win a @sea_celia calendar, Tag a Friend, Like this Post, and Follow Me. Three random winners will be announced in 2 weeks.* This was followed by a whole string of smiley faces and palm trees. There were thousands of gushing replies.

The Instagram page made money sponsoring various brands. Swimsuits. Drinks. Clothing companies. It was strange: you'd think with the amount of followers she had, and considering I was her identical twin, I'd get stopped in the street from time to time. But it had only happened once or twice. People were too busy focusing, fantasizing, and drooling over her butt, the blue of the water, and her dream lifestyle. Nobody recognized the same face wrapped up in gloves and a scarf and a winter coat in New York City. Lately, Cece was advertising a healthy protein shake.

Instagram stars were more worshipped than models or actors these days. Everyone had Instagram accounts to keep them in the public eye. She had found her niche. Sometimes, I had to admit, I wanted people to run up to me and say, "Hey, are you

@sea_celia from Insta? You are *so* beautiful!" But I, Sara, didn't even have a Facebook account. I was just your average woman, almost invisible to most people. I never flashed off my figure or wore short skirts.

That's why Bradley's interest in me struck a chord. *He must be the kind of guy who likes a quiet girl like me.*

"Poppy approves of Bradley," I said after a long hiatus, ignoring Cece's sulk. She was right: what I had said about her not meeting him was cruel. I considered what would happen if she moved to Florida.

"So you haven't upgraded from the park?" she cut in. "No dinner? No real date?"

"No. Just the park. But he does know where I live now. He always walks me home."

"*Bradley...*" she said his name like his name was uncool. "Where does he live?"

"On Fifth and 62nd."

"On Fifth *itself?*"

"Yes."

"Shit."

I laughed.

"Like, overlooking Central Park?"

"A penthouse. With a view to the park," I said. "And a private roof terrace."

"Totally loaded then." She said this as a statement.

"I guess."

"That's what you need, Sara. Finally! A guy with money."

"No. It isn't," I objected, hoping by speaking the words they'd become real. "I don't need a man in my life. At all. Not after how it went down with you."

There was another silence.

Then she said, "Of course you do."

"No, I don't."

"Yeah, you do."

"No."

"Do, too."

"Do not."

This yes/no do/don't banter could go on for hours with Cece. Despite everything, the kid in us had never died. Maybe I would always be locked into childhood with my sister? Because the times when we were young were the happy times, when we were inseparable, when we trusted each other implicitly, when we were one unit. Me and Cece against the world or with the world, we were never quite sure. But what we were sure about was each other. About *us*. About the *we* in our relationship.

"Look," I said. "I have to go. And I don't think these conversations are healthy for me. I need to stop talking to you. We need to stop talking."

She laughed. "Ha! You can do that? Just like that?"

She was right. I'd tried before. And always came back to her, tears in my eyes, regretful for pushing her away. Pleading for her to be a part of my life, whatever the consequences.

"You think you can oust me out?" She laughed again. A childish, girlish cackle. I stared in the mirror of my vanity, brushing my hair, my phone propped up, music in the background: Abba, "Take A Chance on Me," an old favorite of ours.

It was Cece who'd taught me to dance, and Abba had been our go-to music. Our parents had gotten us into Abba. We used to laugh at the way our dad danced like a mechanical robot. He had no natural rhythm. Cece taught me how to move my arms, hands, feet, and shoulders to the beat of the drum, each step, each shake to match the drumbeat exactly, or "you look dumb and uncool," she'd say, "like Dad." She showed me how to bend my head down and sway it from side to side, swishing my hair. "Boys love it when you do the head shake," she'd tell me with authority. Cece knew all about boys and how to attract them. How to play cool: raise an eyebrow, say things like "Maybe I will, maybe I won't," or, "If you play your cards right, I might think about it."

Cece and I were mirror twins, so when I looked in the mirror now, pulling my hairbrush on its long journey from the roots to the tips, I saw her, not myself. Some identical twins have a congenital condition, when major organs, even the heart sometimes, are reversed or mirrored, like one of those wet ink or watercolor drawings when you fold a piece of paper in two and then open it up again. One twin might even have their bladder on the wrong side of their body, or their heart on the right. Not us. We never had any weird medical issues, but our faces were imperceptibly mirrored if you looked closely enough. My right eye a fraction lazier than my left, and the opposite with Cece. The dimple on my right cheek, Cece's on her left. She wrote with her left hand; I wrote with my right. But there was one obvious telltale sign that told us apart at a glance, unique to only one of us: her mole, the beauty spot on her right cheekbone. It appeared when she was about eight. She was a real sun bunny. Lucky for my parents and the teachers at school.

My parents pretended they could easily tell us apart, but the truth was… they couldn't. Or could, later, but only because of Cece's mole. Because their eyes would always quickly flash to our cheek before they spoke. *Which one am I speaking to now?* their gaze would tell us. Once or twice, we tested them with makeup. Cece would cover up her mole, and I would create one in the exact same place with a brown eyeliner filched from Mom's makeup bag. I'd seal it with lip-sealer, the stuff you put on so your lipstick won't smudge. And, yeah, we had them fooled. It would make them secretly furious for being caught out, although they'd pretend they knew all along and were humoring us, coming "along for the ride."

Cece and I knew better.

It came in handy several times, our persona swaps. An exam here or there. A tricky interview. Nobody could tell us apart. But we were kind to them, mostly. We'd dress differently, to help them out more than anything. But our personalities? Cecelia was the movie, the blockbuster, and I was the closed book. She was the storm and I was the breeze. People would know just by speaking to us who was who. But if we wanted to mess with them we could.

Swapping seats in the classroom. That was a favorite.

Funny, I always felt that by having a twin I had more in common with dogs than humans: humans who were not twins or triplets or quadruplets, of course. Every time I looked at Poppy, I was reminded that she was part of a litter, just like me.

"We're like puppies," Cece said to me when we were small. We were lying side by side taking an afternoon nap.

"Why?"

"Because we were born together like a pack of puppies. Mom says some dogs only have two babies."

Cece was right. We were a litter of two.

Poppy and I were the same in that respect.

I didn't have friends in New York, not really. Lots of acquaintances and people I could joke or have a drink with, or work colleagues: the editors and authors for the publishing houses I collaborated with. But really *close* friends? Nobody could ever live up to Cece. When you spend your entire childhood joined at the hip with one person, you forget about everyone else. We were one, she and I. Conceived together: one egg, one creation, one individual and then, at the last moment, we split apart as two identical twins, but we would always be one, always and forever. Nothing could change that.

Not even her.

CHAPTER NINE

Mrs. Scott

Now

I didn't clue into Sara immediately. I have to admit she just seemed like a normal sweet girl with nothing to hide; the perfect neighbor. I took great joy in looking after Poppy Delight, you see, and just loved Sara for everything she did for that adorable little dog. You can judge a person by how they treat animals and children, can't you? And that young woman was an angel incarnate with Poppy. An angel. Even if I wasn't doggy-sitting Poppy, Sara loved to come over and chat. Help me out with all kinds of things. She'd bring me groceries, help me if I was having problems with my computer or the Wi-Fi connection. She was a bit of a whiz with technical stuff. Oh, I can't tell you what a perfect neighbor she was for me. Worth her weight in gold, that girl. Always putting others first. Very warm and giving, always with a smile on her face and a kind, encouraging word.

But when I first spotted Cecelia, I was utterly confused because Sara hadn't told me anything about having a sister. The whole Cecelia thing was a secret. The unpleasant backstory, the truth about what her twin had done… Sara had kept Cecelia well under wraps. I never go on Instagram, you see. I guessed Sara was still in denial because she still loved her sister so much. Anyway, little by little, I did see that things were problematic for

Sara, that the situation had become impossible, especially with Bradley right plumb in the middle, and, no, I do not think Sara behaved in an appropriate manner, and yes, I do understand that she's a criminal and by law she should be behind bars, but it didn't mean I loved her any the less. Would I have turned her over to the police? No way, José. I'm *not* a rat. That sweet girl in prison? Not in a million years.

So, if you want to arrest me for aiding and abetting a criminal, go ahead, make my day.

CHAPTER TEN

Sara

Now

"So let's talk about your sister," the feisty detective said, leaning onto the table so I caught the minty tang of her breath and a whiff of her perfume. I could make out the bulge of her pistol, cross-strapped over her shoulder, under her jacket. "At what point did Cecelia move to New York?" she asked, her shrewd eyes honing in on mine.

My shoulders lifted into a vague shrug. I knew this woman was testing me. I looked down, focusing on her NYPD-approved, black lace-up boots. In my fantasies, I had always imagined myself as a cool, tough cop holding a gun with both hands like they do on TV, and like this detective did in real life. All women should have the smarts and skills to defend themselves. My sister was proof of that fact.

"Would you say it was around June?" I heard a shuffle of papers. I still didn't look up.

"If that's what your notes tell you," I said.

"We see she closed down her Charles Schwab brokerage account on 79th Street, on June twenty-eighth. They have her passport on record that she used as ID. Her distinctive signature."

I nodded.

"She'd been living in Thailand for several years previously?"

"I guess you've done your research."

"Miss Keller, why are you making this more difficult than it has to be? We're simply asking some basic questions about your sister. She has gone missing. If you care about her, you'll help us. That is, unless you have something to hide. If you'd prefer to have an attorney present…"

I shook my head. If I could just get this over with, say little, and between now and whenever they hauled me back in here (because, let's face it, they were bound to catch up with me sooner or later), I'd have time to get an airtight story together. Something that wouldn't incriminate me. I'd bring an attorney with me. A damn good one. I knew one, a guy who had helped me with my taxes when I'd gotten myself in a tricky spot, but this? This was way beyond that. I needed a top-shot criminal lawyer. I wondered if Bradley knew someone in his Wall Street world. A shark. The type of lawyer Gordon Gekko might hire. Then I remembered… asking Bradley was impossible.

"Would you describe your relationship with your twin as a close one?"

"We were inseparable," I said.

"Were?"

Oops, that came out wrong. Tears filled my eyes. The Abba song "The Winner Takes It All" popped into my head.

Cece and I did everything together, always. At one point, I'm not sure how old we were, probably about eight, they tried to split us up at school so we could be more "individual." Grownups became fed up with us talking in our own language; a language they couldn't understand. It was unique to us: our twin language. They call this phenomenon cryptophasia. It's not uncommon, apparently. Not only were we born as mirror images of each other but sometimes, in art class, without even looking at the other one's drawing we would create mirror-image pictures, with a house or the sun, or our parents or whatever. It was the same picture just backwards.

We thought as one, did as one. We were the ultimate double act. It never occurred to me that anything or anyone could come between us.

Especially not myself.

CHAPTER ELEVEN

Bradley

Three months earlier. May.

Spending time with Sara in the park was Bradley's favorite part of the day. It felt almost like a job getting to know her, hoping that with every conversation she was warming to him, little by little. He had made a huge effort, especially with Poppy, because Poppy, he'd noted, was the key to Sara's heart. He'd proffered little treats and gifts for the dog. He'd even gone shopping at FAO Schwarz to buy a cute teddy bear for her. He wasn't sure if that was what you were meant to do, but he didn't have much clue about dogs; he had never had one as a child.

So far, his and Sara's "dates" had been limited to Central Park. Sara was reticent… a little coy, there was no denying it. She seemed cautious and wary, especially of men. But, as far as Bradley was concerned, this showed intelligence on her part, and proved she was absolutely worthy of his attention. Yet there was something… he couldn't put his finger on it… a sort of brilliant simplicity: her mind quite one-track: determined, with absorbed interest in certain topics, especially her dog and her work. She had a mission concerning Poppy's recovery and nothing was going to stop her succeeding. A person who cared about others. She was just the girl Bradley had been looking for his whole life. Straightforward. No games. Somebody he could respect.

And above all, she let him be himself.

The two of them had graduated from long conversations to holding hands like teenagers. He had given her a gentle kiss on the cheek: a lingering one, taking in the scent of her hair, to show her how much he liked her without pushing it too far. He felt like a boy at school with his very first girlfriend. Not that he'd had that type of sweetheart relationship at school. But with Sara he was able to live it for the first time. The innocent excitement and slow-burn thrill of falling in love. He wanted to make this feeling last, savor every drop of anticipation, and he could tell she liked him by little gestures she made: letting her hand touch his, walking so close their bodies brushed, laughing at his lame jokes.

It was a total turn on… a *mental* turn on. Every day he thought of new ways to please her. He had found her a 1944 first edition of Agatha Christie's *Towards Zero*, the dust jacket, with a fabulous illustration, still in great shape. Knowing how much she was into books, he knew it would please her, and it did. He had totally scored on this one! Then he presented her, or rather, Poppy, with a pink diamanté collar. Although he hadn't seen Poppy wear it, Sara had incorporated the collar into one of her book covers, on another dog, a fictional dog, and so Bradley felt his gift had not been in vain. This had never happened to him before: hanging onto every last word or reaction from a woman, anticipating her likes or dislikes.

Sara was not making it easy for him, true. Every time he walked her home to her apartment on 79th and Lexington and saw her off at the building's front door, safely deposited under the green awning, she never invited Bradley in, and would just say "Thank you so much for accompanying me, Bradley, see you around."

Yet he was pretty sure he had a chance with her. Sara was obviously not impressed by wealth or by the fact he worked on Wall Street.

Sara was new, unchartered territory. How refreshing!

Meanwhile, had he stopped seeing other women?

Not exactly.

He wanted to, but he would wait until he'd got Sara to commit first.

It was a Sunday when he finally pinned Sara down to accepting a non-park date. In the end he decided the best thing would be to invite her over to dinner. He'd cook. A girl like Sara deserved the utmost respect.

CHAPTER TWELVE

Sara

This was the first date I had been on—a proper date—in, I don't know how long. The last, I guess, was when I'd tried out a dating app, went for one disastrous drink and gave up.

Slowly, I had changed my mind about Bradley. Dating anyone terrified me, yes, but shouldn't I give this guy a chance? I couldn't carry on forever keeping men at bay just because I was frightened of getting hurt. He seemed genuinely so interested in me and everything I talked about, even when I had verbal diarrhea about my work or Poppy. He was gentle, kind, considerate, putting me first. And he was the right age, too. More mature than anyone I had ever dated before. I pegged him to be in his late thirties. In all our park chats I hadn't asked him his age, nor he mine. The truth was, whenever I saw him my tummy did little somersaults, and when he looked at me a zap of electricity rushed through my body.

It took me forever to decide what to wear this evening. I almost kept on what I had been going around in that day: just jeans and a T-shirt and sneakers, but then thought I should don something nice. Something feminine and pretty. I raided my closet and chose a dress. I didn't wear dresses very often, but since the weather had changed into full-on spring, I opted for something edging on elegant. A yellow dress, why not? But when I looked in the mirror and examined myself, I looked all wrong, because I was rather pale from a long, New York winter.

Staring in the mirror in a sort of daze, I thought about my sister. Her favorite color, at one point, was yellow. Primrose yellow, buttercup yellow, even a garish acid yellow. It suited her, but it didn't suit me. How crazy was that? That as kids we looked identical yet somehow certain colors suited us differently. She could wear anything. I allowed my memory to draw me back in, and I pictured her: Cece in her one-piece gold swimsuit. That was another way to tell us apart: she tanned more deeply and never turned pale in winter like me. I'm not sure why; if it was because I shied away from the sun or if our pigment was actually different. I think the former. She worshipped the sun. Once, I did our astrology charts. Incredibly, the twenty-minute difference in our births placed one of her houses in Leo that I didn't have. I can't remember which or what, but I found that fascinating.

I looked in the mirror again and saw her and missed her, as I did every time I saw my own face. I wished she could be with me. Then I remembered how I had a date to go on and reminded myself how I yearned for emancipation from my twin. For a man to be in love with *me*, and not just half of me, to be accepted, pale skin, pale personality, without Cecelia getting in the way.

I tore off the primrose-yellow dress and decided that no, I would not wear a dress. This was a first date and I should protect myself with pants, not some whimsical flowing thing that could float up in the breeze (didn't he have a roof terrace?) or invite wandering hands. I fished out a pair of black slacks from my messy closet. Tried them on but they seemed so formal and office-like, so I unbuttoned them and hurled them on the bed. Things were piling up fast.

It struck me that Bradley must have liked what he'd seen so far in the park, or he wouldn't have invited me to dinner in the first place. Last seen, I had been in my sneakers and leggings. So that's what he was going to get!

Then I changed my mind again.

My outfit ended up being a pair of skinny jeans, some red, high-top Converse sneakers, and a blue and white horizontal-striped French fisherman's shirt. I applied some mascara, groomed my brows, and smeared on a dab of lip gloss. But then I wiped off the makeup with cold cream. It just wasn't me. Makeup-free, I looked in the mirror. Nothing special, but cute.

Again, against my will, Cece popped onto the screen of my memories. We were in Brittany, on the French coast, and with her pocket money she had bought a shirt just like the stripy one I was wearing now. I'd chosen a bucket and spade so we could make sandcastles on the beach. I wanted to make a princess's palace where our whole family could live, but she said she was going to be self-sufficient (she'd learned that word from Mom… so grown-up!) She'd sail off in a boat, she told me, and catch fish and tour the islands, alone. Me being me, and Cece being Cece, I believed her. She didn't need her family, she announced, because she was strong and independent. In that moment, she broke my heart. There I was, worrying about how we would all fit into the sandcastle I was trying to build, and how I would never ever be able to make it big enough for the whole family because the sea would come in great slapping waves and wash away my work, and meanwhile she, my sister, was slipping away from us all because she didn't need us. In a boat, alone, no less.

I could taste those tears of mine on my lips now. They tasted of betrayal. Then she had laughed her special Cece cackle-laugh and told me she was just kidding, that no, she would never leave me, how could she do that? *How can you even believe that?* she said. But the damage was already done. In my mind, I had her in this fisherman's shirt, on a boat, setting out to sea. Like the Owl and the Pussycat, but alone. And me on the beach pathetically trying to keep my castle together, while rough brown waves washed our home away.

All dressed now in my modest outfit, I found Poppy in the kitchen, snoozing. I hadn't given Poppy her massage. Once a week, we went for her physiotherapy sessions, but I also gave her an intensive massage every day. She loved it. Especially behind her ears. Those hind legs would normally be able to scratch ears and the rest of her body, but poor Poppy couldn't, so every day we'd have a scratch fest and I'd massage her all over. Her thighs were beginning to gain a little muscle though.

I was so grateful for Mrs. Scott: being able to go out and have her babysit. There was no way I would have felt comfortable leaving Poppy alone.

I picked out a camel wrap-coat that belted around the waist, and Poppy awoke with the sound (coat equaled walk), dragging her little legs behind her, eager for her wheels. Even though I was just going down a few floors, I knew Poppy expected her wheelchair. It made her feel autonomous.

We got into the elevator and rode three floors down to where Mrs. Scott lived. I had entertained the idea of bringing Poppy along with me to Bradley's apartment but my voice of reason told me to remain cautious. If I needed to make a run for it, it would be easier and faster if I didn't have to worry about my dog. Crazy, really crazy. The fact I was even thinking that Bradley could be some choppy-choppy freak made me question whether I should go to his apartment at all. But who wants to go through life jaded and suspicious of everyone? I was overthinking it. Worrying too much. I'd let Mrs. Scott know where I was going, just in case.

"And how is my little Popsicle?" Mrs. Scott said, wheeling herself over to Poppy. She had frizzy red hair with a shock of white on one side of her parting. The auburn red was colored, I presumed, but she left this white tail au naturel. It looked very striking. Her kind, twinkly eyes were a beautiful sea green. Her skin even paler than mine. She must have been a great beauty once… well, she still was, especially because she smiled so much.

Not only was Mrs. Scott amazing with Poppy but she insisted on baking me treats. Sometimes I'd find a loaf of homemade soda bread outside my door, or caramel popcorn, or brownies. She was a bottomless well of giving. Always thinking of others. Not once had I heard her bitch about her circumstances, never even a whisper of complaint about having a disability.

Poppy whimpered with excitement and wagged her tail. She tried to jump up but failed, wheels spinning. Wheels seemed to be everywhere: Poppy's, Mrs. Scott's. I unhooked Poppy's wheelchair and laid her into her babysitter's ample, waiting arms. Mrs. Scott nestled Poppy against her large cleavage. She wore purple and strings of colored beads draped around her neck.

"I've already fed her and she had a long walk today so she should be pretty tired. If you could indulge her with a massage and ear scratch that would be great. Thanks so much, Mrs. Scott, I really appreciate it."

Poppy was licking Mrs. Scott's face, tangling her white paws in her strings of giant red and orange beads. "I adore looking after this little munchkin. And I know how much she loves her ear rubs." She turned to me. "You look very pretty, Sara. Come on over and give me a hug. You're the daughter I always wanted, you know that, right?"

She pulled me into a great big bear hug, and we laughed when my hair caught in her beads. After I untangled myself, her eyes took me in with approval, from the clip in my hair down to my red Converse. She knew I was going on a date, I guessed. I fished out my phone. "You know what? I'm going to text you the address of where I'm going. Just to be on the safe side."

Her smile dropped. "You don't know this person?"

"No, I do. We met in the park. I know where he works. We've been on a lot of park dates, but this is the first time he's invited me to his home. He's very nice, I'm being silly even making an issue out of this. I'm just nervous, I guess."

She nodded approvingly. "You've told your mom? About this boy? You know how much I worry about you?"

"No."

Her russet brows knit together in concern. "Okay. If you don't show up by midnight, I'll send a pumpkin or a coach or whatever. You'll be fine. But if it makes you more comfortable, send me a text to let me know you're okay. At around ten o'clock? Who's the lucky guy?"

"His name is Bradley. Bradley Daniels. Works on Wall Street, lives on Fifth and 62nd and wears beautiful tailored suits. He's like someone who stepped out of a film noir movie. I didn't figure he was my type, but then I don't know what my type is anymore." I laughed.

I suddenly felt a little wave of embarrassment. I had hung out a lot with Mrs. Scott's son, Jack, just as friends. He had a girlfriend, although his mom didn't approve of her, because all she talked about was fashion and makeup, but then, Mrs. Scott was so crazy about her son and they were so close, I wondered if any woman would be good enough for him in her eyes. I'd gotten the impression that she assumed he and I had dated for a while, since she was so delighted we were spending time together. Jack and I were still friends but saw less of each other than before, after we'd had a bit of a disagreement. I wasn't sure how much his mom knew about what had happened. I didn't want her thinking Jack was not a cool guy in my opinion, because he was, but… well… what happened between us was a whole other story, and he'd sworn to me that he would not tell a soul, not even his mom.

CHAPTER THIRTEEN

Sara

Bradley's apartment was located in a really amazing neighborhood, and was a penthouse. Right on Fifth Avenue, overlooking Central Park.

After getting out of the elevator, there were two doors on his floor, and I wasn't sure which was his. As I was digging around in my purse for my phone, to see which was his apartment number, the door swung open and there he was. I was glad I had taken off the dress and chosen just jeans. He was barefoot, also in jeans, and a T-shirt. A far cry from the city slicker I had seen every time in the park. It was nice to see him look just like a regular guy. A little butterfly fluttered round in my tummy, against my will. I couldn't deny how attractive he was to me and how excited I was by our first official date.

"Sara, so glad you came. Where's Poppy?"

"I left her behind with my neighbor. She had such a long outing today in the park, I didn't want to make her walk again. As you can see I'm wearing sneakers, I just came here by foot so…" *In case I need to make a run for it,* I thought, only half seriously.

"It's a great walk, isn't it? The weather's been so perfect lately."

"Hasn't it? So glad the cold weather's over. I swear, I'm going to live in a year-round warm climate one day." I wasn't being serious, but his eyes flashed with excitement.

"Hey, me too! You can't imagine how freezing those Minnesota winters were as a boy. And New York in January? I'm done with the cold."

"Minnesota? Is that where you're from?"

He grinned at me, looking so much younger in his T-shirt and jeans than he did in his suits. And here we both were, feeling awkward, talking about the weather, of all boring things.

"Sorry, Sara, come in, come in." He stepped back and ushered me inside. "What can I get you to drink?"

I unbuttoned my coat. "I don't know, what do you have?"

"Everything."

"A white wine spritzer?"

"You don't want something stronger? I make a great cocktail. I used to be a cocktail waiter once."

"Tom Cruise style?"

He laughed. "So you like movies from the 80s too?"

"And the clothes. And the music."

"So, no cocktail?"

"Sure, why not?"

"Come into the kitchen. You can leave your coat on the couch."

There was a velvet sofa in the foyer. The floor was all pale gray marble, the foyer almost bigger than my apartment. The place was beautiful. I shrugged off my coat and draped it over the sofa arm, my purse buried beneath. I followed Bradley down a hallway into a kitchen, *twice the size* of my apartment. The double-doored refrigerator alone was the size of my bathroom. My gaze scanned the place, in awe. An island in the middle of the room, topped with white Carrera marble. A big round table on one side, and wall-to-wall cabinets reaching all the way up to the high ceiling. All was white, the countertops white marble, the floor marble, too. Evening light was gushing into the room through enormous windows. A shiny chrome-edged stove was at one end of the kitchen, flanked by more white marble. Everything was pristine.

Something told me Bradley was no cook; either that, or he had staff, or a cleaner who polished everything to a high shine.

Spotting a blender with something frothy already made, I asked, "Frozen daiquiris?"

"Margaritas," he said. "Tonight I thought I'd do Mexican."

He poured one out for me in a tall frosted glass, edged in sea salt. I was impressed with the effort he'd made. We clinked cocktails and made a toast to Poppy walking again without her wheels. I looked around the room with envy at its tidiness. So unlike the tiny, rent-controlled apartment where I lived, with my piles of books and magazines and dusty corners, and Poppy's toys. I couldn't get over the way everything here gleamed and shone.

He watched my eyes skim the room. "Actually it's me," he said.

"What is?"

"I'm the one that keeps the place this tip-top, this pristine. You could call me a bit OCD. I hate mess."

It made me smile because he had read my mind. "You don't have a cleaner? Someone who comes on a regular basis to help?"

"No, just me. I don't trust anyone to do the job the way I can do it myself."

My gaze landed again on his fridge. No grubby fingerprints. *My* refrigerator had yellow Post-it notes all over it with to-do reminders or book ideas, held there by an assortment of dog magnets. This fridge was like a piece of modern architecture and shone out like an advertisement in a magazine. What kind of man with a full-time job had the time to keep his apartment this perfect? Especially such a large place as this?

In that second, it occurred to me that Bradley must be gay. It all made sense now. His reluctance to give me a real kiss. Bradley was gay and I was his new best friend, was that it? I saw him in a whole new light. My mind, being pulled in opposite directions, wrangled with my new perception of this man. Actually, I reasoned, maybe this arrangement was much better. We'd just

be fun friends. Buddies. It was safer this way. This way I couldn't
get myself tangled into some romantic mess.

"This apartment isn't forever," he said, eyes fixed on me intently,
as if making a promise. "New York's not forever. One day, very
soon, I'd like to move, I don't know... somewhere warm, like you
said earlier. I'm serious about Hawaii. I loved Kauai. It's so wild,
so prehistoric. They filmed *Jurassic Park* there."

"Really? I've seen pictures. All those gorgeous waterfalls and
rock formations. The Napali coast is just beautiful."

He swallowed a gulp of margarita. "Isn't it? That's so cool
you know what I'm talking about. Wall Street's just for now. I'm
planning to move in the near future. Maybe Maui, maybe Kauai.
Want to come with me?"

I felt a flutter of several butterflies freefall in my belly. The way
he was talking made me realize I'd read him wrong: Bradley was
definitely not gay. I hid my enthusiasm with a shy smile and tried
to look unfazed. But I felt like screaming, *yes!* Moving to Hawaii
sounded just perfect. It made me think of those movies, the classics, from the 40s and 50s when a man met a woman and they got
married two weeks later. It was normal in those days. Now people
would think you were a freak if you did that. But my fleeting excitement was just that. A *fleeting* fantasy. I was happy in New York.

"You don't like what you do? You don't like your job?" I asked.
"Is that why you want to move?"

"I do, actually. It gives me a huge buzz and it's exciting, but
it's a burnout job. It won't last forever... it can't last forever."

I sipped my cocktail. It was delicious. Not too sweet. "So
what do you do exactly? Invest people's money?" He nodded.
"Individuals or companies?" I asked.

"Truly? I'm not going to bore you with it. It's not creative like
you, Sara, like what you do with your book covers."

I hadn't given much thought before about Bradley working on
Wall Street, but lately I had been mulling it over and wondering.

Weren't Wall Street bankers cutthroat people who brought whole companies down, making people redundant? Mergers, takeovers, putting poor folks out of jobs? I had zero Wall Street knowledge, apart from what I'd read, and *Wall Street*, the movie, with Michael Douglas playing the infamous Gordon greed-is-good Gekko. I had read that his character was a pastiche of some real people.

I knew about the giant bonuses investment bankers and brokers made; sickeningly huge. Sometimes a cool million for Christmas, not counting their already enormous salary; more than most people made in a whole lifetime from grueling, grinding jobs. I thought about investors' money being powered into fossil fuels, all possible because of investment bankers on Wall Street putting the big buck before ethics, before ecology, even before human rights. I had no idea how it worked and felt too nervous to bring it up with Bradley, because I really liked him. I didn't want to come across as pernickety, judgey or granola-bar soap-boxy. Everybody had to earn a buck; none of us was perfect, whatever you did in life. Whenever I brought the subject of his work up, though, it made him a little edgy. Maybe he didn't want to think too hard about what he did?

Perhaps it was better just to make the money and not worry about its source?

"I hope you like dinner," he said, checking the dish in the oven. "You told me you don't eat meat anymore? I've made *chili sin carne*. Chili, but without the meat."

I smiled. He'd remembered. I'd mentioned it in passing that I was trying to go for a plant-based diet, striving hard. "That's so thoughtful of you." Then I said, as if to excuse myself from all the trouble he'd gone to, "You know, I'm just trying to do my little bit. My tiny contribution. So much of the rainforest is being chopped down for cattle and cattle feed. I'd love to live a sustainable life. You know recycle, not buy vegetables wrapped in plastic, do every day things to make a difference?"

"You eat avocados though, right?"

I laughed. "Of course! Guacamole's my favorite."

"Great, because I've made some." He pulled a big bowl out of the fridge and put it on a silver tray.

"This looks amazing," I said. "Smells yummy."

"It's the cilantro. And chopped red peppers, super, super fine, and I threw in some spicy ones too. So beware. Gives it an extra kick. The trick to preparation is sharp knives. I take my knives very seriously." He nodded at a set of state-of-the-art kitchen knives lined up on a large, horizontal wall magnet.

I tittered nervously. I hated knives. My mind hovered over the bare truth: I was alone in a semi-stranger's apartment. Knowing Bradley somewhat did not make my situation any safer. Had I been a fool to come here? But then I caught Bradley's eye and he was smiling.

I was being paranoid, wasn't I?

He pulled a packet of tortilla chips from a cabinet. I had assumed he didn't cook, but this was looking very promising. The *chili sin carne* smelled delicious. He had just inched himself up several notches in my approval rating.

A boyfriend who cooked? Wow!

Was he a "boyfriend"? I asked myself, as my mind continued with its internal yes/no banter. I still wasn't sure where we stood, what this relationship was all about… if he'd make a move or not. And more importantly… was I ready? Like with all relationships at the beginning, my emotions were yo-yoing back and forth. My life had been going so well pre-Bradley. Simple. Uncomplicated. I felt vulnerable all over again.

"Let's take this to the roof terrace," he suggested. "You up for that?"

I nodded, curious to see the famous roof terrace. "Great. Let me help."

"You bring the margarita jug and the bowl. I'll take the rest on the tray."

He lead me to a living room, where there was a screen taking up one whole wall—movie-theater size. Luxurious couches and armchairs, in white, commanded space. Yet space was not exactly lacking in this extraordinary home.

"I bet you don't serve red wine in this apartment," I joked.

He looked at me, nonplussed.

"All the white everywhere."

He shot me a wry smile in answer.

We wended our way up a wrought-iron, spiral staircase, Bradley balancing the glasses and other snacks on the tray, me holding the big bowl of guacamole and the jug. At the top, was a Victorian-style conservatory, spilling over with tropical plants, and trees in pots flanking the length of an expansive roof terrace.

The sky was melting from purple into orange as the sun dropped slowly behind the Manhattan skyline. Leafy trees in the park made the sunlight come and go in dappled, flickered shadows. It was a huge terrace. The apartment next to it owned the other half, but it was blocked off with a row of Italian cypresses. *I love the way people have gardens on roofs in New York*, I thought. I had a flash of us moving here to live with Bradley. Then I squashed that mad idea from my mind. I hardly knew the man.

"See?" he said, gesturing to his garden. "The irrigation system is pretty complex, so even if I'm not around nothing gets too dry. It's all on timers. It's quite some garden, don't you think? I love it up here. A real retreat from what can seem at times like a concrete jungle below, especially after riding the subway in the commuter hour."

The conservatory had some small orange and lemon trees, purple and pink bougainvillea climbing on a trellis, and palms. The heady smell of jasmine filled the air, also entwined around trellises, tangled and in flower. It was like entering a different world. Double French doors led out on to the garden. *A garden in New York City? On a rooftop?* I had to pinch myself. The garden had real grass spanning across the length of the terrace and small silver birch trees in huge pots, and maples, shimmering in the evening June breeze. The view across Central Park was endless, the expanses of water denoting each landmark. The lake, where people would rent rowboats on a sunny day, flanked by Bethesda Fountain one side and Loeb Boathouse the other, with the elegant Bow Bridge arching over the middle of the water. The Dakota beyond, at West 72nd Street, the famous apartment building where John Lennon had lived, and later, died. To the north was the reservoir, now named after Jackie Onassis, circled by trees, around which some New Yorkers would do their daily jog. It was easy to see why Central Park was known as the lungs of the city. Its beauty, smack in the midst of this urban metropolis, was breathtaking.

More than twenty blocks south of the park I could make out the Empire State Building in the distance. Until 1971, this Art Deco masterpiece was the tallest building in the world. But now a couple of the newer, "Lego" buildings, as I called them, almost blocked the view.

"This place is unbelievable," I said, my jaw dropping. "Like something out of a movie."

"Isn't it? Actually, I think they may have used this for a movie location in the past."

"It must take a lot of specialized work to plan a garden like this, on a rooftop."

"Yup, you have to consider the weight of the trees and earth, and building regulations for height and so on, not to mention the wind. And not all species survive both the cold and heat of New York. The higher up, the colder and windier it is."

"You made this garden yourself?" I asked.

"No, it came with the apartment. The conservatory and the garden were already established. It belonged to a Frenchman. You've heard of the HookedUp guy, Alexandre Chevalier?"

I nodded. The HookedUp CEO was a billionaire. HookedUp was a bit like Tinder, but classier, and had been founded a few years before Tinder. It was incredibly popular in its heyday. My sister had used it a lot. She loved it.

Raising his chin rather regally, Bradley inhaled the air. "Isn't the jasmine amazing? And the datura? It comes out in the evening… in the daytime it doesn't have any scent. Mr. Chevalier bought this apartment for his black Labrador, Rex, especially because of the roof terrace. He designed this garden, apparently. Rex, they said, was used to the high life. Flew around in private jets. There was talk of a big bronze statue being made of him and erected in Central Park, in the dog's memory after he died, but in the end, despite a generous donation to the park from the Chevaliers, the city said no."

I laughed. "That's so cute! He must've really loved that dog. I'm surprised he wanted to ever sell this beautiful place."

"Mr. Chevalier lives in Paris with his wife and children now. And has houses all over the world even better than this place. Why live in New York when you can own islands in the Caribbean, chateaux in the Loire?"

"And you too would be willing to leave this incredible home in favor of Hawaii?"

"All good things must come to an end."

"Must they?" I said. And then thought, *True, all good things in my life have come to an end.*

A devastating end.

But Bradley didn't answer.

We dug into the guacamole; it was delicious. Spicy though. I washed it down with large swigs of margarita to cool my tongue.

"You like the guacamole?" Bradley asked.

"Spicy, but *so* good!"

He assured me the avocados were organic, not grown in countries where the locals' precious water supply was being decimated by farming practices. We chatted briefly about conservation and climate change, and it reminded me that however hard you tried to do the right thing, there was always somewhere where you failed. Being a good person had been drilled into me by my mom and dad. Growing up in Africa, with parents working in medical humanitarianism as doctors for Médecins Sans Frontières and UNICEF, made me view life through their eyes. Seeing people who smiled when they had a simple bag of rice to eat, or a cow as their family heirloom, had trained me to value the essentials that mattered: shelter, food, water, love, family, the ability to eat or pay the bills without fear of losing your home, and anything more than that was icing on the cake. These were the things I never took for granted, and although I too counted my pennies and relied a hundred percent on my salary to support myself, I had never been on the brink of starvation so felt huge gratitude on a daily basis. Sometimes I pinched myself. I was living in Manhattan and had a well-paid job! That in itself proved to me I was living the dream. The Bradleys and Alexandre Chevaliers of this world seemed otherworldly, surreal.

Bradley's eyes were fixed on mine, and even though he was smiling, for some reason that movie *American Psycho* popped into my head. *Rich guy in New York goes on a rampage.* Just because someone has boatloads of money doesn't make them safe. I turned away, hoping he couldn't read the worry on my face, but when I looked back he was still grinning, and I realized that ring of ice in the whites of his eyes was all in my imagination.

I took this opportunity to ask Bradley about his job. "What about your work? Do you vet companies then to make sure they're ethical?"

He rested his chin on his hand, his intense gaze snagging mine. "We're all a part of this whether we like it or not, Sara. As you say, little choices we make every day have their power, make a difference, and I too want to do the right thing. I have stocks in the plant-based Beyond Meat, Tesla, and solar energy and so on. I do my homework."

Hearing this made Bradley look even more handsome to me. A weight of worry lifted from my shoulders, my neck. My fingers, which had been twizzling the stem of my glass, let go their tension. Wine glasses snapping in my hand was something that happened more often than I wished.

"Like you, I care about our planet," he said, giving me a wink.

I had been dreading finding out that Bradley was a major player in the arms industry or something. My happiness felt palpable; the ache in my jaw changed from a teeth-grind to a huge, stretchy grin. I was falling for this guy. But was he too good to be true? I picked up a beautiful linen napkin from the tray to hide my mouth. I was sure I had guacamole all over my teeth. The napkin was monogrammed: V. C. It looked antique. I was about to ask who V. C. was, but his romantic gaze held me captive, and I didn't want to distract him.

He took the napkin away from my face and held my hand in his. His fingers were long and slim. He wore a heavy, gold signet ring on his pinkie. Also V.C.

"And that's what attracted me to you. You *care*. You're a rare bird, Sara. I could see that the moment I set eyes on you in the park with Poppy. There's something pure about you."

I laughed. "No, really, Bradley, don't exaggerate, I'm no angel!"

But he was serious. He rested his lips on my hand. I waited for a real kiss but none came. Did he think me too "pure" to kiss?

Nervously, with my other hand free, I knocked back several large sips of my cocktail to give me Dutch courage. Maybe I should make a move myself? I was timid though. He locked his loving gaze on me, his dark brown eyes intense. All I could think was *how romantic*. He was really *looking* at me, taking me in, absorbing me. No man had gazed at me this way for years. Maybe ever. My stomach flipped. I felt giddy.

Was Bradley *the one*?

"You're beautiful, Sara."

I looked away coyly. I was stumped by what to say. I was expecting him to bring his lips to mine, but he carried on holding hands, almost as if I were too delicate to spoil with a kiss.

To hide my awkwardness I blurted out, "So, how long have you lived here? The location's amazing."

He took his hand away and sat back, his eyes still on me, as if weighing up his options, deciding what to say. "I know," he said. "I was lucky. Contacts, I guess. I always like to be ahead of the game."

The way he said that made me feel, for a second, as if he knew too much about me. That he was onto me. *Ahead of the game.*

I smiled, nervous, and took another slug of my cocktail. I was aware how unladylike that was to knock it back like a truck driver at a bar. Then I let out a little burp. Oops. I hid my mouth again with the napkin. A self-conscious glitch I had from when I'd chipped my tooth after a bicycle accident. I took a long time to find a dentist who could fix it right. I went around with the chip for a long time. A little complex had set in though, and still, sometimes I hid my smile. It must have looked to others like I was afraid to be happy. Perhaps I was. Afraid to be happy in case I lost everything again. Afraid to love.

"Who's V.C.?" I asked, holding up the monogrammed linen square. I was veering away from the intensity of our moment… being blithe.

I was being a scaredy-cat.

Cecelia's voice popped into my head. *Scaredy cat. Scaredy cat. Why didn't you kiss him?*

Bradley's gaze shifted for a nanosecond. "Those old napkins? I found them in an antique shop in Paris."

"I've always wanted to go to Paris."

"I'll take you there one day," he said.

I went all swoony again, the alcohol kicking in, giving everything a dreamy sheen. It frightened me how much I was fantasizing about a future with Bradley. Ridiculous.

"Tell me about your family back in Minnesota," I said.

"Nothing interesting to report. I had a very middle-of-the-road, suburban childhood. Parents still together. I talk to my mother every week, though if she had her way she'd call me once a day." He smiled.

"That's nice you and your mom are so close," I said.

"I better check the chili. Let's go back down."

Dinner, it turned out, ended up burned. I had been right; Bradley was not used to cooking. The local Mexican restaurant was closed for refurbishment, so we ordered in Chinese from some new fancy place a few blocks away.

He led me to the dining room and instructed me to sit while he brought in the food. The dining room was round. It was like walking into an Italian palace or museum. Trompe l'oeil murals adorned the walls with three-dimensional scenes, topped by a painted blue sky around a dome, peeping through wispy clouds. A big bird—a hawk?—was flying through the air. It really felt as if there were no ceiling and we were outside in the middle of the day. Faux double-doors opened onto a picturesque lake dotted with swans, the view reaching to the horizon. The effect was dizzying. Even if I hadn't been so drunk I would have been blown away.

"This place is crazy!" I gasped. "It's like going back in time to another century. So Italian! I can't believe we're in New York City!"

Bradley smiled. "Isn't it a trip?"

Bradley had style. When the takeout arrived he put a giant silver spoon (V.C. initials) into each of the white boxes and we helped ourselves. He had set the table with beautiful china and crystal glasses. He offered me a glass of fine French wine, but I didn't want to mix drinks so stuck with margaritas. There must've been at least ten different dishes: sesame noodles, dim sum, steamed vegetable dumplings, eggplant with garlic sauce, fish braised in soybean paste (for him), mango and arugula salad, scallion pancake. I wasn't sure about mixing margaritas with Chinese, but I was having such fun and had loosened up to the point of saying or doing things I shouldn't, but so far, I hadn't behaved outrageously.

"So delicious," I said, swallowing another sip of cocktail, after eating way too much. Still, I couldn't stop, the food was that good. I was lazy about feeding myself nutritious food and often ordered in but couldn't afford top-end takeout like this.

This food tasted like love. I was on a high.

He watched me as I savored another mouthful of dumpling. It was light and spiced with lemongrass. "Do you like to cook?" he asked.

I giggled. The drink had taken its toll. "You want me to be honest?"

"You can lie if you like. Go ahead, tell me lies. You had me at '*Excuse me would you mind holding my dog?*'"

"No. It was *you*. You offered to hold my dog."

"Really? No, I seem to remember it was the other way round. So, do you?"

"Do I what?"

"Like to cook?"

I laughed. "I'm an *amazing* cook," I fibbed. "And I love to bake cookies and make my own jam. I do a fantastic soufflé, it comes up perfect every time."

It was his turn to laugh. I studied his face. He had deep brown eyes and dark wayward eyebrows that were very expressive and moved a whole lot, as if they were separate entities on his face. His hair was thick and floppy and also brown. His skin had an olive complexion. He looked like he worked out, now that he wasn't covered up in a suit. I could detect defined muscles and the form of his taut abs beneath his T-shirt. I felt a little intimidated and lazy sitting next to him. I never worked out. I counted my walks in the park as my exercise.

"Are you a runner?" I asked, thinking of Poppy and how her owner must have jogged around the six-mile loop in Central Park every weekend, or maybe even every day.

"Nope. I kickbox. And I got into yoga recently, but I think I'm going to drop that. It's not for me."

I was about to tell him that my sister was into yoga but stopped myself. The last thing I needed was for Bradley to know about Cecelia.

We chatted the whole evening, in between mouthfuls of this sumptuous food and sips of cocktail. It started off with small talk about this and that but then developed into chit-chat about his family in Minnesota. He told me a little about his brother and sister. Both older. His sister worked in community service, his brother as a counselor. They sounded so wholesome. Reading between the lines, it sounded like Bradley was the black sheep of the family for coming to New York and making all this money. Not that he mentioned money at all; he was very discreet, but I could tell that money must have been his motivation rather than a love for his job, because he always avoided discussing it or going into detail. Almost as if he were ashamed of what he did. Unlike myself. It gave me great pleasure to talk about my work or bounce ideas off people. Talk about my projects to the point of being a bookish nerd. There had been several moments when I considered kissing Bradley, but I reminded myself how a guy like him had the pick of any woman, and launching myself at him—drunk, to boot—was probably not the smartest move if I wanted him to stay interested in me.

It was around eleven p.m. when, in my margarita stupor, I remembered I had promised Mrs. Scott I'd call or send a text to let her know I was fine and I hadn't been abducted or murdered. I felt so embarrassed and shameful that I'd been suspicious in the first place, when Bradley had hosted this beautiful meal and had been nothing but charming and attentive. He had not tried to take advantage of my tipsiness at all, yet I'd given him ample opportunity. I quickly texted Mrs. Scott and let my host know I needed to get going. But by this time, I was practically seeing triple.

"You've been such a gentleman," I slurred, swaying as I spoke, "not to take advantage of me."

"Sounds like you're disappointed," he said, and laughed.

"Only surprised. Most men go in for the kill when a woman's drunk."

"I would never kill *you*, Sara."

Our eyes met. His humor was dark, but funny. His deadpan expression almost had me fooled. Somehow—and I couldn't remember how or when—we'd made it back up to the roof terrace again: the New York skyline a backdrop to this romantic, warm evening wafting with the scent of jasmine and datura. I saw two of Bradley, though, and for a second I wondered if he too had a twin. *We could double date. Ha!* Evidently it was no longer evening but night. Having a dog waiting for you was like being a perpetual Cinderella; I needed to get home. I reiterated that it was time for me to leave.

Bradley offered me the crook of his elbow and helped me stand up. "Before you go, would you like a tour of my apartment? I'd love to show you the library."

"Sure, okay."

I grabbed his arm—muscle-hard—and he led me carefully down the spiral staircase toward the library.

The floors were parquet, the wood polished to a high shine. It smelled of lemony beeswax and old money. The paneled room was also all wood.

Bradley told me, his voice sounding vaguely rehearsed, as if he'd said this many times before, "This, as you know, is a pre-war building, and this walnut *boiserie* is original 1930s from when the building was constructed. I'm pretty sure this apartment's the only one in our building that has this special paneling, cabinetry, and bookshelves. And look at the view to Central Park! Not bad, don't you think?"

My mind was in a spin, both literally and figuratively. This place was so opulent. The library—*who has an actual library in their apartment?*—had two fireplaces and a double-aspect view to the Plaza Hotel and Fifth Avenue. I scanned my gaze along the display of books. They were the old-fashioned, leather-bound kind: all the classics. It would take a lifetime to read them.

"Behind that bookshelf there's a secret room,' he revealed. "Like a panic room. Soundproofed. Even if you screamed, nobody would hear."

"I can't see it," I said.

"Of course you can't. That's why it's secret. Like in a horror movie, when you take out a book and, abracadabra, it opens."

Was he kidding me? I couldn't tell: he was wearing that poker face again.

My eyes perused the rest of the room. In the middle, two huge sofas faced each other, with a coffee table in between. Also, a grand piano sat majestically at one end.

Bradley noticed me eyeing up the instrument. "I don't play," he admitted. "It came with the apartment. It's a Steinway. You can stay the night if you like."

I was tempted to say yes, but my voice of reason reminded me that jumping into bed on a first date was a dumb idea. "No. I need to get home," I told him.

I made a trip to the bathroom before leaving. More marble. Not a *Scarface* 80s type of deal with gold taps. But classy, elegant.

Rummaging around for some mouthwash to mask my alcohol breath, I dug into some drawers. And then I found something disconcerting, something I hadn't been expecting: a gold charm bracelet. The charms each told a story: the Eiffel Tower, a palm tree, a Schnauzer-type dog, dice, a tennis racket, a bottle of champagne. As if each charm represented a memory. It definitely belonged to a woman because it was very delicate. Gold. Men didn't wear charm bracelets, did they? Whose was it? An ex-girlfriend? His sister? Worse, a current girlfriend?

My heart plummeted. Silly. My little jealousies concerning this man were absurd. Did men ever feel this way on a first date? Picking apart every look, every word, every sign? I doubted it. But a little voice told me to dig around some more. I rummaged through the cupboard to see if there were tampons, lipstick, more signs of a female resident. A laundry hamper sat in the corner of the bathroom. In my drunken haziness, I opened the wicker lid and peered inside. Men's dirty socks, boxer briefs, T-shirts. Black Kevlar gloves. What was it about black men's gloves that sent shivers down my backbone? I stuck my hand in and stirred. A lone woman's sheer stocking lay beneath. The kind of old-fashioned silk stocking you held up with a garter belt, the kind they wore in the 60s, the kind the American soldiers in World War Two gifted to European women, like in the movies. I searched for its pair. Nothing. I gently pulled it out.

"Sara? Are you all right in there?"

Guiltily I shoved it back and hid it with a T-shirt. "Yes, fine, almost done."

"You need anything?" he boomed through the door.

"No, I'll be right out. Thanks."

I flushed the toilet, washed my hands and stumbled out, all in record time, my face hot and flushed. Bradley was standing there waiting for me. I couldn't read him. Concerned? Irritated?

"I just get worried when someone hangs out in a bathroom too long," he said.

What did that mean? I wanted to ask him about the vintage stocking, the charm bracelet, and *those* gloves, but of course I didn't. It would have been shameful to admit I was rifling through his dirty laundry.

Bradley, accompanying me to the street, didn't put me into a cab, since I needed the fresh air anyway and was more than happy to go home by foot. I told him I was quite capable of walking home by myself. I wanted to mull over my latest discovery: the charm bracelet, the stocking… because, in all realistic likelihood, Bradley had other relationships. It made sense. With those looks and all that money? He was a major catch.

He insisted upon seeing me home. He linked his arm in mine and showed, as always, perfect manners. "I refuse to let you walk the streets at night," he said. "I read in the paper the other day a woman got murdered on the Upper East Side."

"But the victim knew her killer, didn't she? I mean, it's not as if someone's going to pounce out from behind a tree." I had read something in the paper, though I couldn't remember the details. A date rape in the man's apartment—or was it the girl's?—that had led to murder.

"It's not safe," Bradley said simply.

I couldn't even open my mouth to answer in case I vomited right there on the sidewalk. Never again, I told myself, would I drink so much. But there was Bradley, by my side, ever the gallant gentleman. I couldn't get over how debonair and old-fashioned he was. Like a modern-day Cary Grant. *Was* he seeing other women? The jealous side of me didn't want to contemplate the possibility.

It was around eleven thirty when, at the main door of my apartment building, we bumped into Jack walking Poppy. Poppy and I always did her late-night walk around the block to do her business before I went to bed. Long gone were the days when New York City was a dangerous place to be out at night, despite what Bradley had just said. I felt totally safe. This neighborhood was fine, and Poppy and I always did our night walks, come rain, shine or post-snow slush. Not once had I ever felt threatened or scared.

I had meant to come home a whole lot earlier, though, and felt terrible for inconveniencing Mrs. Scott. She had told me she was a bit of a night owl, but still, no excuse.

Jack was standing there, holding Poppy's leash.

I rushed up to him. "Jack, jeez I'm so sorry I'm late, I didn't realize what time it was. Thanks so much for walking her."

Poppy was whimpering with excitement. I bent down, kissed her head and rubbed her soft, black, pointy ears. She smelled of perfume: Mrs. Scott's *Ô de Lancôme*, the scent I always bought her for Christmas to show my appreciation. "Hey, Popps, did you have a wonderful time?"

"She's done everything," Jack let me know. "Both poop and pee."

Jack adored Poppy too, and would sometimes join me for the round-the-block walk when he was visiting his mom. Jack was arrestingly attractive, though he wasn't my type. It was his eyes that were so mesmerizing. Green like his mother's, and against his pale skin they shone out. His dark hair dropped into twisty curls, and he was lean and quite athletic. His father was from London. Mrs. Scott had met him on a work assignment there. They'd had a brief affair, but when she became unexpectedly pregnant (she didn't, for even one second, consider terminating the pregnancy), she discovered he'd been two-timing her all along and had no intention of settling down, so they parted ways. However, she still kept in touch with his parents. Jack's grandparents played an important part in his life. His father had numerous girlfriends apparently, and so Jack had a whole host of half-brothers and sisters. His father remained aloof and disinterested, even actively uninterested. Jack took his dad's benign rejection in his stride, luckily, because the rest of his British family was so welcoming and loved him to bits.

"Thanks *so* much for walking Poppy," I said again.

Bradley stood by my side, awkwardly.

I turned, and catching Bradley's eye, said, "Good night, Bradley, thank you for a *wonderful* dinner." He frowned. "Sorry," I added, "where are my manners?" I was slurring, being overly effusive. "This is Jack, Bradley. Jack, this is Bradley." I swayed a little and Jack caught me.

Bradley raked his eyes over Jack: up and down, down and up, a haughty air of disdain. He nodded and said hello. The two of them could not have been more different. Bradley, clean-cut, in immaculate jeans, expensive cologne, even when he was on his time-off, and Jack, a groovy, wanna-be Lenny Kravitz (though Jack was white), all cool and trendy, in his orange velvet, 18th century-slash-70s-style coat and silver Converse. Neither of them seemed taken with the other. These men were from different worlds.

Family was Jack's mantra. He was a fabulous son to his mother. He checked in on her pretty much every day; called her, did her shopping and would arrange for it to be delivered. He generally paid her a lot of attention, without grumbling or any misgivings. He had a casual air about him that let you feel that nothing was too much trouble. Like walking Poppy. He did it with grace.

He stood there now. Confident. Unfazed by Bradley's standoffish demeanor.

Bradley gave Jack another curt nod, but didn't shake his hand. He addressed him coolly, "Nice to meet my girlfriend's neighbors." He swiveled on his polished heels and said to me, "Night, honey," kissing me on the lips in a long linger, as if to stake his claim on me. "I'll call you from work tomorrow, babe."

He hadn't called me "babe" before or "honey" for that matter. And *girlfriend?* That, too, was a first.

At least I now knew where I stood.

Jack, Poppy, and I rode up in the elevator together. I kept bumping into him and tripping over. I was pretty wasted. I hadn't drunk this much since college. The aftershock of the kiss with Bradley lingered. I guess I was smiling, feeling buzzy with a throw-all-caution-to-the-wind irresponsibility.

"New boyfriend?" Jack asked, with a hint of a wry smile. The smile said *the guy's a jerk, can't you see?*

"I don't know yet," I answered, my eyes fluttering in a half-mast haze. "Maybe. Why do you care?"

"Because."

"Jealous?" I joked.

He laughed.

I swayed, had to hold onto the rail of the elevator for balance.

Jack gripped my elbow. "Easy, tiger."

His touch felt caring. Nice that we were friends again after what had happened. One thing I could say for Jack: he had been a good friend in the loyalty department, despite what had gone down between us.

He had kept my secret.

Hadn't told a soul.

CHAPTER FOURTEEN

Mrs. Scott

Now

Yes, I was aware that my son Jack was seeing Sara at one point. And I was pleased about it. Did I know he was guarding her secret? No. But then that doesn't surprise me because he's such a loyal kid, a really great person. He and Sara had been hanging out for a couple of months when everything went south. When I asked him what had gone wrong, he told me they'd had a dumb argument about a show on Netflix she thought was sexist. I laughed and told Jack he should get over it, that life's too short to waste on silly disagreements and that he should apologize to her. He told me that Sara was so sensitive, like a bird with a broken wing, and he was worried he'd blown their friendship, and it was too late. *Just apologize already*, I said. *Don't you know anything about women?* And then he said something interesting. He said, "*Sara's not the person you think she is, Mom.*"

CHAPTER FIFTEEN

Sara

Two months earlier. June.

Not *again*. I tossed around in my bed and grabbed my phone. It was three a.m. I groaned. I was so not in the mood to have my sister's voice prattle in my ear. Why would she not let up? I genuinely thought I'd put an end to this.

"What now?" I moaned.

"I'm thinking of being with you in New York," Cecelia told me in a voice so quiet I barely heard her.

My eyes flew wide open. "What do you mean, 'being with me'? You're in Thailand."

"I'm thinking of coming to stay with you. Living together. Sharing clothes and makeup like we used to. Really being part of your life."

My heart missed a beat. What I wouldn't do to have her with me. But under *normal* circumstances. The way it used to be. I snapped back, "No. No. You can't. You can't just move in on me. This can't happen again. No."

"Why not? You just said you missed me."

"No, I didn't. I did not say that."

"But you thought it." I heard her distinctive laugh. Husky and throaty, all in one.

"I do miss you. I miss what we had, what we were."

Silence. I thought she'd gone and I could go back to sleep. But her voice whispered in my ear, "It's Bradley, isn't it?"

Another silence. I would *not* go there. I would *not* let this happen!

More insistent now. "Isn't it?"

I found the appropriate song, "Knowing Me, Knowing You," on my playlist. As if in answer to her question, I pressed play. This time, I wanted to be through with her, I really did.

It was true. I didn't want Bradley to even know she existed or let her anywhere near him. He and I were really connecting. The truth was I was falling pretty hard for him, and I knew Cece would screw it all up.

"Why can't you forgive me?" Cecelia asked. Her voice was a ten-year-old's. "How many years has it been now? Don't you think it's time for you to move on?"

I couldn't answer her. Tears were blocking my vision.

"You haven't even told Bradley about me, have you?"

No, I hadn't. I didn't want to. Bradley and I might be getting serious. I could feel it in my bones. He liked me for *me*. He was attracted to me because of the person I was. There was no room for three in our relationship. There was no way I'd let my twin muscle in.

CHAPTER SIXTEEN

Sara

Now

"Would you say you were… how can I put this… 'watchful' of your twin's outgoing personality?" Detective Pearce asked me. "Her ability to attract men, for instance? Funny that. That you two look so alike but have such distinct personalities. At least, from what we can ascertain from Cecelia's social media page."

I mulled over the question. Was the detective insinuating that I was jealous of Cece? I wondered where that had come from… our unique character traits. And the irony that was bestowed upon us: Cece always yearned to be someone else, and I yearned to be Cece. I hankered after being everything she intrinsically was by nature yet, at the same time, I abhorred it.

Perhaps her role-playing had something to do with our lifestyle. We had seen more countries by the age of ten than most backpackers. My parents were not just doctors, they were humanitarians; they were believers in good and measured the world by how many lives they could save. We lived in so many different countries in Africa, I lost count. My memory is a medley of dusty red villages and little thatched roofs. Flip-flops and poisonous snakes, tents, water wells, skinny cattle, colored woven rugs and smiley black faces and children with swollen stomachs like perfectly round footballs. Flies on snotty faces creeping into the corners of their dark eyes. Waterfalls. The Bush. Laughter. Scrubby yellow grass. Blood-red sunsets and sprawling, wild savannahs. Riding in Land Rovers along bumpy, ravaged roads. Bathwater the color of bricks after our mom would scrub us clean. And my sister—her starring role as doctor—with a stethoscope around her neck, pushing it against my chest and listening to my heart. Cece told me she was a surgeon—she must have only been seven years old. Then she told me she was a UN ambassador, and then president. I believed in her and every role she played. And in the heat of the African sun, I took solace in her cool protective shadow.

She was the sun and I was the shade.

And then we ended up moving to Switzerland. Cece and I hated it. Or I said I hated it because she did. It was cold and white. So very white. The people, white. We had never seen so many pale arms and legs, so many washed-out faces. Privilege didn't sparkle in their eyes the way it should have, so dull and uninspired we thought they were. It was a strange thing that they had so much yet showed so little happiness. We noticed something interesting: the more money people had, and the more perks and creature comforts, the less they appreciated it. We begged our parents to go back to Africa. Cece and I were miserable in Switzerland. Especially Cece, and I latched onto her unhappiness like a limpet to a rock, because that was how our dynamic worked.

It was as if without full sun Cece could not be photosynthesized. That's when we reverted to our twin language. We understood French all right, and we had to write it in class—and German too—but we had *our* language, in our own world. If I had been alone I probably would have blended in, blended into the school and made friends, but being with Cece, I didn't need anyone else. Even our parents took second place. I followed along because that's what I always did; she was my guiding star, my full moon, my sun, and I felt completely lost without her.

It's a strange thing to have parents who are humanitarians working in third world countries. Because whatever your needs are, there is always a child whose needs are greater, who is struggling between life and death, and so your "needs" are just *desires*: a cuddle, a glass of milk, help with your homework. All these non-life-threatening wants must have seemed vacuously insignificant to our parents.

This drew us twins closer together because sometimes we felt the only one we could really rely on was one another. My mother was this far-off ethereal beauty in a white coat, with long tan legs and a ponytail, somehow untouchable, somehow unreachable. My parents' precious time was allocated to *special* children. Cece and I shrank into ourselves. We were like a walnut in a shell; two halves making up one whole, and the shell a tough nut to crack.

We were our own protection.

But I wasn't about to mention my parents to the detective. That was the last thing I needed; for her to be digging into that can of worms. If she knew about my parents and what happened, my number would be up.

So I sat there and said nothing.

CHAPTER SEVENTEEN

Sara

Two months earlier. June.

A couple of days after the drunken dinner at Bradley's, I had an important meeting with clients; I was nervous. I selected an old suit—a pant suit—so retro I could get away with it and still be in style. I had already arranged to take Poppy down to Mrs. Scott's.

When we arrived at her bright, sunshiny apartment, decorated with walls of all different colors: one wall yellow, another cerise pink, she opened the door and, as usual, Poppy was all excited to hang out with her. I unclipped Poppy from her dog-wheelchair and bundled her into Mrs. Scott's waiting arms. Her large ears folded back with love and she whimpered with happiness to see her doggy godmother.

"Sara," she said. "That man Bradley, oh my word, he has the best manners in the world. What a *nice* person! He sent me these flowers to apologize for you getting home so late the other night and to say thank you for looking after Poppy. Isn't that nice of him? He really didn't have to do that."

"I had no idea! That *is* nice," I agreed. There was a huge vase of flowers on the hall table with a note attached. Bradley's perfect manners were going almost too far. "That was very thoughtful of him, but it wasn't really his fault. I felt terrible about being so late. I messed up your evening, Mrs. Scott, I'm sorry."

"Nonsense, you're young and you need to go out and have a good time. You've been cooped up in that apartment, and you know it's my great joy to look after Poppy." Poppy was covering her face with kisses, while Mrs. Scott massaged her behind her pointy ears, and all over. "Those hydrotherapy sessions must be making a real difference. The other day she hoisted herself up and was doing really well, almost standing completely on her own!"

I grinned, watching the pair of them. "The sessions really are making a difference, aren't they? The therapist thinks Poppy should be walking within the year."

"That's simply marvelous. Aren't you a strong little girl, Poppy!" She turned her gaze to me. "You look fabulous in that outfit, Sara. You know, you remind me of Diane Keaton in *Annie Hall*."

"Oh, I haven't seen that movie."

"She was all the rage in the seventies. Everybody wanted to look like Diane Keaton and dress like her. You've managed to get the Annie Hall look without even trying. Good luck with your meeting, honey."

"Thanks so much. You know, usually I do everything by email and send all my work digitally or give them my website to look at, but when you meet people in person it makes such a difference, I think. The personal touch. So when they invited me in to meet them, I jumped at the chance. There's nothing like a one-to-one meeting to build trust. You need to see someone's face. You can always tell if someone's a good person from the look in their eyes, don't you think?"

"I do. I really do. And by the way, I hope you'll introduce me to your charming young man."

Sending flowers to Mrs. Scott? It made me wonder about Bradley… it was as if he was too good to be true.

I was about to find out my instincts were right.

CHAPTER EIGHTEEN

Bradley

This slow-burn dating thing? Bradley had never done it before, not like this, not since he was practically in kindergarten. The tentative kisses, the holding hands, the old-fashioned-style court-ship. He usually got them into bed on the first or second date. Sometimes with no date at all.

But there was something about Sara that made him believe he had to go slowly, because she was shy, and even, dare he say it, a little cautious of him. He didn't know why she was so skittish, because he could see it in her gaze: her guarded passion for him. Her eyes spoke to him of a woman in love. But he didn't want to blow it. He really liked her and wanted to make it work. They'd had quite a few dates now and he still hadn't fucked her yet. No, that was the wrong word to use; Sara was *not* the kind of girl you "fucked," she was the sort of person you made love to. He wanted to impress her and make her trust him, yet at the same time he stifled guilty feelings deep inside himself knowing he wasn't good enough and knowing, at some point, he was bound to let her down. As if the whole thing was an act, and yet he hadn't done anything wrong by her.

But he could feel it coming. Brewing inside him.

It was tough for him… being perfect.

She was hard work, Sara was. Not high maintenance or anything like that, just a good, nice girl, and he didn't want to disappoint her. Maybe that was why he had been trying, with all his skills, to impress her. They were such different animals, the two of them. He wasn't artistic like her. Creation seemed to be her driving force. Sara was her unique self, her own true person, without caring how she came across to others, which disarmed him because, unlike most women, he had to use his imagination with her. She kept him on his toes. He had taken her to the Metropolitan (it sounded cool to be "Friends of the Met," and to have membership to all the major museums). Each time he'd read up on various artists and art history so he could prepare his little spiel about whatever or whomever. The memberships were not cheap, but it was worth the investment.

See the way he handled the paint here? That was pretty avant-garde in its day. See how loose it is? How free? Nobody was doing that back then. Or, notice the symbols here? That peach represents fertility, that feather, divinity and spiritual growth.

The other day he had taken Sara to the Japanese wing at the Met and talked for over half an hour on such and such. He couldn't even remember half the bullshit that poured from his mouth, but it seemed to have had its effect. Sara even decided to create a new book cover for a client with a Japanese inspired kimono.

His hard work paid off. She finally invited him to her apartment. A modest, rent-controlled one bedroom on the Upper East Side. Messy, arty, a little cramped. She made him dinner. Her cooking wasn't as bad as he expected. An Indian vegetable dish with rice. Pretty good actually. It was strange the way there were no pictures of her family in her apartment. He hounded her somewhat about meeting them, and she reluctantly agreed. He wasn't quite sure what Sara was so secretive about, but she was hesitant. Kept telling him that her family no longer played a role in her life, that she was, for all intents and purposes, alone.

It was the tail end of June by the time they set off for dinner to meet her family. It was one of those sweltering New York evenings, the sidewalks giving off a whiff of garbage, the heat sultry in the air, ambulance sirens, car horns bleeping more often than usual: angry people caught in traffic jams. Bradley didn't keep a car in New York City. He knew only too well how road rage could creep up on him. Yes, he had a temper that could flare up if his buttons were pushed. If he went anywhere, he took the train or a plane and rented a car the other end.

On the walk to Sara's mom's apartment, he bought a bunch of flowers at one of the corner grocery stores, and as he and Sara were walking into the lobby, Sara holding his hand, she told him, with a slight tug, "I have a confession to make."

"What?" he said, curious.

"You assumed you'd be meeting my mom?"

He nodded.

"We're not meeting my actual mom tonight."

"What do you mean by 'actual'?"

"Well, she's been like a mother to me, but she's actually my aunt. Robbie will be there too: he's my cousin but kind of like a brother."

"So what about your parents?"

"They're not around."

"Do they live in New York?"

"No."

She didn't elaborate, and he didn't care to push it further. She had mentioned her parents before, in conversation. Had told him that they were both doctors and she'd spent much of her time in Africa when they worked for Doctors Without Borders—Médecins Sans Frontières. Not like doctors in the States who make a fortune, but the kind who eschew healthy salaries and live simple lives in out-of-the-way places to help those in need. Admirable. It sounded as if Sara had led a fairly humble childhood without much money or comfort. Yet there was a lot about Sara he didn't know. She was hiding something, and he hadn't found out what yet.

As they rode up in the elevator, she was nervous and fidgety, kept twiddling her hair and looking at herself in the mirror. The elevator was an old-fashioned, wooden kind, paneled, with a rickety old mirror. The building was pre-war.

"Did you know," she said breathlessly, "people never complain about an elevator taking too long when there's a mirror? It's a trick companies use: if you put mirrors in waiting rooms, people don't notice how long they're waiting because they can entertain themselves."

A little boy and his mother were also in the elevator. The child fixed his innocent gaze on Bradley, peeping at him from beneath a set of lustrous long lashes, then looked away and clutched his mom's skirt. Bradley felt uneasy. These days, what was a man meant to do with a child he didn't know? Smile back? Say something? Anything could be construed as inappropriate, so he didn't smile. Sometimes being a grown man sucked. When he was a boy, things were different. Now you had to watch every move you made, every word you uttered. Instead, he shot Sara a grin that said, "Cute kid, one day that'll be us." The kid and his mom got out at the eighth floor.

Seconds later, the elevator door opened and they arrived at the twelfth floor. Sara held Bradley's hand and gave it a little squeeze. He wasn't sure if she was reassuring him or needed reassurance herself. Then she leaned up and kissed him, bringing her other hand over his as if sealing a deal, as if to silently say, *You are my boyfriend, here we go, good luck.*

The door to their apartment was open. Sara's aunt was waiting for them and immediately took Bradley's coat and hung it up on a coat stand. She was cold, brisk but very polite. A WASPy type. Blonde, tall, her features quite like Sara, but without the smile and without the softness of face.

"How do you do, Bradley, I'm Jenny," she said, in an efficient tone.

The cousin, Robbie, was nowhere to be seen. Then Bradley spotted him through an open doorway, slumped on a couch in the living room, playing with his phone or some kind of gadget. The apartment was tidy but pretty cramped. Normal: most regular people in New York lived in small spaces, especially in Manhattan.

"Robbie!" Jenny called out to the living room. "We have company, put that thing down, learn some manners. And take off that ridiculous baseball cap. I've told you a million times it's rude for men to wear hats inside."

Robbie's feet were on the couch. The loafer heaved himself up and ambled toward them with a kind of roll-like swagger as he walked, his purple Lakers cap turned backwards. He must have been around nineteen or in his early twenties. Robbie reluctantly took off the cap to reveal a shock of red hair and freckles and a surly scowl on his face. Bradley wished he hadn't ingratiated himself into their home. These people weren't even Sara's immediate family. He wanted to grill her, to find out what her backstory was, and why she didn't see her parents. He handed Jenny the bouquet of flowers with an awkward thrust of his hand. They were nothing special, just a mixed bunch of whatever—but he hated turning up empty-handed to a home.

"How sweet of you, Bradley," Jenny said. "I'll put them in a vase right away."

"I'll fix you a drink," Sara said. "What would you like?"

Bradley replied without hesitating, "A scotch on the rocks."

"Coming right up." She headed toward the kitchen, and Bradley followed Robbie into the living room. There were two large windows and the early evening light was flooding into the room. Despite this being a pre-war building, the furniture and décor gave the place a contemporary, Nordic touch. Everything was pale gray. Two old sofas that had seen better days faced each other; a coffee table piled with *National Geographic* magazines in between: nothing out of position except a big dip in the sofa where Robbie had been lounging. Bradley imagined how Jenny must be itching to plump up the cushions but she was in the kitchen with Sara. He got an instant feeling that Jenny had almost given up on her son, the way some mothers do when they can't stand the admonishing nag of their own voice anymore. There was a heavy, unhappy, family vibe in the air. Strange how he was so attuned to that. Getting away from his own family had been the biggest priority of his life, especially his mother. He'd been avoiding her calls all week. He imagined how hard it must be for Jenny to have a teenager living with her in this small apartment.

He already wished he were somewhere else. He could discern low mumbling voices and had a strong suspicion Jenny and Sara were talking about him. This apartment was a far cry from Sara's messy home that doubled up as her workplace, overflowing with books, clippings of magazines, and newspapers used for inspiration.

"So how long have you known Sara?" Robbie asked, a red eyebrow raised. His eyelashes were pale blond. He was deathly thin, his shoulders faintly stooped, and Bradley wondered if he dabbled with drugs.

"Just over a couple of months now."

"Oh yeah?" Robbie said, with an ironic curl of his mouth as if he knew something Bradley didn't: a nasty little secret. Bradley disliked him instantly. It made him wonder. What was Sarah not telling him? He wandered around the room and browsed the bookshelf. There were books on philosophy and psychology. Art and architecture. No novels. Placed lovingly here and there were photos in large silver frames. A picture caught his eye: two Saras in one.

"Who's this?" Bradley asked Robbie, pointing at Sara number two.

Jenny appeared holding a tray of canapés. "Why that's Cecelia," Jenny said, bemused, as if Bradley should have known all along. "Sara's identical twin."

Bradley felt as if he'd been punched in the gut. Two months nearly, of dating Sara, and she'd never mentioned a twin? "I had no idea," he mumbled, and then felt embarrassed. He couldn't recall her ever mentioning a sister, let alone a twin. The picture had been taken a long time ago. Sara and her twin looked around fifteen years old. That moment in life when a girl is not quite a girl anymore and isn't an adult either. They really did look identical.

"I had no idea," he muttered again, studying the photo. They were standing by a Land Rover, dark hair sweeping over Sara's face—or was it Cecelia's face? half-hidden.

"Sara's been telling her little lies again?" Robbie said with a smirk.

"Robbie," admonished Jenny, setting the tray on the coffee table and slipping back out of the room.

Robbie swaggered up beside Bradley. His acrid breath was close enough to smell. Bradley stepped aside.

"Look," Robbie began. "You seem like a nice guy, but I'm not so sure Sara's ready to date right now, so…"

Sara glided into the room holding a scotch for Bradley. She didn't have a drink herself.

Bradley took the glass, ice clinking. He threw back a large gulp. "I was just looking at that photograph of you and your twin. How come you never told me about her?"

"Oh, didn't I?" Sara said breezily, with a nonchalant shrug of the shoulders. Sara, too, slipped out of the room, and Bradley was left with Robbie, alone once again.

"You really do *not* wanna get involved with Sara and her other half, believe me," Robbie said. "My advice? Stay clear."

Bradley shot a look at Robbie to gauge whether he was pulling his leg or not. It didn't seem so. Robbie stood there, his gangly frame uneasy, as if he'd had a growth spurt; his arms too long for his body, his legs somewhat bowed.

"Why?" Bradley asked. "What's Cecelia like?"

"You haven't seen her Instagram page?"

"No. Hell, I didn't know anything about her until five minutes ago."

Robbie held back another in-the-know smirk. "You will. At sea—as in ocean—lower dash Celia with an e. Check it out, it'll blow your mind, she's a total babe. She's like uncorked champagne. If you un-pop Cecelia, watch out, she'll be all over you in a hot sticky mess."

What a weird way to describe someone, Bradley thought. Robbie, despite his snake-like personality, had an inventive way with words.

Bradley was so stunned during the course of the evening by what he'd heard about Sara's twin that he hardly concentrated nor even tuned into what people were saying… making small-talk about this and that. Jenny asked him lots of questions about his family. She was obviously vetting him, wondering if he was good enough for her niece. He felt like he was on automatic pilot.

"My dad owns a chain of hardware stores and my mother's a teacher," Bradley told her. "My sister works in community service and has two kids, my brother's a counselor. You know, suburbia-land, nothing out of the ordinary."

Jenny nodded politely at everything Bradley said, telling him how she too was a teacher at a local private school—she taught math—but he could feel how stilted the conversation was, how uneasy, and he doubted she was taken with him. It was just a feeling he got. And when the women were in the kitchen again and he had made an excuse to go to the bathroom (so he didn't have to suffer Robbie's bad breath and inane grin), just as Bradley was coming out, he heard Jenny and Sara talking in angry whispers.

"Why did you have that photo out?" he heard Sara say.

"I didn't put it there," Jenny hissed back. Then Bradley heard, between clanking of dishes, "Crazy stuff" and, "Do you hear me? Get a grip, young woman."

Bradley made out the words "Midwestern boy." He couldn't fathom what she was on about, but it sounded negative in some way. Negative about him. Bradley was pretty sure Sara was falling for him, and he didn't want this prickly aunt getting in the middle of their relationship. He hoped Jenny didn't wield too much influence over her niece.

He couldn't wait to leave and check out Cecelia's Insta account.

CHAPTER NINETEEN

Sara

Taking Bradley to meet Jenny and Robbie was a huge, fat mistake. What had I been thinking? Robbie, with his sly, devious ways, always trying to bring me down and get the better of me. I could tell Jenny did not like Bradley one bit, yet I didn't understand why. I thought she'd be pleased.

Poor Bradley chatted away as best he could, aware, obviously, that he was not liked by Jenny (or Robbie, but then Robbie doesn't like anyone). Although I did notice Robbie eyeing up Bradley's tailored suit and talking to him in an obsequious suck-up way after he spotted his Patek Philippe watch, as if Bradley's riches might rub off on him.

Jenny spent most of her time in the kitchen, avoiding Bradley. I had no idea why she took an instant dislike to him considering he was being perfectly polite. He told her about his job, his long hours, how work was just a means to an end. And all the while his eyes passed over me as if we were a real item, he and I, and that our relationship would be moving onto the next level soon. "Of course, Sara and I hit it off immediately," he'd said. "She understands what's important in life. Look at her with Poppy. Sara's a keeper," he'd said.

And he had spotted that photo of Cecelia and me in the living room. It hadn't been there before. Robbie must have put it there. I felt like the world was spinning off its axis, changing into slow motion and I'd topple off, be disconnected from everything I had called mine, and that Bradley, fascinated by what he saw, would start digging. Meddling with something he should stay away from. I could see it wash over his good-boy, salt-of-the-earth face. Curiosity. Fascination. Disappointment.

His expression told me: *You have betrayed me. You have lied by omission.*

I knew, after this moment, there was no turning back. My heart did a nosedive. He had won me over and now things would be really screwed up. And then, just as expected, Robbie admitted to me on the phone yesterday that he had told Bradley all about Cecelia's Instagram account. Robbie's voice was jeering, teasing me. He let Bradley know that Cecelia was "a hottie" and to look her up.

"It'll be just like last time"—Robbie laughed—"Bradley will see that ass and get all hot under the collar."

"No," I said. "That won't happen."

"You think you got her under control? You're kidding yourself," he sneered. "Are you going to *see* her when she gets here? Hang out with her? How about a family photo of you two together all coochy-coo just like the old days?"

"Please, Robbie," I snapped. "Stop being cruel."

Robbie was untrustworthy. Unpredictable. He knew my secret, and I was terrified he'd do something to compromise me, to ruin my life. Letting Bradley anywhere near him had been like playing the lottery. But then Robbie was family. And with family you often forget, don't you? You gave your family second chances, and third chances, to your detriment.

Robbie was a live mine.

Bradley hadn't called for three days. I kept thinking I'd bump into him in the park, but no. I was beginning to wonder if he had ghosted me. I knew what men were like; if you chased them, it just made them run further away, but still, I could not resist sending him a text message.

Coffee in the park?

No answer.

I could feel it in my bones. Things were going to go wrong from now on. He had seen Cecelia.

Sensing that my world was sinking down around me, I flung all my energy into Poppy and my work. Luckily, I had a commission to do a romcom book cover, which was the perfect distraction and pick-me-up for how I was feeling. The brief was an illustrated couple and a basset hound.

I brought out my gouache paints, mixed up all sorts of beautiful pastel colors and, after a whole bunch of sketches—of a cute couple in the park with the dog, the bench, and some trees—I felt like I was getting the image I wanted. *Light! Fun! Happy! Love!* the cover cried out. All these things that had been taken away from me by introducing Bradley to my family, or what was left of them anyway. I wondered what my real mother and my dad would think of Bradley. Maybe he was all wrong for me. If he was, it didn't make it any easier. I was in too deep now. Then I was reminded of something: how you can't have love without pain, so it was easier not to let love in. Like a fool I had let my guard down. Opened myself up to love.

Out of the blue—because I *was* feeling blue, the darkest blue—my phone buzzed. I grabbed it, thinking it would finally be Bradley, but it was Robbie again. I willed myself to ignore the call, but curiosity made me pick up. I still couldn't believe I'd taken Bradley over there for dinner.

"What?" I said. "What do you want?"

"Bradley texted me. He asked me for Cecelia's number."

I knew this would happen. "How did he text you? You gave Bradley your number? Why?"

"He said he could find me a job in finance."

Robbie was unemployed and living off his mother. He was supposedly job-hunting, but I knew all he was doing was loafing around, playing videogames and going on porn sites.

"What should I tell him?" Robbie asked.

"Anything. Tell him she's dead, for all I care," I barked at him.

He laughed. "Hey, I forgot to ask. How did you get the rich boyfriend anyway? You used the deformed dog as bait so he'd feel sorry for you?"

"Don't ever call me again, Robbie."

The idea of Bradley drooling over Cece's Instagram account made my stomach roil. He was angry with me, I deduced, for not being honest with him, for not letting him know about my twin. But surely he'd forgive me?

I wondered if he would be able to tell us apart.

Unlike Cece, embracing my sexuality, my sensuality, was something I had shied away from. Her Insta pictures were me... but tan. Me... but pouty. Me... but hotter. Suddenly I felt inadequate as if I, Sara, was not enough for him. Surely now he knew about my twin, I'd fade into the background?

I had been tempted to jump into bed with Bradley soon after I'd met him. I mean, who wouldn't? He was handsome, very sexy, his physique strong and muscular... a total catch by any woman's standards. But... something held me back. I felt like I was in an airplane wearing a parachute and somebody was telling me to jump. I just wasn't ready for it. I was standing at a precipice of decision-making, and a voice was warning me *No, you're not strong enough for this!*

I had met him at an awkward moment in my life when I had sworn myself off men, at least, in a romantic sense. How I would have loved to just have fun with a man without getting hurt. Maybe some women can separate sex with love, but I wasn't able to do that. At least I *had* never been able to, not after what I knew, what I'd seen. I would have loved to be the no-strings-attached type, but I wasn't that person.

I thought of Cecelia.

I always wondered what it was like to be her.

CHAPTER TWENTY

Sara

My mother used to call Cece and me her "little soldiers" because when we walked we did so in synchronicity: the same foot forward, the same pace. We might even start skipping at exactly the same time, or running. Like a flock of birds who veer to the left or the right, just knowing instinctively what the other is doing, Cece and I needed no words. We would drink simultaneously at the dinner table: pick up our glasses in unison at the same precise moment, put them down with one single clunk. Or we'd stop for breath together, or widen our eyes at the same time, doing everything as one unit. It wasn't that we wanted to be like this, it was just the way things were. The way *we* were.

You would think that Cecelia, being the leader out of the two of us, was the smart one, but that wasn't the case. She didn't have much interest in her studies the way I did. She felt ambivalent about history or geography, or math. She said that if she didn't experience it firsthand, it meant nothing to her. So while I was reading Jane Austen and learning about love, she was doing it for real. Cecelia was the one who had the first kiss, the one who told me what it was like to have a boy's hands on her naked waist. "It tingles," she said. "Makes me funny inside. And boys dribble when they kiss."

I tried to live vicariously through her, but I felt the chasm. I couldn't be her, but I wanted to be. I envied her, even if I no longer understood her. I wanted to feel the same: think what she thought, feel what she felt. But Cece and I were sipping our breaths in unison less often. We were slowly becoming individuals, and it confused me.

I was no longer swimming in her slipstream, and when I veered away, Bobby came into the picture. She was this gangly beautiful creature with long legs, elongated arms that hung cool by her side, hair in dreadlocks, her ebony skin smooth as velvet, eyes hazel and huge. She was possessive about Cece. And she didn't want boring old bookworm me hanging around tainting Cece's coolness. Then a boyfriend appeared on the scene, which sent Bobby wild with jealousy. Cece had another life, lived in an alternative world that didn't include me. They were fighting over her: boys, girls, all of them. I sank into myself, relied on my inner strength, more than ever.

It was the prelude of what was yet to come.

CHAPTER TWENTY-ONE

Sara

Now

"Would you say you and your sister are identical? I mean, technically, yes, you're identical twins, but apart from the mole on her cheek, are there other body marks or physical differences between the two of you?"

I shook my head. Our toes were somewhat different, but I wasn't about to share that with Detective Pearce.

"And your personalities?"

Wiggling on the chair, I thought about what the detective had just asked me. Our personalities? Memories are strange, elusive things. You can't pin them down or bring them to you at will: they live with you in some hazy form and pop in and out of your consciousness at unbidden moments. As I sat there during this interview, lights glaring, eyes glaring, Cece came to me as a mermaid, deep under the water moving her tail the way a dolphin moves her tail. Of course Cece must have been pressing her legs tightly together, her toes pointed, her arms undulating to make herself look so authentic, so convincing to me. But I remembered how I truly believed that my sister was a real live mermaid. I did. I believed her. Was it the sea? A swimming pool? Blue, blue water, anyway. The water felt bottomless. Brittany? No, it was warm water.

"Cecelia was the extrovert one, right?"

I nodded, a lump in my throat, tears spilling down my face.

"Get her some water," Detective Pearce told the good cop. "Take your time," she said in a softer tone. "Recollect your thoughts, Miss Keller."

I tried to remember. I couldn't recall how old Cece and I were when we began to develop individual personalities and roles. She was the gregarious one, the showoff, the one who attracted—and demanded—attention. I was her quiet shadow, her thought keeper. She'd tell stories, by flashlight, as we hid under the sheets at night, and I would illustrate her stories—fairy tales or spooky ghost stories—with pastels or my colored pencils the next morning. I'd awake at the squawk of dawn, while Cece remained sleeping, so I could surprise her with my handiwork. Dragons or witches or whatever crazy tale she had invented. She'd make up voices for her characters. Deep cavern-like growls for gremlins, raspy witches with rabbit teeth. She was quite a little actress. She loved to perform in front of any audience. When it wasn't me, it would be our parents or their friends. Cece would create costumes from old T-shirts, even bits of trash, or dishcloths from the kitchen. Then I would draw her in action. Put her zaniness down on paper with my pastels as fast as I could, rendering her into some tangible form, because she flitted here and there in her ethereal fairyish way, and it was so hard to capture her in the moment before she'd change into another character, change her role.

Mercurial was the word. I could never pin her down.

Yet she was mine. She'd always belong to me, would always be the one half my soul. A bond like that could never be broken.

Whatever I did.

CHAPTER TWENTY-TWO

Sara

Two months earlier. Early July.

Finally Bradley called. The dinner at my aunt's had been over a week ago.

From the tone of his voice on the phone, I couldn't read him. I wasn't sure if he was furious with me for keeping Cece a secret, or hurt. A wild rush of happiness ran through my body when I heard his voice, even though there was a tinge of doubt plaguing me: would he want to split up with me? I could fix this, I told myself. I'd explain everything. I liked him too much to let this problem fester.

He invited me to dinner that evening, to his apartment.

This time, he hadn't made so much of an effort. That in itself told me how he was taking this. A little betrayed, no doubt. And I didn't blame him.

It was raining outside, so we didn't sit in the conservatory, or in the roof garden. The patter of summer raindrops on the kitchen window smeared the view into a haze of green and cubist blocks of gray: the swaying trees and profiles of apartment buildings. I looked out, contemplating my situation. Suddenly everything felt sad. No cocktails, just white wine. Bradley was still dressed in his work clothes: a charcoal-grey pinstripe suit. He wore a silver tie pin that clipped a silk scarlet tie—probably Italian—in place.

The faint crescents under his eyes indicated tiredness. I knew he put in long hours on Wall Street. I wanted the romantic Bradley back, the one who gazed into my eyes.

I broke the ice. "Everything okay at work?"

"Dealing with a big merger right now. Crunching lots of numbers." He didn't elaborate.

"Late nights?"

"Too many."

"Is that why you didn't call?"

"No."

His "no" was clipped. I was dreading what would come next, so I said, "I'm so sorry I didn't tell you about my sister."

Silence. He shrugged. Then he said, "It's not just that. It's like… your family, too. I thought I was coming to meet your mother for dinner, until you let me know at the last minute it was your aunt and cousin I'd be meeting. I just don't get it. I don't get why you didn't tell me the truth."

"I never lied to you, Bradley. I said we'd be going to meet my family. And I did fill you in before we arrived. A little late in the day, true, but I—"

He interrupted, not buying my excuse. "I have to admit I felt… I don't know." He sighed. I could see the hurt emanating from his gaze as he held my eyes. *Please*, I thought, *don't let this come between us.*

"I wasn't ready," I replied, in my defense. "I didn't know if I could trust you. I mean, you know, one hundred percent."

"Trust me?"

"Jenny has tried really hard to be like my mom—"

"Well, where *is* your mom? Is she dead or something?"

"Yes."

He grimaced. "Oh crap, I'm sorry, Sara. Damn, that sounded so callous the way I said that. Sorry, honey."

The "honey" felt nice. I could tell he cared. Did I trust him enough to tell him everything? The whole truth? No. Not all of it. No way.

He let a few beats go by then asked, "You want to tell me what happened?"

I hated reliving the events of that day. Never spoke about it, because every time I did a series of gruesome images flashed across my mind. I took a deep breath, and on the exhale said, almost in a monotone, just stating the facts, "My parents died in a car crash, in Africa. Cecelia was driving. She was high."

Bradley took my hand and weaved his fingers through mine. "Oh my God, I'm so sorry. That's horrible. When did this happen?"

"Nearly ten years ago."

"Yet your sister survived. Shit, I can see how upset you must've been with her, but at least she's—"

"We don't speak," I said, clipping off any ideas he may have had about meeting Cecelia, or persuading me that I needed to be more forgiving. I had forgiven her, I had, but forgetting was another thing altogether.

I wanted to make it clear to Bradley that Cecelia was not part of my life anymore. He didn't need to know the gamut of craziness that was me and my sister. That even though I no longer saw her, we still had a very screwed-up relationship. "My aunt has been my family. And Robbie. For what he's worth."

Bradley shook his head. "I can't say I warmed to him at dinner the other night, to be honest."

"No. Few people do," I said. "Yet you gave him your number?"

He frowned; his dark eyebrows knitted. "No, I don't remember doing that."

"He said you did."

He let go of my hand. "He wanted to know if I could get him a job and asked how much money I made."

"Seriously?"

"I told him I had signed a non-disclosure agreement with my company that prohibited talking about my salary and bonus."

"That is so tacky," I said, ashamed of Robbie.

"I just wish you trusted me more, Sara."

I looked down at my wine glass, rolling its stem between my fingers. "I've had to fend for myself for a long time. I guess I'm a little tough on people when it comes to trusting them. It's not personal, I promise."

He pushed an errant strand of my hair away from my face. "I think we could have a future together, you and I. Look, I don't want to rush anything or put pressure on you, but I really like you. I mean… a lot."

I smiled. Felt my cheeks heating, sweat gather behind my knees and all the creases in my body. I was thrilled but nervous. I felt exactly the same way, but if I gave him all my heart, what if he broke it? "But you don't even know me," I said, savoring his sweet words. "Not really. Not at all."

"I know enough. I know you're kind, Sara. You try, and you want to do the right thing. You put others first before yourself. You're a little quirky, true, but I like quirky. How many women your age would look after a dog who's handicapped—"

"Handi-capable…"

"Handi-capable, my apologies. You care about ecology, about making the planet a better place. You care about your work. You take pride in what you do. I looked through your website. Your designs are exquisite. Unusual too. A sense of fun and beauty. Honey, I know this sounds crazy to say this… we haven't known each other very long… but I think I'm falling in love with you. Real love. A respectful kind of love. That's worth so much more than just having a good time in bed. And before you came along that's what I'd gotten all wrong. I'd pursued women for the wrong reasons. Half the time I didn't even like—"

"Please!" My hand, fluttering in a kind of panic at the thought of Bradley with another woman, knocked my wine glass over by mistake, and it shattered to the floor. I didn't want to know about his exes. I stared at the broken mess I'd made, and mumbled, "I'm sure your ex-girlfriends were all very beautiful and sexy and hot, but I'd rather not think about them." I actively forced away the memory of the charm bracelet and the sexy silk stocking. It was past. Done and dusted. Bradley was into *me* now.

"Sorry. Let me clean that up," I said, getting up, wondering where Bradley kept a pan and brush in this pristine room where nothing was out of place.

But he leaped up. "Stay put, let me do it."

A calm filled the atmosphere. He presented me with another glass and filled it with more white wine, then went about his business, retrieving a broom from a closet. Quietly, he swept up the mess I'd made, the sound of broken glass clinking, as I held my thoughts together about my unbidden moment of jealousy. Just picturing Bradley kissing someone else made my skin prickle, let alone him being on top of some gorgeous, gregarious brunette or blonde, or anyone who wasn't me. I wasn't naive; I was aware of how he must have played the field, with all his money and good looks, but I didn't want to delve into that. Being a very visual person I already had a slideshow of images in my head.

It brought my sister to mind. *No. Just… no*, I scolded my active imagination.

He was on his knees, sweeping every skinny shard up, almost with glee. My outburst hadn't fazed him one bit, just the opposite. "I've been controlling myself, Sara. Saving myself, if you like. You're *perfect* for me," he said. "Perfect."

CHAPTER TWENTY-THREE

Sara

It was the middle of the night. I was spinning, drunk in my bed. I had ended up quaffing quite a bit of white wine at Bradley's. Now I'd ended up deep in conversation with Cece again, phone by my side. Most of what I said didn't even make sense.

"You're full of shit and you *know* it," she hissed. "I'm destined to be part of your life, *our* life, stop trying to push me away."

What were we discussing? I'd lost the thread of conversation at some point.

I rolled over in bed. "Why can't things just stay as they are?"

"You need to stop lying to yourself about you and me. And by the way, you should stop seeing that OCD freak Bradley."

This was a one-eighty. I couldn't believe I was hearing this! I had told her what a gentleman he was. How we hadn't even had sex yet, and how respectful he was of me. "Stop bullying me! Stop trying to get the better of me," I said.

Cece snickered. "When I meet him you'll see what he'll do, how he'll behave. Remember that charm bracelet you found? You should've taken that bracelet."

"Stolen it?"

"Used it as evidence. That's not stealing."

"Evidence? Why are you so suspicious? Always digging around for the worst!"

"I'm only looking out for you because you're not listening to my voice of reason."

"No," I slammed back at her, "you just don't want me to have a life."

I put my head under my pillow to block out any more. Let myself be soothed by white noise in my ear instead, the pillow pressed against my head.

I needed to ignore her mean words, ignore her crazy advice.

CHAPTER TWENTY-FOUR

Sara

Jack and I sat at a simple wooden table, in a Japanese restaurant on Third Avenue. Jack never had any money on him, so this place was perfect. Cheap, but with great food. We ordered. Jack, sushi, and for me, vegan maki rolls. Then miso soup, salads, and jasmine tea for two, all for less than fifteen dollars a head.

Jack had a job in a local architect's office. It looked good on paper, but his pay wasn't the greatest. He had stuck with it though because he hoped it would lead to a better, higher paying job somewhere down the line. A love of art, architecture, and design were the main things we had in common. His passion was bridges, the Brooklyn Bridge being his favorite of all. He had enlightened me about Emily Warren Roebling, the wife of the chief engineer who built the Brooklyn Bridge, Washington A. Roebling, and how, when he fell ill, it was she who oversaw its construction—the longest spanning bridge in the world at the time—in her petticoats and dresses, with her genius for calculations and so on. These were the kinds of conversations Jack and I had. We could chat into the wee hours of the morning. In fact, this rapport about art and design was what had attracted me to Jack in the first place. Why we had become friends.

But he looked preoccupied today. Even jittery. I wondered why he had been so insistent about having lunch, last-minute.

"What was so important you needed to see me in person?" I asked, moving my purse from the tabletop and hooking the strap onto the back of the chair.

He poured us both some tea from a pretty pottery teapot and opened the lid, giving the steam a quick sniff. "Did you know they put roasted rice in here? That's why it has a nutty flavor." He was wearing a voluminous shirt, a sort of pirate shirt, and a bright red silk scarf, his dark hair long but less unkempt than usual. He had a pretty cool style.

"What did you want to talk to me about so urgently?" I asked again. I had a deadline. Needed to get an author's logo finished by five o'clock. Poppy was safely with Jack's mom but I was juggling my timeline: collect Poppy for her walk in the park, the logo… or vice versa, get the logo done and then the walk, or would it be too late?

"You're not gonna like this," Jack said, leaning in conspiratorially.

The waiter arrived with our salads and soup.

"Shoot," I said. "Tell me what's on your mind."

"Your boyfriend."

"What about him?"

"He has a shady past."

"Shady? And you know this how?"

Jack brought his voice down to a hoarse whisper. "Look, his ex-girlfriend Cassandra Ross killed herself. A year and a half ago."

I let the information sink in. A thump in my heart. "That's… awful. How do you know this? He never told me this." I brought the miso bowl to my lips and slurped, but it was too hot.

Jack speared a lettuce leaf with his chopstick. "Have you asked about her?"

"No," I admitted. "I don't think it's healthy to get into details about exes. Everybody has a story and baggage, and I don't think it's great to drag that baggage into new relationships. All it does is cause jealousy and hurt and anger. Even when people pretend they don't care, they do care."

He finished his mouthful then said, "Yeah, well, Bradley has *baggage* all right."

"I've purposely avoided asking Bradley about his exes. Are you sure about this? That she killed herself? Jack, how do you even know this?"

"A little birdie."

"What birdie?"

He looked around the room to make sure nobody was listening to our conversation. The restaurant was half empty. There was a wall of giant bamboo cane between the eating part and where the wait staff went, behind the reception desk. A couple sat at the other end of the restaurant engrossed in quiet chatter. Jack flicked his red scarf behind his neck, away from the table. "Cassandra's boss... she worked as a paralegal, is good friends with my boss. Small world, huh?" Jack lifted the miso bowl to his mouth and sipped.

"That's a pretty weird coincidence."

"It is," he said. "Bradley was the last person to see Cassandra alive apparently. In fact, he as good as watched her die."

"*What* are you talking about?"

"One day Cassandra just ended up dead. Bradley was the one to find her."

I flinched. "How horrible."

Jack raised his eyebrows and gave a knowing shrug.

"What are you trying to say?" I pressed.

"She was young."

"How did she die? Did she take her own life?"

"Your guess is as good as mine."

"My guess is that he must've been devastated."

"If he was devastated I think he would've talked to you about her, no?"

"Maybe not. That's a very private thing. Maybe he feels guilty... maybe he let her down in some way, or didn't lend her money, or... look there might be a thousand reasons why—"

"You're making excuses for him."

"You think it was his fault?"

"More than just his fault. One minute alive, the next dead, what do you think?"

I snickered. Unable to believe Jack's conspiracy theory. "This is crazy! What... you're making out he *murdered* her?"

"Shush, keep your voice down, Sara. Maybe. Maybe he did."

"*Who* is saying this? Was there a case about it?"

"There was no suicide note."

"Well that proves it must have been an accident!" I took a sip of tea, and after Jack didn't respond, I added, "You still haven't told me how she died."

"Her death seems to be surrounded in secrecy. Weird, no?" His voice was low and quiet.

"Who told you all this, anyway?"

"I heard."

"Well, surely they looked into this? The police. They must have done an autopsy? If they thought anyone was behind this there would have been an investigation, a court case. And if she did kill herself, who says a suicide note is obligatory anyway?"

"I'm just saying. Be careful." His green eyes held mine with urgent warning.

"She took pills or something?"

"Maybe," he said. "Nobody seems to want to talk about it."

"Jack, why are you so suspicious? Sadly, a lot of people overdose, and yeah, it's usually their partner who finds them, that's normal. You're reading way too much into this." I pushed the rest of my salad away. I had lost my appetite, just picturing Bradley's dead ex-girlfriend. Her stone-cold body lying on the floor… Bradley bending over her.

"Your call," Jack said.

"What do you mean 'my call'?"

"Whatever. Just thought I should let you know."

"Well…" I said, a spike of anger in my tone, "thanks for the heads-up. For whatever it's worth."

"It could be worth your life."

Jack met my irritation with a look of pain in his eyes, like he really cared but also felt sorry for me. I imagined Bradley and Cassandra, a couple in love, and now everything made sense. The way our relationship had never moved onto the next level, the way he had been so tentative, respectful. He was probably traumatized at the thought of losing someone again. Terrified to open up his heart.

Jack was just looking out for me, knowing how much I meant to his mother, but somehow I felt violated, like he was trying to hurt me with this nasty, spiky information. I refused to let this come between Bradley and me. No, this would *not* come between us or our relationship.

After I left the restaurant, rolling all this over and over in my mind, Jenny called asking me to come over. And she too had things to say about Bradley. "Stuff you should know," she said.

What the hell was going on?

CHAPTER TWENTY-FIVE

Sara

So I went to Jenny's apartment for dinner, just the two of us. Robbie was luckily not home. Poppy was cozied up on the couch, asleep, splayed out on her back, little white paws in the air, snoring softly. Jenny and I had ordered in Ethiopian food. The luxury of living in New York City: so many diverse cuisines are available from all parts of the world and nearly all restaurants are happy to deliver. We were feasting on wonderful curries, and *shiro* (a chick pea stew), *gomen* (collard greens) and a whole assortment of dishes, all spread on one big platter, eating everything, as is tradition, with our right hand, scooping the food up with *injera* (a sort of spongy flatbread). It made me homesick for Africa.

It was a high-octane life for Cece and me with parents working in medical humanitarianism, often out in the field, wherever they might be sent. It was a life for a single person, doing this dangerous work, yet my parents would not give it up, even after we were born. They would supposedly take turns, so one of them would always be at home with us, but "home" on occasions might even be a mud hut somewhere in a forlorn village, far away from amenities.

Ironic, really, that our mom worked for UNICEF, yet her own daughters were so often left to fend for themselves. We knew no different though, and loved it. We thought our nomadic life normal.

It took a long time after coming to New York, after their deaths, to feel like it was home here. Even the way I spoke was different to regular, "real" Americans. I imitated people so I might use the same intonation, the same expressions, to feel like I belonged in America. Everything was alien to me.

When I arrived, the choices in the grocery stores were so dizzying that sometimes I would just stand there staring in a trance, not knowing where to begin, and might even walk straight out again because I was so overwhelmed. I took to shopping in smaller stores, more manageable for me, or ventured to the farmers market in Union Square on weekends, taking the subway down with one of those old-lady trollies on wheels so I could stock up on fresh vegetables or farm honey. Other than that I didn't venture very far away from the Upper East Side but stayed within the realms of Central Park and my neighborhood, except for going to school. At art school, I tended to gravitate toward other foreigners in my class because that's how I felt: a foreigner in a strange land even though I was American.

At least my passport said so.

I never braved Brooklyn or the Bronx but kept my new world small. It was all I could manage after losing so much. It felt more like a village in this neighborhood. Routine was my stabilizer. Without routine I was lost. I remember the vet warning me, a few years later when Poppy came into my life, that if I wanted to be a good mom to Poppy, "dogs like routine, especially ones with special needs. You'll need to work around *her*, not the other way around, are you ready?" she said.

"I've always been ready," I told her.

It was interesting, ironic too. I had never known routine during my whole childhood. Routine was a luxury.

And now, when I thought about Bradley and his plans for Hawaii, and his throwaway invitation to join him (had he been serious?), though the idea of doing something different excited me, it had taken me so long to settle here in New York, I had to admit I wasn't ready and maybe never would be. I had fought for what I had now. I couldn't give it up.

Jenny had been so welcoming when I came to live with her after I arrived. But Robbie? What do you say to a parent who has a mean-spirited child? When they just don't want to see what is staring them in the face? I lived with Jenny and Robbie for six months but had to get out as soon as I was able to. Jenny's apartment was so small, and having Robbie in such close quarters was impossible.

It was with all these thoughts in my head that Jenny and I sat at her dining room table, in silence.

She finished a huge mouthful of food and, after smacking her lips, raved, "This is *so* good."

"Isn't it?" I agreed. "I think Ethiopian might just be my favorite food. When you live in New York you get spoiled for choice, don't you?"

Jenny, her eyes watery, obviously reminiscing about my mother, said, "You know, I promised Lulu I'd always take care of you." The look she gave me was of pure love. People got Jenny so wrong sometimes, with her brisk outward manner. When she cared, she cared, and would do anything for those close to her.

"I know," I said. "I know how much you miss Mom."

It had been tough for Jenny. Robbie was her stepson. Her husband's child but not hers, at least not by blood. And when he died, at only fifty-eight, Jenny was left as a single mother. So often she threatened to leave New York, move abroad and do something crazy with her life. But here she still was.

"Sara, something… something ju-just came to me last night." Jenny was hesitant.

"What?" I took a sip of beer.

"I couldn't sleep all night and was worrying and worrying about you, because something was jarring in my mind about Bradley and I couldn't think what. And then I remembered. He came to my yoga class one time."

"Oh, really?" I coughed and grabbed some water; my food had gone down the wrong way. "But you didn't recognize him when I brought him here for dinner?"

"I knew I'd seen him before but I just couldn't place him. You know, in yoga class he was probably in a T-shirt and shorts. When he came to dinner he was in a suit. I just didn't put two and two together."

"Why didn't you say something? Like, I don't know… '*Hey, Sara, his face rings a bell.*'"

"I thought maybe I'd seen him at the grocery store or something. No big deal."

I shrugged. "He mentioned to me he'd done yoga for a while but didn't like it."

Jenny finished her mouthful, her eyes on mine. "I think he might've just been there because of all the women in the class. You don't get so many men doing yoga."

I felt a sting. What Jenny was saying about Bradley only being in the class to meet women was hurtful. Why say that? Not the nicest thing to infer about your niece's boyfriend. But I knew where this was coming from: her need to protect me. "So why is it such a weird thing? He's into keeping fit. He also does kickboxing."

"It's not that, it's the fact that, well, he really flirted with our yoga instructor."

"I'm sure he was just being friendly. When was this?"

"A few months ago. Before she stopped teaching at the studio."

"So. He was single then. Before he met me."

"It's just… soon after, she just kind of vanished."

"Vanished?"

"Left the studio."

"So what's that got to do with Bradley?"

"I think they might've been dating."

"How can you be sure it's even him? If you'd known for sure, you would've known it was him at dinner."

"I'm not a hundred percent sure it *was* even him, you're right." She hesitated, took a long gulp of beer. "Just pretty sure. But you say he was into yoga, so that makes sense, doesn't it?"

"So how come he didn't recognize *you* at dinner?" I remembered how formal the conversation was between them, how Jenny had avoided Bradley most of the evening, fussing around in the kitchen.

"The classes are really big," she explained. "I'm in leggings and a leotard and one of so many other women, why would he?"

"I don't know."

"Just so odd our instructor stopped coming," she mused, taking another mouthful of curry.

"Did you ask the yoga studio about where your instructor went?"

Jenny blotted her mouth with a napkin before replying, "They said she went back home to Australia."

"Well, that's *it* then, isn't it?" I gave her an Italian-style, what-the-hell shrug. Why was Jenny reading so much into this?

But she persevered, wouldn't let it rest. "It's just… it didn't feel right because she loved her classes so much and was a really popular teacher. To suddenly stop like that."

"She must've had a reason. Maybe she had a problem with renewing her work visa or something?"

"Maybe. But the real thing that bothers me is that she has an Instagram page. And it just petered out. One moment she was posting all kinds of cool pictures of her doing different asanas and the next saying she was really busy and she'd be back when she could. You know what those Instagram people are like? They don't just stop posting all of a sudden."

I went silent, thinking of Cece's Insta. Jenny and I rarely discussed Cece. It was too upsetting for both of us. Cece was a no-go topic of conversation, and Jenny would have hated that Instagram account if she'd known about it, would have thought the bikini pictures gratuitous and tacky. Robbie had promised not to tell her.

"Anyway," Jenny went on, "it just felt *off*. All of us thought so. All her students."

I took a sip of beer, taking in what she was saying, wondering why she was making such a monumental deal out of nothing. "Are you still going there? To the studio?" I asked.

"Yeah, of course, you know how I like to keep fit? But I really miss my teacher, it just isn't the same without her. In fact, I've swapped over now to Pilates because I prefer the instructor to the new yoga one they gave us, who I just don't think is any good."

I mopped up the last lot of sauce from my plate. "I just don't get what all this has to do with Bradley, Jenny." The idea of Bradley seeing some sexy yoga instructor made me uneasy. Especially considering how lazy I was when it came to exercise classes. I had always hated sweaty, crowded gyms: people watching me, judging my body or my fitness level. Yet this all sounded like something that had happened before Bradley had even met me, so what was the big deal?.

"So when was the last time you had a class with this woman?" I asked. "What's her name?"

"Jacinda. About three months ago."

It was around the same time I started seeing Bradley. When we met in the park, in April. He must have stopped seeing Jacinda after he met me. I had nothing to worry about whatsoever. "What's her Instagram handle?"

"At Yoga Babe hyphen Jace. J.A.C.E."

"I pulled my phone from my purse and went onto Instagram. There she was: @yogababe-jace, last post two months ago. She had nine thousand followers, following just over a thousand. Not a big following, but still, enough for it to be strange that she just suddenly stopped posting. She was pretty. A little disconcerting, I had to admit, because she looked a bit like me.

I flipped through a few of the pictures. They were not beautiful like the glamorous Cecelia posts. Still, I knew how proud Instagrammers were about their accounts. Jenny was right, you didn't just stop posting unless you had a good reason. A flash went through my head of some wild, passionate affair between the two of them—Jacinda and Bradley—Jacinda going home to Australia with her heart broken, tail between her legs, humiliated that America was not the paradise she had supposed. I sort of wondered why Jenny was making such an issue of this though. I thought back to the dinner at Jenny's, when she was so offhand with Bradley to the point of being rude. And that was before her light bulb moment tonight when she realized she definitely knew him. Why had she been so weird with him at the dinner?

"What was it about Bradley you didn't like?" I asked her. Was Jenny overly judgmental? Too protective of me? Though I was being cautious, I had to admit I was falling for him, or worse, already *had* fallen for him. Let's face it, the guy was gorgeous. And he had only been kind to me, and had forgiven me for lying to him. The thing was… could I trust him? Jack, and now Jenny, were now seeding doubts in my mind.

"Just my gut feeling," Jenny said, clearing the plates.

"But he was so polite to you."

She raised a cool brow. "Too polite." She slipped out of the dining room. I heard her load the dishwasher but didn't feel inclined to help after all she had said. She reminded me of my mother: the impassive, "for-your-own-good" tone. The way she spoke before she thought. Before wondering if her words could wound others. I was aware it was just her protective streak, but it still hurt.

Jenny was forty-seven, the same age my mother was when she died. They were ten years apart. Half-sisters, with the same father but different mothers. Cece and I never even met Jenny till we were sixteen. Like Mom, Jenny was also a blonde and very attractive. Her face a little sharp, chin pointed, high cheekbones, skin so glowing it made you stare, and eyes like shards of sea-blue crystal. Sometimes I found it hard to be in the same room as her because their personalities were so similar. Like Mom, Jenny had a clipped manner, and like her often absent in her own, faraway world. Far away, at least, from you. Detached. Aloof. Yet she had been so kind to me. She had lost her husband when she was really young. Never married since, and though Jenny did date, she was discreet. She had welcomed me to New York when I arrived here from Botswana, bewildered but ready for art school. But I only lived with her for a short time, because treading eggshells around spoiled and contentious Robbie was exhausting. It was easier to go solo. But Jenny still kept an eye on me and called every week. She cared about me. I could call her in the middle of the night if need be. I could rely on Jenny.

She came back into the room with two small bowls of ice cream and set them on the table. I was still sifting through everything she'd said about Bradley in my mind, trying to figure out what her motivation was—if any. Was she just looking out for me?

Why did I feel so skeptical?

"Jenny, why did you tell me all this about Bradley?" I tried to keep the sharpness from my voice, aware I might be doing a pretty bad job of it.

"I just think you should be careful of him, that's all. I hate to say this, he's the first guy you've dated in so long, but there's something creepy about him."

My mouth agog, I replied, "I'm sorry, but I do *not* see that. He's drop-dead gorgeous, great manners, kind, makes an effort. I think he's a *great* guy. A super-nice boyfriend."

"Have you introduced him to your friends?"

"No, not yet."

I didn't have so many friends, just work colleagues. One close friend had moved to Los Angeles and had kids, another to Europe. Perhaps I should, I thought, introduce my work friends to Bradley? Yet, our relationship wasn't really like that. I separated work from my private life. So did Bradley, it seemed. He had never mentioned his friends, just an old buddy from home he called now and then, and work people. We were happy with our museum visits, walks in the park, our weekly Sunday brunch. We didn't need an entourage. Some couples thrive in groups, and without them their relationships wither. In truth, some couples can't really stand each other's one-on-one company for very long at all. But Bradley and I even enjoyed each other's silences. We jelled. We were serene together.

"Just be careful," Jenny warned, reaching out to touch my hand.

After I left, Poppy and I went for a nice evening walk near Jenny's apartment building. Past Madonna's house(s), where I had seen a trio of handsome dogs emerge with the dog walker, down the steps. Like real stars themselves, unaware, I supposed, they lived in the lap of luxury. We wheeled and walked past the best Mexican on the Upper East Side, past a little front garden with a bird feeder, where a night bird now chirped, past a row of chic brownstones, chandeliers lighted like low glowing moons in their front living rooms. As we wended through one block after another, heading toward Park, before turning back on ourselves, Poppy barreling along at great speed after her nap at Jenny's, my anger percolated. My trust in my aunt breached by her attack on my choice of boyfriend and her snide insinuations. I decided, as I trotted to keep up with Poppy, not to see Jenny for a while, mainly because I didn't want to hear what she had to say.

As for what Jack had told me, that was absurd.

Strolling along breathlessly, Poppy sniffing this and sniffing that, it occurred to me that Bradley was just a few years younger than Jenny. Did that make her jealous of our relationship? Did she imagine herself dating someone as charming as he was? Was that possible? My own aunt feeling jealous of what I had and what she didn't? No, that was nonsensical. She loved me.

I felt more lost than ever, and I couldn't shake this premonition about Bradley, as if our relationship was in jeopardy, hanging on by a thread. Like when your very-loved jeans fall apart. You wear them despite all the holes, despite when your butt starts showing, your knees, your crotch, all your vulnerable places exposed to the elements, but then one day you have to throw them away.

CHAPTER TWENTY-SIX

Sara

"I'm ready," she breathed into my ear.

Again, the middle of the night. What time was it in Thailand? Or was she in Florida now? Cece always was a night owl.

"Ready for what?" I groaned, rolling in my bed.

"Ready to meet him."

"Oh no, you don't."

"Oh yes, I do."

Seriously? Was she going to indulge in childish banter at this hour?

I said snappishly, "That won't work, Cece. That won't work at all."

"Why not?"

"You *cannot* get involved. Keep away from Bradley. This is not the answer."

"I want to test him."

"Test him?"

"Yeah, to see if he buckles."

"This is ridiculous. I really don't want to play games."

"Yes you do, admit it."

I laughed. This conversation was absurd. "No, stop this stupid game."

"I need to meet Bradley."

"You don't *need* anything."

"No, but *you* need me to do this."

"I don't. I just want to get on with my life in peace."

I heard the Cecelia-laugh, though it was distant and echoey. Full throated and almost hysterical. Like this was all hilarious. "So how are you going to explain that your twin's coming to New York and you're not even inviting her to stay with you and you don't even want to see her? How will you explain that to Bradley?"

"I won't explain it to Bradley because you're *not* coming."

"Oh yes I am."

"Good night," I said. And then, not wanting to end things on a bad note, "Sleep tight, don't let the bedbugs bite."

I stared at the ceiling and into the blackness, pondering over this surreal little conversation. Why did it have to be this way with twins? Why was it so hard to be separate, to be different entities, even when it came to relationships with other people?

Unable to get back to sleep, I threw my face into my pillows and heaved out huge sobs. Windy lurches hiccupped from my diaphragm—or some deep fathomless part of my body—as I tried to suck oxygen into my lungs. I hadn't had an ugly cry in a long time. I was making so much noise, Poppy woke up.

I felt so fragile, so split in two, wondering who the hell I was.

Poppy dragged her little self over to me and licked my face, cleaning away the salty tears, which only made me weep all the harder. Clasping her in my arms, I craved to be my own person, to have a grown-up relationship with a man. Was I sabotaging any chance I had?

In the sooty, grubby little recesses of my mind, I knew my twin would split us up before Bradley and I had a chance to even get started.

CHAPTER TWENTY-SEVEN

Sara

Our relationship—mine and Bradley's—had been going along in first gear, or sometimes cruising along in neutral, and now it had, by necessity, shifted into fourth. I could feel it. Reverberating beneath me. It wasn't a premonition or an eerie feeling, it was a fact.

Things were about to change into fifth.

I waited for my cue.

It came when Bradley asked me if we could have dinner together with Cecelia.

"You've been looking at her Instagram page, haven't you?" I shot out, not able to hide the accusatory tone from my voice.

It was early evening and we were in the park strolling around the boat pond, Conservatory Water, watching people's remote-controlled sailboats glide over the water. You'd think it would be kids playing, but most of the operators were grown men. I nursed a hot chocolate, Bradley a coffee. It was one of those freak, climate-change days when the temperature had suddenly dropped. Yesterday had been roasting hot.

"Of course I checked out her Instagram," Bradley said. "What do you expect? She's your twin. Your *secret* twin, I might add. Someone whom you tried to keep hidden from me. But she's a part of you and I was curious. How can you expect me to ignore her, how can you blame me for being curious?" Bradley was trotting to keep up with Poppy, who had seen a dapper husky ahead, all intact, and she wanted to check him out. We were both zipping along, her wheels flying.

"Why are you so fascinated by Cecelia?"

"Who says I'm fascinated?"

"It's obvious or you wouldn't be asking to meet her. Am I not enough for you?"

"Of course you're enough, that's crazy."

"Don't call me crazy."

"I didn't mean it that way."

"Then what way did you mean it?" I tried to rein Poppy back with the extendable leash I had bought for her, but she was now at nose level with the handsome husky's butt.

"I just don't see the big deal if we all go out together for dinner."

"That's not going to happen," I told him, "so get that idea out of your head." I said to the husky owner—an elderly man all in black. "Please excuse my dog."

"Are you jealous of her?" Bradley fired out, as Poppy sped toward an impossibly small Chihuahua in an orange jacket.

We moved along, and veering her away from the yapping dog, I thought about Bradley's question for a long while. I finally replied, "I *used* to be jealous of Cece, I guess… if I have to be honest with myself. But it's hard to be jealous of someone you love so much. You know, when someone's identical to you, how can you be jealous of them? It's like being jealous of yourself. It's impossible really."

"But… but, you're so different," he stammered.

"How do you even know that?"

"You're not flashing yourself off on Instagram. You're—"

"You should check out her TikTok page," I said facetiously, "if you're really that interested."

"I just want to meet her, as your sister. As part of your family."

"Don't you get it? Don't you *get* that she broke my heart into little pieces and she *cannot* be part of my life anymore?"

Bradley looked down at his polished shoes.

I fired out, inexplicably fierce, my emotions getting the better of me, "Look, if *I* want to see my twin, I will, but I don't want *you* in the middle of us."

"You're worried I'll fall in love with her or something?"

I nodded. "To be honest, it's my greatest fear." I trudged over to a trash can and chucked in my empty cup.

He followed me, laughing. "But I'm crazy about *you*, Sara. I love you for who you are."

"How do I even know that for sure?" I said.

He strode toward me. Took Poppy's leash out of my hands and reeled her in closer. He leaned in toward me, his hands on my shoulders, pulling me toward him. I wet my chocolatey lips aware of my raspy breath coming faster. Nervous, I almost laughed; his eyes were serious, intent, only on me, one hundred percent, his attention on me. I wondered who was watching us: two lovebirds in Central Park with their cute dog. We looked like one of my romcom book covers, minus Poppy's wheelchair, of course. Bradley's head tilted down as he lorded above me—he was tall. He pressed his lips on mine, sealing them over my mouth, and my heart thumped wildly. I crumpled into him as he drew me closer. I dared to open my mouth a little, and his tongue flickered against mine, tasting me, exerting just enough pressure yet gentle at the same time. I breathed into him. The kiss was full of confidence yet devoid of aggression, but his free hand that wasn't holding the leash had moved to my waist, now clinching me in a fast hold, so I was helpless to move. I became aware of his strength for the first time, his power—he was a pretty muscular man—and I melted into his grip. This was the kiss I'd been dreaming of. The raw emotion, the electricity zapping through my body. I raised my own hands and pushed back his thick dark hair from his forehead, weaving my fingers through the soft strands, our heads touching until he broke away from the kiss.

"I love you, Sara." His heart tight against my chest beat to the rhythm of a fast drum.

"Me too," I whispered, so faintly I wondered if he heard.

But then that pesky little voice inside my head told me something was about to go monumentally wrong, and if I knew what was right for me I'd better watch myself.

CHAPTER TWENTY-EIGHT

Bradley

Bradley left a private message on Cecelia's Instagram account. He wasn't surprised when she didn't respond. She must get millions of them, thousands every day from men drooling over her pictures, he assumed.

Her account, obviously, was public. Pretty much all her pictures were of her in a bikini, hot as hell, absolutely gorgeous. It was true that she looked identical to Sara, yet they were two different people altogether. It was weird. It would seem logical, he thought (because he found these pictures of her twin so sexy) for him to throw Sara down on his bed and screw her brains out.

But he couldn't. It would ruin everything. He had deliberately gone slow with Sara, terrified to mess anything up.

Sara was the sweetest, loveliest girl, and he wanted to marry her. And yet he treated Sara completely differently from all the others, because she *was* different. She hadn't spent the night, and he hadn't pressed her to. She wasn't the pushy kind either, and he certainly hadn't exerted his powers of persuasion, even though he found her gorgeously attractive. Because he suspected she would succumb and then regret it afterward, and he needed their relationship to be perfect, wanted to savor every last minute he was with her. Every smile. Every time he touched her it sent shivers through his body… the good kind of shivers, the beautiful kind.

Sara was what his mother would call "a keeper."

He scrolled through Cecelia's pictures again. She always had her bikini bottom hoisted high so you could see the cheeks of her ass: round and perfect. She must work out every day, he surmised. In all her posts there was a sort of pseudo-spiritual jargon about being kind to others and having positive thoughts. *Such bullshit.* He'd heard so much of that in his yoga classes, especially from the instructors, but few of those people were sincere. He suspected Cecelia was the same. But his curiosity was piqued. He *had* to meet this woman! Her last post was on a beach in Florida. Evidently she'd moved back to the States from Thailand. He knew what he was doing was wrong but wrong had always been his driving factor.

Like it or not, wrong was what made the world go round.

Finally, Sara's sister responded to Bradley's Instagram message.

Hi, Bradley, Sara has told me all about you. So pleased she's seeing someone as nice as you! Would really love to have dinner with you guys. But she's not responding to my emails. Is there any way you could arrange this? Would love to hook up with you both. Am in NY.

He replied: *I'm sure I can persuade Sara for us all to have dinner together. I'm not quite sure why she hasn't answered you. Have you two spoken on the phone?*

Cecelia texted back: *We used to speak every day almost but now she's gone all cold on me.*

Bradley: *Why?*

There was silence. No answer. He had obviously hit a nerve with Cecelia. Had she done something to upset Sara?

Two days passed and still no answer from Cecelia. It was really bugging Bradley yet he didn't know why it got to him. He wanted the first time that he and Sara slept together to be really special. And now he wondered why he was deliberating so much. They needed to take it a step further and move onto the next level of their relationship. He'd been dithering, because deep down he knew he wasn't good enough for her. He kicked himself for giving the wrong message to the twin, and for his dirty thoughts, so he sent another text via Instagram.

> *Never mind, if Sara doesn't feel comfortable for us all to have dinner together, I respect that. Maybe I'll meet you one day. Maybe the next time you meet me will be when I'm your brother-in-law!*

No answer.

A week later a message popped up: *OK. We can meet. But not dinner. Where and when? Check with Sara if it's OK.*

Bradley was not going to check with Sara, because she had already made it clear it wasn't OK. He didn't dare answer her message so said nothing.

A new text came in from Cecelia:

> *Is it OK?*

Bradley replied with a thumbs-up emoji. Somehow, an emoji made it un-lie like.

And then Cecelia did something he thought a little coquettish. She wrote: *Are you curious to see what I'm like in the flesh?*

That was an understatement! And he wanted to find out why Sara had been keeping her twin secret from him. He thought of the saying, *Curiosity killed the cat* and couldn't help but wonder what might happen next.

CHAPTER TWENTY-NINE

Bradley

When Cecelia appeared in the Japanese wing of the Met and walked through that door in a little skirt and red tank top, Bradley felt goosebumps crawl up his arms. It was the strangest thing: Sara but not Sara. In the light of day it was impossible to tell Cecelia apart from her twin, but the minute she opened her mouth she was intrinsically different.

"Hi," she said. Her tone was husky and deep, her cadence so unlike Sara's. She seemed less innocent, less hesitant... as if she owned the place. There was an arrogance to her step, a self-assuredness that told him she thought the world of herself and not so much of him. The fact he was meeting her at all, on the sly, without Sara here, made him feel like a real douche. But he had done everything he could for them to all hook up together, hadn't he? So what was he supposed to do?

He tried to justify his actions, though, in truth, it was curiosity that spurred him on. He convinced himself it was because he needed to get to know *Sara* better, the woman he was crazy about, and surely by meeting her identical twin he'd have a window into the psyche of her soul?

At least, this is what he was telling himself.

She flicked her hair, Cecelia did, and lowered her eyes to look at his shoes, as if appraising him. Her gaze trailed up his body, hovering somewhere in the middle. He felt a frisson of uneasiness but also excitement... he couldn't help himself. Was she aware of what she was doing?

"You like this shit?" she said, dragging her eyes around the museum, landing on Old Plum, a work of art on four panels of an ancient plum tree, all gold leaf.

"J-Japanese art?" He was aware of his stuttering. It was ridiculous.

"Yeah, you're into art?"

If someone had asked him this a few months ago, he would have said no, but since meeting Sara he'd made such an effort to try and please her, to show he was worldly and educated. He had done crazy amounts of research on art and artists and different periods of history, that yes, actually, he was beginning to *enjoy* art.

"You know what? Yes, I do," he replied, almost as if apologizing. "I think it's very beautiful, and every time I see blossom now in the park I think of Japanese art, the way it depicts a sort of yearning and a kind of melancholy. Blossom's a huge deal over there in Japan. Full blossom and also when it's falling from the trees. It has a name, even: Sakura. For them it's symbolic of the Japanese spirit. Beauty, life, and then... inevitable death."

"Death?"

"Death can be beautiful too," he said, smiling.

Cecelia looked at him blankly.

"I have to say that yes, yeah, I love all this artwork," he confirmed, feeling awkward. Did this woman have any idea what he was talking about?

Cecelia listened to him with benign boredom. "You wanna go get something to eat?"

He couldn't believe how different from Sara she was. Sara would have hovered here for hours looking at each intricate detail. She would have lingered over each sculpture, each painting and waxed lyrical about the waves, or the shapes of the branches of the trees depicted in the works. Or the flicker in the deer's eyes of the painting in front of him now, or the beautiful Japanese characters—the writing. It was strange to be with this woman who looked identical to Sara yet she had nothing of her magic or intelligence. He could tell this after just five minutes of being with Cecelia. Still, something about her impelled him to dig a little deeper, get to know her.

She changed her weight from one foot to the other. No wonder, she was wearing heels. A sure sign of someone who wasn't a New Yorker. "Let's go and get a beer somewhere."

"A beer?" He couldn't disguise the surprise in his voice. Sara never drank beer during the day.

"Sure, you have anything against beer?"

"No, not at all. That would be great." He was about to say they could get a beer here at the Met, because having a Friends of the Met card meant he had a membership to the private café, but then he thought, *no, these people know me… well, they might know me by sight, anyway*, and suddenly he felt embarrassed of being with a woman who looked like his girlfriend but wasn't, in her tight little miniskirt. Still, one part of his body was denying what his head was warning him. Something was egging him on, urging him to be adventurous, to get to know this woman better.

"Where would you like to go?" he asked.

"No idea, you tell me. You live here. I don't even know this city. I was born here but I've never lived here. I like beach life, you know? Cities are not my thing."

He racked his brains trying to think of somewhere he could take her. Somewhere discreet. It suddenly made him realize how dumb it had been to ask Cecelia to meet him here at the Met. As vast as the Metropolitan Museum was, he felt as inconspicuous as a dog in the midst of upset trash: this is where he and Sara came. He couldn't believe he was sharing their special spot with her twin whom he didn't even know.

"There's a luncheonette diner place on Lexington and 83rd," he suggested. "It's like a really old-fashioned place with a soda fountain, like walking into a time warp. It's fun. One of the last of its kind in Manhattan, a real New York City landmark. Do you want to go there?"

Cecelia gave an unenthusiastic half shrug. "Sure."

He knew the diner, the Lexington Candy Shop, was safe because it was a burger, fries, ice cream and sodas joint. Stuff Sara wasn't into. They walked a block, but with Cecelia's heels they ended up taking a cab, even though it was just around the corner. Bradley was nervy. He kept looking behind him, thinking, with his luck, he might bump into Sara. Ridiculous, since he knew she was at home with Poppy and had a work deadline. When Sara was doing one of her cover deadlines she thought of nothing else and would lock herself away for hours at a time. He was sure he'd be safe until around six o'clock when she went to the park with Poppy for their afternoon walk.

He felt so shifty, so guilty.

He and Cecelia sat side-by-side in the diner, at the counter, eating hamburgers and drinking iced sodas, because they didn't serve beer here after all. Except Cecelia took just one bite and picked tentatively at a couple of French fries, like a finicky child not wanting to eat her greens.

"I've got to watch my weight," she explained. "Being in a bikini's my job, you know?"

He asked her about Thailand and about her Instagram world, not feeling at ease with her the way he did with Sara. He had expected, because they were identical, to… the truth was, he didn't *know* what he had expected. Maybe what he was doing was crazy, meeting her here, in secret.

Wrong, wrong, wrong!

Cecelia slurped the last of her Coke through a straw. "So why did you want to meet me?"

"Well, you're Sara's sister so it stands to reason doesn't it?"

"Not necessarily."

"If this is awkward for you…"

"No, it's fine. In fact, I wanted to ask you some questions anyway."

He finished his mouthful. "Questions?" The way she said it made him feel like he was about to be interviewed for a job. He shifted on the bar stool, finding space for his long legs so they didn't touch hers. Her legs were bare, her skirt hiked high up her thighs.

"Yeah," she said. "I need to know if your intentions with my sister are honorable."

Honorable? He was lost for words. Maybe Cecelia was kidding?

She drilled her blue eyes into him. "Well, are they?"

No, she isn't kidding, he realized. "Of course my intentions are honorable. Totally honorable."

"So you want to marry my sister? Is that where this relationship's headed?"

He considered it for a second and said, "That's my intention, yes."

"You got her a ring?"

Another, out-of-left-field question. "No, not really."

"Not 'really'? In other words, no. Would you like me to help you choose a ring? Maybe we could go to Tiffany or something?" Sliding her gaze over his gold signet ring, over the folds of his suit, down the length of his moneyed silk tie, she said, "A solitaire diamond would be nice."

"That's very kind of you to offer me help, and I have thought about Tiffany, but… well, I think that Sara would really appreciate a vintage ring."

"Vintage? Like secondhand?"

"She's always going on about conflict diamonds and children working in mines and… well, I think she'd appreciate a vintage ring."

Cecelia pulled a face. "I'm not so sure. Diamonds are a girl's best friend… you know that, right?"

"I think she'd like *vintage*." Standing his ground with this pushy woman felt good.

"You mean, like something you might find… well, what are you talking about? Where would you find this ring? Like in a *pawn* shop?" Her mouth twisted like she'd sucked a lemon.

"No, of course not, what do you take me for! I don't just mean any old ring: I'm talking about my *grandmother's* ring, that's what I'm talking about."

He decided in that very moment, the emerald ring would be perfect. He pictured it sitting on Sara's slim engagement finger and how exquisite it would look. He hadn't imagined, before now, that he'd ever pass this ring along. But since Sara was going to be a part of his forever-life, and he'd see the ring on a daily basis, well…

Cecelia cocked her head as if weighing up his intentions. "Oh, I see, that's a different story then."

He nodded emphatically. "Yeah, that's what I intend to do, give her my grandmother's ring." He took a bite of his burger.

"And you don't think you two should move in together first, before getting married? You have a big apartment, right?"

Bradley swallowed and considered her question. "We've talked about moving to Hawaii."

"Oh, really? Sara never mentioned that to me."

"I thought you two didn't talk much."

"We did, actually, before you two got serious. Now I'm getting crumbs of conversation." She sounded a little accusatory, a dash of bitterness to her tone.

Neither spoke for a while. Cecelia plucked a cold French fry from her plate and dipped it into some ketchup. Shoving it into her mouth, she asked, "Before Sara, did you have a lot of girlfriends?" The question hung in the air for a few beats, and Cecelia quickly added, "Actually, no, don't answer that, it's a dumb thing to ask. I just want to make sure you're not the kind of guy who would cheat on her."

It irritated Bradley that Cecelia was talking with her mouth full. But when her red tongue popped out and she licked a drop of ketchup from her lips…

"Oh no, no, that's not in the cards," he assured her.

She threw him a skeptical look. "In the cards?"

"Not going to happen. I love her. I've never met a girl like Sara before." He leaned forward on his elbows. "But listen, it's impossible to promise anything one hundred percent, but as far as I can see into the future, I love her, and I want to be with her forever."

Cecelia nodded as if she understood that nothing could be fixed in life, nothing in this world was sure.

"OK, it's my turn now to ask you something," Bradley said, but with caution. "I'd like to know more about what's gone on between you and Sara. More about your past."

Cecelia's brows shot up—cool, dark arcs. She straightened her back. "I'm sorry, but I don't feel comfortable talking about anything that Sara hasn't already discussed with you. That would be really weird."

"I just can't understand why she kept you a secret from me."

"Maybe she wants to keep me for herself?"

Arrogant much? Bradley thought.

Cecelia opened her mouth to speak then closed it again. Then began tentatively, "We have"—she paused and shot out a puff of breath—"a bit of a history, put it that way. But I think that's for Sara to tell you. I'm not here to defend myself or make a case against my sister or anyone in my family."

"No, course not. Sorry if I've made you uncomfortable."

She shrugged. "It's fine."

"Can you give me your phone number, just in case?"

She crossed her long legs. "In case of what?"

"In case I need to talk to you about Sara or, you know, if something comes up."

She laughed. "No, I don't think that would be appropriate."

"You have no idea how weird this is for me." He felt himself clenching his teeth to stop his jaw twitching of its own stubborn accord.

"What's weird?"

"Sitting here next to you, when you might as well be Sara yet you're so different from each other… it's an odd sensation, but still, I feel like I know you."

"Listen, don't feel bad. Even our parents couldn't tell us apart."

"I *can* tell you apart. Your voices are different. The way you hold yourself, the way you walk… pretty different. Plus, you have a beauty spot," he pointed out.

"That's because I'm the beautiful one." Cecelia tossed her head back and laughed as if it were a joke, but he wondered if she was serious.

"Sara is *very* beautiful," he said, in his girlfriend's defense.

"Of course she is, she looks like me!"

If that was meant to be funny, he didn't laugh.

As Cecelia scrolled through her phone, he studied her. Her pronounced clavicle. Around her delicate neck—so delicate it looked snappable—she wore a silver chain, and on the end, a fat little bird. Above it, the word *Rock*, all in silver. Ha! He got the joke: *Rock chick*. That was rather apt. There *was* something rock chick-like about Sara's twin. Perhaps she was a groupie. Cecelia had a rawness to her and tangibility that Sara didn't. He couldn't figure out what it was he found so alluring, couldn't pinpoint it. Because his head was telling him to stay away from her. Partly, she disgusted him, partly, she… she affected the wrong part of him.

"What's it like having an identical twin?" he asked, forcing his eyes to stop focusing on her lips. Sara never wore lipstick. But Cecelia was pouting, the way a French girl might pout. Eating with her mouth full, puffing up her lips when she spoke. Drawing attention to herself on purpose, to her mouth... on purpose. As if she was well aware of the effect she was having on him.

He refused to rise to her bait.

"If I asked you what's it like having brown eyes or being six foot two, what would you say?"

He smiled. "I'm six foot *one* actually. But I get what you're saying."

Cecelia tilted her head to one side again. Evaluating him. "Are you for real, Bradley?" Her tone wasn't playful, but dead serious, probing.

He pushed himself a few inches further away from her, feeling horribly under scrutiny. "What do you mean?"

"You seem to be crazy about my sister, but you've been checking me out all afternoon. Do you fool around behind her back?"

"No, I swear! You're the first woman I've hung out with since I met her."

She shoved another French fry into her rosebud mouth and chewed. "Good. Keep it that way."

CHAPTER THIRTY

Sara

After that kiss in the park, I imagined Bradley would have wanted to move things along with me. Sex, up until now, had certainly not been the number one thing on my agenda, so not sleeping with Bradley, not making love to him, didn't worry me too much. He hung onto his old-fashioned values and that was just fine by me. Sometimes, I did question why he didn't insist on pushing things further like most men would have. It almost felt as if he had put me into the "chaste" box. The good girl box. The no-sex-before-we're-married box.

Like he thought I was somebody I wasn't.

But throwing myself a hundred percent into our relationship was something I kept going back and forth on. I was driving myself nuts with my own indecision, vacillating endlessly between wanting all of Bradley, yet simultaneously pulling away from him. Perhaps I was being cowardly. A "scaredy-cat"?

I think getting involved sexually is risky, if you like the person, that is. If you don't see a future with them or don't care one way or the other, it's no big deal, or if you're up for a bit of recreational sex then it's easy, simple. But if you want them to respect you and care about you, and you hope for a future with that person, sometimes sexual relationships can really ruin your self-esteem, your sense of autonomy, because you are opening yourself up (literally), making yourself vulnerable. And until your partner has committed and is all-in, it's best to keep something back for yourself.

Keeping men at arm's length, I decided, was the way to go. So after meeting Bradley I made up my mind to keep him at a physical distance until I knew what exactly it was I wanted from him, and for myself. He made it clear he was really into me. But in my experience of dating so far, the men who came on strongest were the ones to be most wary of. Kissing and fooling around, maybe, but right now, I just wanted to concentrate on Poppy and my work until I was completely sure.

Separating the two: love and sex, felt like a happy medium, a way I could protect myself. I wished I could be different, wished I could be more adventurous.

Yet I couldn't help but be curious. I wondered what was going through Bradley's mind. We were puttering along just fine. We got on well together. We enjoyed each other's company. There was no rush. I wasn't the kind of woman who hankered after marriage and babies. There were enough unwanted children in the world and I wasn't sure I'd make such a great human mother. Dog mom, maybe, but changing diapers? I was only thirty. I had time to mull it all over. And the sex thing did complicate relationships, it did. I wasn't ready for all that at this stage.

So when Bradley presented me with an antique ring belonging to his grandmother, I was really taken aback. I had only known him for a few months. This proposal was not something I had imagined would happen for real. I didn't understand how anybody could want someone to marry them and spend the rest of their lives together after such a short time dating. We hadn't even slept together. But the romantic side of me was jumping for joy, of course. I was flattered, I couldn't deny it. This kind of thing only happened in fairy tales. But it also put me on my guard.

Too fast, too soon. Was this normal?

"It's gorgeous," I said after he had opened the box, without indicating anything other than it belonged to his grandmother. We were at his apartment. All three of us on one of his soft white couches, covered in a special rug he'd bought for Poppy. It was a sweet gesture, that rug.

It was Bradley who opened the box. He took out the ring with reverence then popped the box back in his jacket pocket. I hardly got a glimpse, but enough to see it was faded and had the name of a Paris jeweler I didn't recognize. He obviously did not want the box to be a part of the gift. He slipped the ring onto my finger before I could say anything, and amazingly, it fitted. Actually, it was a little bit tight and not easy to get off. I tried to dislodge it.

Gazing at me, a flicker of hurt in his eyes, he said, "Just leave it on, why try to take it off? When you take rings on and off that's when you lose them. Don't take it off to wash your hands, just keep it on. It's yours now, Sara."

Jittery, I brought my left hand up and inspected it. The emerald—flawless—was almost square, with two little diamonds on each side of the gem, set on a gold band: simple but elegant, the emerald raised up by prongs. "It's stunning. Even more special that it's your grandmother's."

"Yes, isn't it beautiful? I did think about getting you a new ring—"

"No," I cut him short. "This is…" What could I say? At least he hadn't spent any money on it. I guessed this was a proposal, yet he hadn't asked me to marry him in words. But this ring spelled out *Engagement*. This was no friendship ring. I needed time to decide. All I could say was, "It's gorgeous."

"Isn't it?"

I sat there nervously, still unsure of what else to say. Maybe this *was* just a regular gift?

And then the question came. "Will you marry me, Sara?"

It was the strangest thing: I had been convinced, a couple of weeks back, that if Bradley ever asked me to marry him I would say a resounding yes. I had *prepared* myself to say yes. The "yes" was still hovering on my tongue. But when those words *Will you marry me?* hung in the air between us, I floundered, my mind wavering with indecision.

He noticed the worry in my eyes. "Look," he said, after an embarrassing pause that made me feel cruel for not answering him immediately. "You don't have to let me know straight away. Take your time to think about it."

I got the impression he was waiting for me to jump in and say, *Yes of course I'll marry you, Bradley, of course I will,* but I just couldn't. I couldn't form the sentence.

I tried to take off the ring again, feeling that by wearing it I'd be committing myself, but I needed soap and water, or even oil: it was pretty tight on my finger.

"You don't need to take it off. It's not as if the ring and your answer have to go hand-in-hand"—he laughed—"that play on words was unintentional. Marriage is a really big deal, it's not something you just race into. I understand."

"We haven't even slept together," I pointed out.

"No, I realize that."

I remained on the couch, immovable, staring at the ring. Not knowing what else to say. Not wanting to wound him, I couldn't look him in the eye.

I wasn't sure if Bradley had sensed this over the past weeks: my reluctance about a committed relationship, and because of that he was only asking for my hand to seal the deal, pin me down. Or did he genuinely love me? Up until now, he had certainly respected the tentative approach I was taking concerning the two of us. I wasn't being frigid or pushing him away at all, but perhaps he intuited that he needed to hold back when it came to sex in our relationship. I gave him full marks for that.

But this whole proposal felt off.

"I think we need to spend more time together first," I said waveringly. "Maybe move in together? Live together first, see how we do for a year or two before getting married, don't you think?"

Even as the words dropped from my lips, I wasn't even sure I wanted to live with him anyway. I loved my chaotic apartment, Mrs. Scott safely below. She was like Poppy's godmother. Always there. Dependable. How would I manage without her if I were in Bradley's humongous apartment, alone with Poppy when he was at work, not able to be my messy self? His OCD nature would be at odds with the person I was. It wouldn't be long before we'd start fighting about what a slob I was.

The look on his face was contemplative, as if he didn't agree but was too shy to speak up. I heaved a sigh of relief like I'd been let off the hook.

"Well,"—he hesitated—"I know we're both happy in our apartments, for now anyway, but I was hoping we could move to Hawaii, start afresh."

Thank God, I thought. *That things can continue as they are. For now, anyway.*

I said carefully—I didn't want to hurt his feelings—"When I told you I'd love to live in Hawaii one day, I was thinking of the future, not right now. I have my work here, and as for Poppy, she has everything here... her hydrotherapy and physiotherapy sessions, Central Park. To be honest, Bradley, I couldn't even imagine us living elsewhere, at least not for a few years. Moving's a monumental change. My work, my—"

"Poppy could adapt. And you don't need to work, I have enough money for both of us."

"It's not the money, it's my sense of independence, and I adore my job. It's creative... I'm a creative person, and I have no intention of stopping work. Even if I were a millionaire, I wouldn't stop."

He looked down at his tie, pulling at it and smoothing it with his elegant fingers. "You could work just as easily in Hawaii. You work from home anyway."

"I know 'technically' I can work anywhere, but I meet people here. One-on-one meetings and stuff. It's important for relationship building. New York feels like my anchor." I touched his hand with my emerald-ringed finger. It glinted, reflecting the windows of the apartment in its big, square face, the diamonds like little eyes looking at me expectantly. I finished by saying, "Anyway, the long and short of it is, I'm not ready to move away yet."

With his gaze still fixed downwards, he muttered, "As you wish."

As you wish? That sounded so formal, so antiquated. But then that was the kind of guy Bradley was, decked out in his smart, three-piece suits, his shiny shoes, his elegance. Always immaculately dressed, always polished. I'd wounded him. Rejected him. It so wasn't my intention, but I needed to make my stance clear.

Picking up his hand—to stop his fidgeting or as a loving gesture, I wasn't sure—I said, "I feel like I'm stringing you along. I should give you an answer soon otherwise it's just not fair."

He shook his head. "It's fine. Honestly. Take your time, there's no rush. I want to be with you… forever. This isn't a race, you know."

He was being so reasonable it made me feel guilty.

"And you're really happy for me to go around wearing this priceless ring that belonged to your grandmother? Even if we're not officially engaged?"

"Even if you told me you never wanted to see me again, honey, you could still keep the ring. I'm not the kind of guy who's going to ask for an engagement ring back. You're the love of my life, so see this as a token. Take your time, like I said."

Why was I hesitating? The niggling thought swirling around my head was:

Bradley seems too good *to be true.*

But I could read the look in his eye. The way he'd just said what he said, I knew he was lying. This emerald ring meant the world to him. If I continued dating him he expected me to wear it. And if we went our separate ways? There was no way he'd let me go around with this ring on my finger. He didn't come across as a materialistic person, but there was something almost living and breathing about this ring. As if I brought back to life his grandmother. Personified something dead and gone.

It gave me the chills.

CHAPTER THIRTY-ONE

Sara

I had been avoiding asking Bradley about his ex-girlfriend, Cassandra, the one who mysteriously died young. It was for him to open up to me about it, not for me to push him into something he wasn't able to share, or ready to share. Yet we had been together for enough time now that his not mentioning it was beginning to perturb me a little.

There were lots of things about Bradley I didn't know, mainly because I hadn't asked. His work, for instance. I had never visited his workplace or even had lunch with him on Wall Street, partly because of my own laziness, and partly because of Poppy and work. It was a bit of a schlep all the way downtown when I knew how busy he was anyway. And whenever I asked him about his work, he was reluctant to talk, said it was "dull" and would change the conversation around to what *I* was doing. That was the thing about Bradley: he was interested in other people, didn't talk about himself so much, unlike most men who used the word "I" too frequently in conversation. Bradley was always curious to know about others: their likes and dislikes, their work, what made their minds tick.

We had gone to a private cocktail reception for a Friends of the Met do, and mingling with the other members, he was so animated chatting to everyone, asking each and every guest enough personal questions so they lit up and talked voraciously, all evening. Bradley had enough intellectual curiosity that he drew out the best in people, without putting anybody on edge or sounding nosey. He really was a charmer.

Too bad my aunt and Jack were both so negative about him.

And now here we were having a picnic in Central Park, all prepared by Bradley. He kept looking at me in a strange way, as if to gauge what was going through my mind. Something had changed, but I couldn't figure out what.

He had totally surprised me with an old-fashioned picnic hamper, replete with lovely plates, not plastic, beautiful silverware and glasses, not plastic either. Bradley was a very traditional but vogueish kind of guy. He had bought a bottle of Pol Roger champagne, had even spread out a gorgeous Scottish tartan blanket on which we sat, Poppy's leash hooked around my ankle, so she didn't zoom off with her wheels somewhere, because once she started, there was no stopping her. Bradley had even packed special treats for Poppy, too. It was a beautiful sunny day and not too crowded. We had commandeered a spot at Cherry Hill, overlooking the lake, beneath a Japanese cherry tree. Couples in rowboats were gliding about on the water. A light breeze had picked up, perfect for this warm July day.

I unhooked Poppy from her wheelchair and settled her on the blanket, got out her collapsible water bowl and filled it up.

As I watched my dog drink, I turned the subject of Cassandra over in my head; something I had so wanted to talk about but hadn't yet dared bring up. It felt wrong, really, wanting to do so on today of all days, considering Bradley had organized this romantic picnic, but I prepared the sentence in my head, determined not to let this topic slip by any longer.

I waited until he had quaffed the lion's share of the champagne, which he seemed only too pleased to do. Like he was nervous about something. Like some question was on the tip of his tongue, but he was too nervous to ask. I was taking it very easy, had only a few sips myself. The alcohol loosened him up, until he became merry, relaxed, stretching out his long legs, lying back, his head upturned to the sun, dappled shadows dancing on his handsome face, his head resting on his laced-together hands, elbows out, looking up at the trees. Some squirrels were scurrying around. Poppy was gazing rapturously at them. As if to say, *Just wait till I get my wheels back on!*

"Did you and Cassandra ever come and picnic in the park like this?" I asked tentatively.

Bradley half sat up, resting himself on his elbows, his expression one of shock. "How do you know about Cassandra?"

"You mentioned her to me once, didn't you?" I tested, seeing if I could get away with my fib.

"No, I don't remember telling you about her."

"Oh, I thought you had," I said vaguely. I took his empty glass from his hand and topped it up with more champagne. I had ruined his serenity I was well aware. Too late now.

"I really don't remember saying anything about Cassie. But I guess, if I did, I did," he said.

I couldn't tell him I'd heard through the grapevine, i.e. from Jack, about Cassandra.

"At the time, she was the love of my life." He was gazing up at the trees when he said this. I followed his eyes flickering between the leafy branches, blinking at the sun peeping through the trees. We could see the rise and fall of the buildings in the distance—beyond the lake—the cityscape so pretty in the light. A dove fluttered across our field of vision.

"So why did you split up with her?" I asked dishonestly, because I knew the truth: Cassandra had died.

"We were going to get married," he said, and sighed.

I had not been expecting him to come out with that. I was expecting him to tell me that she had killed herself.

I gave Poppy a morsel of my cheese sandwich and took a bite myself, chewed, and swallowed my mouthful. "So what happened?"

"We were engaged," he said, still looking up at the sky. "But then, well… perhaps we'll talk about this another time, Sara, I don't want it to ruin our day."

"Okay," I agreed. "But I'd love to know more about her."

"Why? You told me you didn't want to go into detail about ex relationships, and I get that. The past is the past, and there's nothing we can do. I think it's best if we just think about our future, that is… if you want to have a future with me. Do you, Sara? Do you see us having a future together, the way I do? Me, you, Poppy, Hawaii, maybe kids too?"

Uh-oh, I'd reignited him again on the marriage topic, or at least, the forever-after topic. I stuttered, "I g-guess. Maybe."

He sat up straighter, his eyes flashing at me. "Maybe?"

"I think so," I said, "but I just don't know if I'm ready for all that now."

"Will you *ever* be ready?"

"I don't know, Bradley. That's the thing. I just can't say, can't make any promises."

"If you were into me, you *would* know. You would know you wanted to be with me. Good things take time, great things happen all of a sudden."

Was that a quote? I absentmindedly stroked Poppy's ears. She had calmed down about the squirrels and was half dosing. "I feel like I need to give you a straight answer: yes or no. Is that what you want?"

Silence. He drained his glass, then rested himself back down on the rug, closing his eyes as if in defeat. A long while passed while we didn't speak. A soccer ball came bouncing our way, and poor Poppy, now roused, wanted to run after it, but couldn't. At moments like this, my heart bled for her. She probably didn't understand how one minute she could race around with her wheels and the next she was immobile. She had never not had her wheelchair on in the park, and suddenly this "romantic" picnic seemed like the cruelest thing ever. I had ruined both her day and Bradley's. It was time to leave. I began to pack the hamper up and get Poppy ready.

"*Cassandra* died," Bradley piped up. He emphasized her name. Strange.

I stopped what I was doing. "I'm so sorry," I said, trying to sound surprised. "What happened?"

"She… she decided to end her life."

"Oh, no. How awful, I'm so sorry. Why on earth would she do such a thing?"

Bradley was still lying down, hardly moving a muscle. "She was riddled with cancer. She had terminal cancer and only six months to live. That's what the doctors told her. But she refused treatment. Refused to even try. Said she wanted to live her last months having fun, not in a hospital. She wouldn't even give treatment a go. Nobody could persuade her. She said it was her choice and she didn't want to be bullied. But it felt to me like she was opting to kill herself."

I knew it, I knew it, I knew it! Jack had gotten it all wrong! Made it seem as if Bradley were somehow to blame, yet there was a perfectly good explanation all along!

"I'm *so* sorry, Bradley, you must've been devastated, really devastated."

"Yes, I was. But now you see why I want to move on." He sat up all of a sudden and set his eyes on me. Intense, unrelenting. "I didn't think I'd find love again, but I have, and you're the one, Sara. You. Are. The. One. I'm so clear about that now. I don't want to wait any longer, I want us to get married. Stop packing up, sunshine, I haven't finished here. Would you pass me a sandwich, please?"

He had taken to calling me "sunshine." He'd tell me I was "the light of his life." It was something any woman would long to hear, long to be, yet… it seemed like, instead of being the light—and feeling light—I was full of heaviness, as if I were carrying a burden. As if I had to live up to this ideal person he had created. This sparkling, *light* woman.

I undid the picnic basket and rustled around for the sandwiches. Poppy groaned, bored, so I gave her back her chewy toy and she reluctantly settled down, the whites of her eyes shining like a sulky child, as if to say, *Five more minutes only, Mom, you promised.*

My heart went out to Bradley, it really did, but I just didn't feel ready for this. Was there something wrong with me? Here was Bradley, such an eligible bachelor — most women would have fought tooth and nail to have a such a great boyfriend — and I was being all… not indifferent, exactly, but like I didn't care *enough*.

"What if I can't give you an answer, Bradley? It feels odd you want to jump into a marriage without living together in your apartment first."

The old argument, which I had already turned over in my mind. Yet I said it anyway. This beef about us not living together in his huge Fifth Avenue palace still didn't make sense to me, despite my own reservations anyway. Was I being disingenuous pretending it was a deal breaker? Yet this all-or-nothing attitude of his confused me.

The muscle of his jaw twitched. I noticed this happened when he was quietly angry. Bradley didn't do rage, just soundless, simmering wrath. "I'm trying to be patient, I really am," he muttered.

He edged himself closer to me and took my hand, his fingers absentmindedly stroking the emerald of the ring. The truth was

I wanted this ring *off* my finger. It gave me bad vibes, but I didn't want to bruise his feelings. It was wrong for me to be wearing this ring when I had not agreed to marry him yet. It wasn't my style, anyway. Who goes around with a big green emerald on their finger? It was too tight, too constrictive.

"I'd like to give you this ring back," I said decisively.

"That's a no then, isn't it? A definite no," he grumbled, his lips turned down.

Poppy started pulling the leash, desperate to play, bored out of her wits. She began to bark in a shrill staccato. Woofed at my face, her eyes fixed on mine as if to say, *Let's get a move on already, what the hell are we doing sitting down on the grass?*

"We've got to go. Let's pack up. I need to get Poppy home."

Bradley rose to his feet, his long legs looming above us, his giant shadow blocking my light. Poppy barked even more frantically. Onlookers were beginning to stare.

"It can't always be about Poppy, you know," Bradley griped. "There are other factors to take into consideration in your life, as well as this dog."

"*This dog?*" I barked above Poppy's cacophony. "*I* am the one to decide whether there are other factors in my life, Bradley." I stood up, too, and got Poppy into her chair, not looking Bradley in the eyes. I'd been mean. Snappy.

"I'm here for you, Sara, I'm offering you my heart, my everything," he said forlornly.

I wondered… was what he was saying true? Perhaps if I'd trusted him I would have said yes to his proposal… but there was something holding me back.

As always, it was Cecelia.

CHAPTER THIRTY-TWO

Bradley

Ever since he had proposed to Sara, she had acted not cool, but a little aloof, as if deliberately keeping him at arm's length. He got it; he had come on too strong.

He'd bide his time.

Meanwhile, a carping voice chattered on at him, whispering in his ear, telling him something was off-kilter. They carried on seeing each other: their walks in the park, brunch every Sunday, the odd movie, but nothing about their relationship had been cemented. Bradley couldn't figure out why Sara was not willing to take that next step. Any time he tried to bring it up, she'd change the conversation.

Then one evening, happening (accidentally on purpose) to walk down Sara's street, Bradley spotted her and Poppy on their evening walk, accompanied by that jerk, Jack. *Okay, okay, Bradley did know her hours, her routine*, he admitted. He almost wanted to warn her: *Do you realize you're setting yourself up for a mugger, a rapist, your schedule is so predictable?*

Maybe that's why Jack was now with her. Because of Bradley berating her about her evening walks around the block.

Well *that* had backfired.

He followed them. It was a pretty bustling, busy, Friday night, plenty of people on the streets, the air warm. A group of teenagers, merry on liquor, ambled down the sidewalk in a wobbling weave, oblivious to those around them. Bradley overtook them but kept himself close to the shadows, his eye fixed on Poppy's wheels, his distance calculated.

Not too close but close enough.

Sara and Jack walked together, fingers not linked, but hands grazing, touching. They laughed and chatted, carefree.

A flare of jealousy raging inside him, Bradley sucked in a deep breath and carried on his stalk.

At Third Avenue, they turned. It was busier. Restaurants open, people spilling into the street. Bradley, wearing a raincoat and fedora hat, like he'd stepped out of a Mickey Spillane novel—even though it was far too warm for a coat and hat—glided ahead, dodging a yellow cab, unseen.

Sara and The Creep stopped outside a bar, deliberating. Bradley slipped behind a parked car, also unseen, but within earshot. Close enough to hear their conversation. If they spotted him, so what? He'd act like it was meant to be, that he was coming to say hi, all along. Sara, busy arranging Poppy's harness, crouched down.

He heard Jack say, "You need to tell him."

Sara replied, "I think he might've already guessed."

"You need to find out for sure. If he knows."

"And then what?" She was still fiddling with the arms of Poppy's wheelchair.

"Get rid of Cecelia already," he said in a hiss. "For good, this time. You can do it."

She stood up, luckily looking ahead. "Not so easy."

Poppy was peeing, so they carried on standing in the same spot.

"It is, of course it is, Sara. Get her out of your life."

She heaved out a resigned sigh. "I know. I know I need to get rid of her for good."

"So why are you stalling?"

"It's complicated."

Jack snapped back, "No, it's not!"

"I will. Soon. I promise. But not quite yet." And then they moved on, their voices muffled by the rowdy commotion coming from the bar.

Bradley stood stock-still, stunned. He couldn't believe his own ears. Sara was not the person he thought she was, not by a long shot. "*Get rid of her for good?*" she'd said. What did that even mean? Was it as bad as it sounded? He needed to see Cecelia. He'd invite her to dinner. Warn her to keep away from her twin.

CHAPTER THIRTY-THREE

Sara

I watched Bradley from afar with fascination, waiting to see what he'd do next.

Sitting patiently at the snowy-clothed table, set with an assortment of fine silverware and wine glasses—a different wine for each dish—he was waiting for Cecelia to come back from the powder room. His eyes were uneasy. He kept glancing at his watch as if every second counted… his guilt ticking away. He had invited her to have dinner with him at this Michelin-starred restaurant.

I saw him say something to the deferential waiter, look at his watch again, then across the room. I slunk into a dark corner, avoiding his gaze and slipped off to talk to my twin for the very last time.

The bathroom was beautiful. All marble and mirrors, which gave the place a sort of dizzy, Versailles effect. I raised my eyes and got a shock when I saw her suddenly in the room with me, looking all in love, her eyes glazy as if she'd found happiness for the very first time. I ignored her, pretended I hadn't seen the sex siren in her red, borderline-slutty dress. Cleavage… availability written all over her. If I'd been a man, I would have wanted her. I couldn't blame Bradley for that.

I still loved my twin. Felt a rush of empathy… of understanding, of forgiveness for all she'd done, despite myself. I sat down, rested my elbows on the marble vanity and moisturized my hands with some L'Occitane cream they had, biding my time. Perhaps she was too preoccupied to talk. Perhaps she would pretend she hadn't seen me. Wasn't ready for this conversation.

I remembered her sadness, recalled the ugly tragedy that had ripped us apart. Remembered that none of it was her fault. That everything she later did stemmed from one thing.

I love you, Cece, I said, under my breath, bracing myself for what I was about to do.

I rewound, ten years back. The first indication that something was wrong with Cecelia was when she chopped off all her hair. I found great swathes of her locks, like dark, bronzed Grecian ropes, lying in the trash bin, her beautiful long hair hacked off haphazardly. She had done it herself with no care to how she looked. My first reaction was personal; I couldn't believe she wanted to be so different from me. We had always prided ourselves on being identical, our shiny long hair our signature. She was breaking away from me. She became quiet, her usual talkative self clammed up. When I asked her what was the matter, she just said, "I'm different from you now. And don't you dare cut your hair off too."

I felt my body go numb, as if my fingertips had no sensory perception, my arms and legs made of paper. I asked her what the matter was, begged her to tell me if I'd done something to hurt her, to anger her.

Her eyes were stark, empty, as if a piece of her had been scooped out. I had never seen her so devoid of personality; her "Cece-ness" sucked out of her. It was the eeriest thing I had ever known. Anything that hurt Cece hurt me too. You couldn't divide us, yet this hair-chopping had done just that.

I tried to piece it together; the moment when Cecelia changed. Ever since the party, she'd been moody. At the party, she'd danced, done her famous Cece head swing, her dark hair flying, whipping anyone in her wake. The next day I assumed she was just hungover. Snappy and surly, and the mood would lift. But two weeks later... that's when she lopped off her hair.

"If you can't guess what happened, I'm not going to tell you," she said, her tone barbed.

Up until then I had always been able to pretty much read her mind. It was like when we'd swim in the sea and a current would take one of us out in a dangerous direction while the other stood on the sandy shore, watching helplessly. When that happened there would be a grownup to rescue whoever had strayed, beady eyes nearby, a great hand to pull us out of the water—whichever one of us had been swept off—but somehow the grownups (namely our parents) were too busy to even notice anything amiss this time around. We were no longer children, but sweet sixteen. We could look after ourselves, they told us.

"Oh, you've decided to go short," our dad remarked to Cece. "Sensible, easier to manage short," he added. He didn't notice the spikey knobs of hair, all uneven, the DIY job that wrenched Cece away from her own essence. It wasn't just her hair. Her eyes looked void, I thought, like one of the devil's minions had come in the night and stolen a piece of her soul. In fact, that is, I found out, exactly what had happened.

Because finally, after weeks of this, kneeling beside her bed, I begged Cece—curled in a fetal position, swaddled in sheets, her eyes ghostly, the blue now great holes of black—to tell me what was wrong. Gone was my ego of the past couple of weeks, having assumed her character change was personal, somehow, against me.

Watching her tuck into herself like a mollusk in a shell, I knew she was hiding some terrible, unspeakable thing.

"It was my fault," she whispered, as I held her hand. "I shouldn't have egged him on at the beginning. My dancing, my short skirt. I made eyes at him. I never imagined..."

"Obinze?" I said. He was her sort-of boyfriend. He'd been harboring a closed, private love for her, even though they were just buddies. Obinze helped her with homework, would do anything for her. But he was shy, retired, and reverent of her.

There was a slight rustle of the pillow; she was shaking her head. "No, he would never hurt me."

"Someone *hurt* you?"

Cece said nothing.

"Look, you can tell me anything. You cannot keep holding this inside you, Cece. Who hurt you?"

"He started off with the neck of the wine bottle then…"

"Someone hit you?" I scanned my eyes over her body for bruises but saw none.

"You see? You can't even imagine it… you're that naïve." Her words were scornful, but her tone sad. So *sad*. As if she and I were oceans apart, and I was too dense to understand.

"Down there? He…?"

"Now you're getting it," she said, and exhaled so there was nothing left inside her lungs.

"That's not nice."

She sucked in a new breath. "Not nice?" she repeated, and laughed; a scornful chortle that told me how pathetic my choice of the word "nice" was.

"Who?" I asked.

"He told me it wouldn't hurt. I was drunk, I didn't realize what he was doing and then it was too late. Then he forced himself on me, shoved himself inside me, told me I had been begging him with my eyes."

"Have you told Mom?"

"She wouldn't believe me."

"Yes she would. You should've shown her, she's a doctor, she could've examined you."

"Ugh," she said. "Gross."

"Melissa then."

Melissa was a fellow doctor whom we adored. She worked with the team. She always brought us candy, even now we were teenagers. Or little presents. A handmade, carved elephant from a market or a pretty woven rug for our room. Always one present for the pair of us like we were one person. Up until this happened, Cece and I *were* pretty much one.

One happy family.

Now we were divided by what had happened. I had an overwhelming urge to hurt myself in that moment so we could be even, so I could take away some of her pain.

Now there was this chasm between us, and some nasty man had done this to my sister, my twin, my other half. He might as well have done it to me.

"I feel so ashamed," Cece sobbed with quiet tears, then closed her specter eyes.

"I'll tell Mom, so you don't have to."

"She won't want to hear it."

"She'll have to listen," I shouted, anger rising. "She'll *have* to!"

I didn't ask Cece the sordid details, because my imagination had now been ignited. She had been raped, in the guise of consensual sex, and she felt like she was to blame. Cutting her hair to punish her self-loathing self. The consequences were what mattered, the fact that whatever this man had done to her had broken her spirit. And that was what rape was. Not just an unspeakably violent physical act, but a breaking of the spirit.

"He needs to be punished," I said. "Who is it, Cece?"

Silence.

"Who did this to you?"

"Doctor *Atkinson*." She didn't say his first name because it was too shocking to say out loud. But we both knew the ramifications.

"Are you serious?"

"See? Not even *you* believe me."

"I do! I do believe you, it's just… oh, my God! What will Mom and Dad say? They think he's so great!"

"Exactly," Cece mumbled. "He's such a great fucking guy."

Dr. Atkinson was handsome, and we had flirted with him in the way teenagers flirt with older men, in innocence, in comradery. He had just gotten married to someone who also worked for Médecins Sans Frontières; someone very special to our mom we had heard all about but hadn't met yet. But because the organization rarely sent couples out together in the field, the newlyweds had been spending time apart. His wife hadn't been at the party. Dr. Atkinson was popular with everyone. I had felt, before this hideous revelation, almost envious that he had taken a shine to Cece. Joked and laughed with her more than he did with me. And now I remembered. At the party he had asked her to dance with him, and then they had slipped outside "to look at the moon." He had, evidently, interpreted Cece's sexy dancing as something more than it was. She was only sixteen.

I told my parents. I had to, despite Cece's shame. She was furious: yelled at me that she didn't want her name forever linked with his, that by coming forward she was taking two steps backwards, that the last thing she needed was to be a "rape poster child."

Cece refused to speak or hear the man's name. Privately, I found out that he had been dismissed from MSF, but because Cece also refused to testify against him in court, and because, at sixteen, she was considered an adult by law in Mali, where we were living at the time, there was no prosecution concerning underage sex. My father went to work on the Ivory Coast, and my mother took me and Cece to Mozambique. My parents were both in denial. I wasn't even sure if they believed my sister. That was the most painful thing of all. The double-whammy. Cece told me she wanted to die she felt so bad.

She was never the same. Contrary to what you might expect, she flirted all the more and became quite sexually active with a variety of men, none of whom loved her. It was as if she no longer respected herself and couldn't care less about how men treated her, because she was treating herself so much worse. Mom and I endeavored to intervene, but Cece pretended she was having a good time and told us to stay out of her way. Once or twice, I ended up in fights with her "boyfriends" as I tried to keep them away from her. I became known as the "handbag basher" for whacking men in the chest when they grappled at my sexy sister. Or the FBI ("fucking bloody idiot"). I was the laughing stock, as I followed her around, tried to get her to dress modestly, even went so far as to confiscate her phone sometimes. She'd find ways of escaping from me, sneaking off behind my back, to take drugs, to "party." Whatever names they called me, Cecelia's was worse: "Maneater," "Sister Slut."

It crushed my heart.

As for myself, it was then I vowed to never let men get the better of me, because they were a destructive force. At least, that was how I saw it. And as for sex? Only if you, as a woman, were in control.

I heard a sniffle and was brought back to the present. Sitting at the restaurant bathroom's vanity, wiping my creamy hands on a monogrammed serviette, I looked up.

There Cecelia was. Her hair long now. No drugs. But back to what she once was.

"You think three's a crowd, don't you?" she whispered, even before I'd had a chance to say a word.

I levelled my gaze with hers. "I met Bradley first," I said.

"But you don't even want him. He told me so."

"I made a mistake. I didn't think I could handle it."

"Sex?"

"No, not the sex itself, all the arsenal that goes with it. The pain, the heartache. The loss of self. The vulnerability. I didn't want that."

Her eyes locked with mine. Her beauty spot highlighting her cheekbone, which brought our individual identities to light.

"Why can't things stay as they are?" she said. "I fuck him and you two hang out. He doesn't care. In fact, that's what he wants, can't you see?"

"Stop it!" I bit back.

She laughed. "Stop what? Telling it like it is?"

"This has to *stop*. I wish… I wish you were…" and I whispered that last chilling word beneath my breath, closing my eyes to avoid her blue-eyed gaze. I could no longer bear seeing her. What kind of a person was I? Was I capable of putting an end to this? Bradley was crazy about Cecelia, not me.

"Three *is* a crowd," I confirmed, convincing myself I was doing the right thing.

The only way to deal with my twin was to do the unthinkable and never look back.

Jack was right. This shit had to end. Once and for all.

CHAPTER THIRTY-FOUR

Bradley

Bradley: *Can we meet again?*
  Cecelia: *Why?*
  Bradley: *I'd like to talk to you about Sara.*
  Silence.

Bradley found himself torn in two by the twins. He shouldn't care about Cecelia, but he did. Sara was the woman he loved, but Cecelia was an extension of Sara, so how could he deny her twin? How could he pretend she didn't matter? Cecelia *did* matter. He played the words over and over… the strange things Jack and Sara had said to each on the street. There was no way he could confront her because then he'd have to admit to stalking her, which was something he had been increasingly doing. But he had warned Cecelia at the dinner he invited her to, hadn't he? At that beautiful restaurant, he was pretty sure he had. But they had drunk so much, it was all a blur. And even now he was wondering if what he'd heard between Jack and Sara was his overactive imagination, or maybe he'd misheard? Eavesdropping on conversations could do that to you: confuse you, wrap you up like a fly in a spider's web. Trap you into a place you shouldn't be. Unwittingly, he had stepped into some warped love triangle, although it wasn't himself at the pinnacle, but Sara. The love/

hate relationship between these twins had eclipsed him, as if he was their useless pawn and whatever he thought or did held no importance; he was inconsequential.

It stung.

His emotions were wrangling with him, pulling him this way and that. He tried to keep his ego in check about Sara, he really did try. But no woman had ever rejected him like this before. It was a paradox. One of the reasons he liked Sara so much was for that very thing: she was cool and didn't gush all over him, had a mind of her own, knew who she was and didn't see herself or measure herself through her relationships with men.

But he thought by now he'd have broken through her shell to savor something sweet inside, but he hadn't. Her sweetness was not reserved for him. She was not in love with him, nor did she even love him. She kind of *liked* him. Why couldn't he break through? The only being who melted her heart was Poppy. Bradley was beginning to feel jealous of a disabled dog. And where did that schmuck Jack fit into all this? The Creep?

Yet Bradley couldn't deny that it might be all his fault; he had put Sara up on a sort of pedestal. He needed her there. This woman he could love but not touch. He didn't want to sully her. His feelings were distorted, all screwed up. He knew that.

Did Sara instinctively feel this? That she was too good for him? He should have been angry, yet it only made him want to fight for her harder.

That damn ring. He shouldn't have bared his soul like that. It was as if Sara were doing him a favor by wearing it. He'd given her a little piece of himself, so close to his heart. It seemed like they had been on a path to marriage, but perhaps that was *his* fantasy, only; she had zero intention of falling in love with him, even *trying* to fall in love with him.

Because that's what love is, isn't it? A choice, a decision. It's all about timing.

And somehow his timing was off. Was it his fault she'd spurned him? There was no way he was going to invite her to live in his apartment… that was impossible. He wanted a fresh start in Hawaii where they could begin a life together and he could put his job behind him.

Would he be able to give up his work? If he was in a different town, maybe. A different place, yes, he believed he could. He *could*. He would.

He could do it.

He got a message back, via Cecelia's Instagram.

Cecelia: *This better be good. I don't like seeing you behind my sister's back even if she's not speaking to me. It's just not right.*

P.S. I'm going back to Florida tomorrow.

Bradley: *Please. Can we meet later?*

Cecelia: *OK. Meet me at The Empire Diner. 1 p.m.*

CHAPTER THIRTY-FIVE

Bradley

After the last time, at that dinner at the swanky restaurant, Bradley swore he wouldn't see Cecelia again. But here he was meeting her a third time, at The Empire.

This old diner had been Cecelia's choice. Bradley had passed it before and always wondered what it was like inside. A tiny, old one-story Art Deco thing as small and low as a train carriage, dwarfed by tall skyscrapers towering above, incongruous in its metropolis setting. He wondered about the real estate value of this postage stamp of a place and assumed it wouldn't stay here much longer. These types of venues hardly existed in New York anymore. How did Cecelia even know about it? He had always asked himself, when he passed this place in a cab, what kind of person would eat here, and now here the two of them were as if they had stepped into some pulp fiction novel and Cecelia was the femme fatale.

He could hardly remember that Michelin dinner last week. So much vintage wine, it was a haze. He remembered they'd both eaten steak tartare. Apt for the raw behavior that followed—that they'd both reveled in—and then pretended hadn't happened.

Or did the kiss take place *after* they'd eaten? He tried to string the events together. He had caught Cecelia when she was coming out of the ladies' room, pinned her against the wall, his lips on hers, tentative at first, teasing, brushing them lightly against hers, all the while cupping her pretty face with his hands until he slid his tongue into her scarlet lipsticked mouth; all that wine he'd imbibed—while waiting interminably for her come out of the powder room—had made him wild with desire. It ended up being a tangle of limbs and lips, his hands frantic around Cecelia's body, around her waist, slipping down her lacey underwear, touching, exploring, grabbing.

Then he pulled back as suddenly as he had started, a flame of guilt about Sara flaring up inside him. *What was he thinking?*

They had both walked back to their table, calmly, quietly, as if none of it ever happened. Sitting opposite each other, he drank her in, but spoke, not of their stolen kiss—shameful and filthy and greedy—but of Sara.

But that kiss had changed everything.

There was no turning back now.

And here the two of them were again, a week later, at this clandestine diner downtown. The same old ruse: he wanted to discuss his relationship with Sara. Discuss it with Cecelia. He had convinced himself of this. Even *he* half believed it. Bradley was pretty sure, last time they were together at the restaurant, he'd warned Cecelia about what he'd heard between Sara and Jack. He couldn't remember what they had talked about now. It was all a blur. The kiss is what had stayed with him during the past week. The kiss had spun him out of control and now he was steeped in a lusty, guilty, twin-turmoil again.

The diner waitress came and took their orders. Bradley just asked for a beer, which appeared a few minutes later.

"So why did you want to see me again?" Cecelia asked, jiggling her sky-high-heeled legs into the booth and setting her purse down. Lipstick. Limbs. Hair. Pout.

Bradley planted his elbows on the table and took a gulp of beer to try and calm himself down. "Like I said, I want to talk to you about Sara."

Cecelia played with a packet of sugar. "Are you sure?"

Bradley focused on her long, red-painted nails, nails he imagined ripping along his back, marking him, drawing blood. "Course I'm sure. Why? What are you suggesting?"

"You warned me about her last time we met. Said Sara was planning to get rid of me?"

"Yes. But, you know, I could've heard wrong."

Cecelia flicked her hair off her face, revealing her beauty spot. "Well, that's why I'm going to Florida. I know when I'm not wanted."

He ached to tell her, *But you* are *wanted*, but bit his bottom lip to control his tongue. The tongue that clamored to do things to her.

"It was *me* you wanted to see again, wasn't it?" she said. "You don't want to talk about my sister, you simply wanted to spend time with me again, isn't that the truth, Bradley?" Cecelia lowered her eyes and raised them again. Her lashes longer than Sara's they made soft shadows on her face.

Bradley felt that familiar zap in his solar plexus, the way it happened every time he was in Cecelia's company. He replayed the secret kiss, which they both pretended had never occurred. He averted his eyes.

"Sara keeps me at a distance," he said. "I want to marry her. I think she and I are right for each other."

Cecelia ripped the sugar packet in two. Cheap white sugar spilled onto the table. "Have you thought about the fact Sara might not be ready? That she's incapable at this moment of giving too much of herself, that she's still nursing her own heartbreak? Losing her parents and…" Cecelia didn't finish her sentence.

"Of course I've considered that," he said. "I'm not made of stone. But it still feels like I just can't *get* to her, you know?"

The waitress came by the table and plonked Cecelia's order in front of her. A Coke float and a burger. Bradley hadn't ordered any food; he didn't feel like eating.

"Can I get you two anything else?" the waitress asked.

"No, thank you, we're good," Bradley said.

Cecelia launched her teeth into the cheeseburger, ketchup dripping down the sides of her lips. Like a vampire attacking flesh, she was so *into* the meat. Bradley deliberated how this twin chewed meat, the other eschewed it.

He watched her eat like she hadn't eaten anything in days. After she had almost finished and uncovering his shirt cuff, Cecelia's bare arm brushed against him as she looked at his watch to see what time it was, stroking his wrist briefly with the tips of her fingers. A shiver ran through his body like someone was dragging a cube of ice down his front.

"Fuck," he said, "we really shouldn't do this."

Her eyes widened. "Do what?"

"It feels wrong without Sara."

Cecelia rolled her eyes like a surly teenager. "What am I supposed to do? She doesn't want to see me. And it was *you* who insisted on meeting."

"Where have you been staying in New York?" he asked her, wondering if her host had fed her.

"With a friend," she said. "My sister didn't want me to stay with her." She took the straw in her mouth with her pink tongue, hands-free, and sipped her Coke float, vanilla ice cream swilling over the bubbly brown liquid. Who still drank that stuff as an adult? So unlike Sara. Cecelia's lips drawing on the straw was doing things to him. He tried to wipe away his filthy thoughts of her naked, sprawled across a bed, as he ravaged her from behind, her sweet Instagram ass in the air, her bikini bottoms still on. He felt himself swell, and winced, straining to push his thoughts back into the sewer where they came from.

"You're sleeping with this friend?" he asked, attempting to sound nonchalant, a sudden flash of jealousy escaping his lips. It was none of his business. This was crazy!

She sucked on that straw again and answered coolly, "Yes, I am."
Sleeping with some guy and flirting with me.

"She and I go back a long way," Cecelia let him know.

"'*She?*' A woman?"

"Yeah, a woman. So?"

Cecelia was doing this to him on purpose. Winding him up. He imagined her making love to a woman and felt that excited chill again tear right through him.

"Bradley, I don't have much time. I'm not sure why you brought me out here. If something's on your mind could you please share it with the class?"

He smiled. She had a sense of humor. She knew what she was all about. She was playing with him. Then he said seriously, "Sara doesn't want to move with me to Hawaii. She's not 'ready.' You know what? I don't think your sister will ever be ready."

"Sara's not a sunshine and sandals girl like me."

"How do you know? You two grew up in sunny Africa. She might love a beachy life. Aren't you going to give me some sort of advice as to how to warm her up, how to win her over?"

"The rate you're going, I don't think you'll ever win her over."

"What's that supposed to mean?" But he knew what she meant, and she was right. She didn't need to read his mind; his desire for her was written all over his face. The beaded sweat on his brow, the muscle ticking in his jaw, the way he couldn't stop licking his lips. *This woman* was doing this to him!

And she knew it.

"Wow thanks for the vote of confidence," he answered, not knowing how else to react, washing his guilt down with a swallow of beer. "And what makes you say this? Have you spoken to her about me?"

Cecelia shrugged in a noncommittal way.

"You talk, right? What does she say about me?"

"This and that."

"Good or bad? What does she *say*?" he pressed, his eager voice a plea.

"She talks about the disabled dog more than she talks about you, if you really want to know." Cecelia sounded as cynical as Robbie. She shuffled through her purse, distracted, as if she were getting ready to leave. "Anyway, Bradley, I've gotta get a move on. Maybe I'll see you around sometime, maybe I won't."

It was the kind of thing a teenager might say. *Maybe I will, maybe I won't.*

"What do you mean?" he said, his eyes passing over her long legs as she stood up. He took what she had said as a double message. He stood too, holding her by the wrist. She couldn't just leave! They had just sat down.

"Please don't go. Sit. We need to discuss stuff."

She plunked herself back down almost like she enjoyed his manhandling of her; the physical restraint while he'd held her too hard, too fast. Or was she just deigning to give him a second chance? Amused, perhaps, by his desperation?

Cocking her head, her mahogany hair flopping over one shoulder, she regarded him with a smidgen of interest, or was it pity? Looking up from under those long silky lashes, ketchup still lingering like blood on one corner of her mouth.

He'd come here to talk about Sara so why did he have an overwhelming urge to lay his finger on her mouth and wipe away the ketchup from her lips, then pop his finger into his own mouth and taste her leftovers?

His breathing became forced and heavy. She was eyeing him peripherally—or so he imagined—while she drew her tongue across her lips, looking through her purse again. Ignoring him, yet giving him those damned double messages. She knew what she was doing, and she knew he knew. Then she looked up. Their gazes locked in a standoff. She caught her bottom lip between her teeth and pulled on it. He glowered at her, heart pounding, every organ in his body... pounding. He felt a flash of shame and covered his crotch with the menu to hide the embarrassing, telltale sign.

All his nonsense... needing to talk to Cecelia about her sister was only a fraction of the truth, wasn't it?

Was the real, one hundred percent reason because he desired to spend time with Cecelia herself? He wasn't in love with the woman, no. How could he be? He didn't even know her and, quite frankly, didn't even want to know her. It was something else he desired... something that drew him closer...

He had no idea what was going through her mind.

"Do you want to come to Florida with me?" she suddenly said. Her voice was cool as if she'd just asked him to pass the salt or something. "Because I should get going. And I can't stay here anymore bullshitting about Sara. My car's round the corner, and I don't want to get a ticket. I'm leaving in, like, five minutes. If you want to talk some more, you'd better come with me."

This was out of left field. Whoa!

He gaped at her, open-mouthed. "But it's like a nineteen-hour journey! At least to Miami, anyway. You have a car? In New York?"

"My friend lent it to me. I'm doing a road trip. Three nights."

"You coming back to New York anytime soon?"

"Why would I?"

"I don't know... to see"—his voice stumbled—"Sara?"

"Bradley, get this through your head. Sara does not want to see me anymore."

"Because of the car accident? Because you were driving when your parents died?"

"Other reasons."

"What other reasons?"

She glanced at the clock on the wall of the diner. It was nearly two. "Look, I've got to go. I've made a booking for tonight at a hotel in Virginia Beach and I need to get there before dark."

"You're packed?"

"All in the car."

"And you're inviting me to come along with you, just like that?"

"You wanted to talk, I've got to leave. It's the only way."

"What would Sara say?"

"I have no idea, ask her."

Bradley's heart was thundering in his chest. He felt like Michael Corleone in that scene in *The Godfather* where his whole life changes, when he's in the restaurant and is deliberating whether he's going to do what he came in there for. Kill the cop. Like Al Pacino, Bradley's eyes were darting frantically about the room as if someone, somewhere, might come to his rescue. Cecelia had put some sort of spell on him. He could say no.

He. Could. Say. No.

He could just say no.

"Okay," he said. "I'll come."

Cecelia let loose a rip of girlish giggles. "Don't be stupid, I was just kidding. As if I'd invite my sister's boyfriend on a road trip with me."

A flare of fury. Bradley's breathing shifted into tight, short, fuming puffs, humiliation coursing through his veins. *Who the hell does this bitch think she is?* Playing these crazy head games. *No wonder Sara doesn't want to see her.*

Cecelia blinked at him. As if she were expecting to be forgiven in an instant. "In truth, I'm not leaving until tomorrow morning. Tonight I'm staying in a motel and leaving first thing."

He could hardly get the words out. His lips a thin, taut line. "So why lie?"

"I was testing you," she said, and flicked her hair. "And teasing you." She elongated the word *tease*. Again, those conflicting feelings of fury and being turned on raged through his body.

Bradley caught her by the wrist again. He didn't care if his grip was ironclad. "Look, all I wanted was to meet and chat to you about Sara. I really don't appreciate these childish games you're playing."

Cecelia looked down. Her thick fluttery lashes reaching just above the high points of her cheekbones. "Sorry."

"Just… no more silly games," he reprimanded. His grip released slightly but he still hadn't let go.

She raised her eyes. Blue, blue, blue, with flecks of silver. "Can I make it up to you?" she said, her voice all soft and seductive.

Jesus.

He couldn't wrench his gaze away. "What did you have in mind?"

"Come with me to the motel. We can talk on the way. Ask me anything you like."

"Where is this motel?"

"Not that far."

"Here, in Manhattan?"

"Yeah, like a twenty-minute drive."

"There's a *motel* in Manhattan?"

"Last one standing. A bit like this diner. A dying breed. I like the anonymity of it. Come with me, why not?"

Just like that, Bradley said yes. As if someone else was speaking through him. He had to have Cecelia. Just one night, he told himself. Or afternoon. Get out of there before dark. *Whatever.* Get in the car and go to this seedy motel with Cecelia. Get it over and done with and then he'd stop obsessing. He knew himself so well… the chase, the fixation. But once he'd done the deed he'd be able to put it behind him.

Nobody knew where he was going. Nobody would see him getting into her car.

He'd not tell a soul. Least of all Sara. And since the two sisters didn't speak to each other there was no risk of Sara finding out.

CHAPTER THIRTY-SIX

Bradley

Bradley felt so awkward and devious, sitting in the passenger seat while Cecelia drove this old car.

For a while, neither of them spoke. All Bradley could think about was Sara.

It was Delilah Scott who had come up with the idea of matchmaking Bradley and Sara. And what a mess Bradley had gotten himself into because of it!

Before Sara came along he'd found it hard to commit... because he couldn't face getting his heart broken again. When Cassandra died his whole world had collapsed.

With guilt.

That overwhelming tirade of emotion knowing he could have done everything differently, and that it was all his fault. His remorseless guilt followed him twenty-four seven, pursued him into his dreams at night, turning them into garish nightmares.

Cassandra.

She had destroyed his life and her own in one fell swoop.

But guilt is a useless emotion unless it pushes you into a different direction to make new choices. Yet, at that point, Bradley wasn't ready for change. At least, he didn't think so.

Cassandra was no more because of him. He couldn't deny it, not even to himself.

He pictured the emerald ring he had given her, lifeless and dull on her dead body. It tore him in two, slipping it off her finger and into his pocket like a thief in the dark, his gaze fixed on the chill of her lips; silent, gone. That ring had represented so much: his future as a family man, and with her death that dream had been snuffed out. What was the point of her wearing the ring, six feet under? When she hadn't loved him anyway?

Because… if she had loved him, she never would have done what she did.

Yes, he took that ring off her finger from her still-warm body. Like a bird that had just died, when you believe you might be able to feel a pulse in its skinny frail neck, a pulse of faint life. But considering he had purchased the ring in the first place, what was so sinful about his actions? The ring was his now she was dead, wasn't it?

Wasn't it?

He took it as a keepsake, a reminder, a trophy, if you like, of a love that never was.

He liked collecting trophies.

Cassandra had gone and destroyed everything.

So why *not* pass on the ring to Sara? It made sense to him. But now he thought about it, that stupid ring seemed cursed. Every time a woman wore it something would go horribly wrong.

His mind backtracked to the moment when Delilah Scott had suggested that he find Sara in the park and start a conversation with her.

"You can't miss her, Bradley. She's there every day with her special-needs dog, Poppy. She sticks out like a sore thumb! I'm sorry, I don't mean that in a bad way, just, seriously, you can't miss her. Sara's very beautiful and very lovely and you will absolutely fall for her. What I mean is, you seriously cannot miss this girl."

"But I walk through the park all the time," Bradley said, "and I've never seen her."

"That's because you're preoccupied with work, probably, or caught up in your own thoughts, with your head in the air and you're not noticing what's going on around you," she reasoned. "Have you ever struck up a conversation with anyone in Central Park?"

"No, come to think of it, I haven't. It would seem… I don't know, a little bit rude almost."

"Nonsense, people do it all the time. Great friendships are made in that park. Love affairs, marriages, divorces, business deals, you name it, everything goes on in Central Park."

"What if I don't find her attractive?"

Delilah tittered, her eyes crinkling. A crumpled, white paper bag that never saw the sun; how did she know so much about what went on in Central Park?

"That's ridiculous," she said. "Sara's so lovely any man would be attracted to her."

Bradley made a face. "Well, I'm pretty picky about my women."

Delilah waved her hand dismissively. "Sara's a goddess. You should be so lucky. Long, glossy dark hair. Slim. Although, I have to admit"—she raised her chin—"it might be very difficult for you to gain her trust or even her interest. She's just crazy about that dog and not much else. Oh, and her work. Talk to her about her dog and her work."

"She sounds kind of boring."

"Trust me, she isn't."

"What does she do? For a living? Is she a New Yorker?"

"I'm not telling you anything about her. That's for you to ask and for you to find out. There's a very deep human being that lurks behind those whimsical eyes. You'll find her fascinating."

"So what should I say to her? That Delilah Scott suggested we hook up?"

Delilah laughed. "Don't you know anything about women? If she gets wind of the fact I have anything to do with this, she'll ignore you and brush you off. No, you cannot let her know I'm at the crux of this. Just engage her in conversation somehow, but don't let her know you know me. If anything comes of the relationship, maybe in the future you can joke about it, pronounce me the greatest matchmaker since Jane Austen's Emma. But Sara's the last person who would be game for matchmaking."

It wasn't the dishonesty that worried Bradley—he was hardly a saint—but this woman with a disabled dog sounded like the last person who would catch his eye.

"You're not getting any younger," Delilah reminded him. "You can't go around playing the bachelor forever. How old are you now? Thirty-nine? Remember, if you don't do something about finding the right woman you'll end up having a midlife crisis and spending all your money on a Porsche."

He laughed. "Sounds like a good idea to me."

"I promised your dad I'd keep an eye on you as long as you were in New York. And you need a woman who you can take home to your family, someone who has good values. Please tell me I'm making sense here."

Bradley nodded. He had lied to his family. A lie of omission more than anything. Why he lied, he wasn't even sure. Maybe it was a kind of F-you thing to make himself seem bigger than his siblings, to gain respect from his parents. It had sort of backfired and now he was entrenched in the non-truth. Lying came easy to him. Sometimes fibs just tripped off his tongue. Uncontrollably. He even believed his lies most of the time. There was no logic to them either. No logic at all. His friends and family back home all thought he worked on Wall Street as a banker. Well, he hadn't exactly *lied*, because he did work on Wall Street. Not as a banker, though. He was a managerial accountant. And it was boring as hell. But he had learned a few things from watching those bullish broker guys and hedge fund managers come and go from the office building. How they dated glamorous women.

It was a piece of priceless luck when, one morning, an old client from abroad sauntered into the office and Bradley was called in for a meeting. The client had wanted to go through the accounting concerning his French tax returns and domicile status. Not really Bradley's job, nor his company's, but this client was uber-important, so Bradley obliged.

The Frenchman, who had been dealing with Bradley for years with email exchanges and the odd phone call, was Monsieur Vincent Claire, and happened, in that moment, to be looking for someone to house-sit his apartment on Fifth Avenue but didn't want to hire anyone through an agency because, despite his extraordinarily wealth, the man thought the fees exorbitant. Typical. Rich people were not rich by accident. It was amazing how they'd quibble over bills and hoard what they had for a rainy day. Monsieur Claire was willing to pay a nominal fee for someone to live in his apartment, mainly to keep an eye on the lush garden on the roof terrace and all the exotic plants in the grand conservatory. He envisaged someone there full-time, but who would also be willing to leave for two weeks, once or twice a year when Monsieur Claire would visit. That ruled out renters. He didn't want a family there with messy kids, or "some neurotic female," but was looking for a neat and tidy non-smoking bachelor who would keep it immaculate.

Bradley fitted the description to a T and offered himself up as the perfect candidate, and because of the trust Monsieur Claire had with the company (millions invested and they'd done a meticulous job), Bradley was hired at a much lower pay rate than any professional house-sitter would have charged, yet all household bills paid without question, so it was a no-brainer. Bradley would save a fortune in rent and be able to put the money aside for his Hawaii home.

An accountant… nobody was more honest than an accountant, surely?

Bradley was *perfect*.

So the next thing he knew, Bradley had full rein—and reign— of this multi-million-dollar apartment on Fifth and 62nd Street. The very same apartment Monsieur Claire had bought from the HookedUp billionaire, Alexandre Chevalier, a few years before.

Monsieur Claire had bought the place mostly as an investment. His wife hated it so never came, and his children were all grown-up and never came either. They had small kids and preferred to summer in the Cote d'Azur and spend the winter skiing in Gstaad. New York was the last place his young grandchildren wanted to come.

At first Bradley was reverent of his new surroundings, terrified to touch anything in case Monsieur Claire appeared out of the blue. But once Bradley had gotten into the swing of it, it was like a hand fitting into its own warm glove. He began to believe that the apartment and everything in it was indeed his.

Although Monsieur Claire had locked the closet of his bedroom, where all his suits were hung in meticulous color coordination, ranging from black Merino wool to pale blue seersucker, Bradley had found the key.

Of *course* he had found the key. Lock a door and you're begging people to open it, aren't you?

And lo and behold, the suits fitted Bradley perfectly, as if they had been tailor-made especially for him. He favored the tamer, more classic styles. True, it was pretty expensive getting them all dry cleaned before Monsieur Claire arrived for his two-week sojourn in New York every year. But then, Bradley got to wear the suits, the ties, the cufflinks, and even the beautiful Patek Philippe *Grand Complications* (that was nestled in a safe behind the closet) for approximately three hundred and fifty days a year. Monsieur Claire, evidently, was not a combination-loving man but one who favored keys. Again, the key to the jewelry safe was "hidden." There was another stunning watch: a Vacheron Constantin, but Bradley just loved the Patek Philippe. It suited his character.

He drew a line at the man's shirts and shoes and bought his own.

It was the beginning of a beautiful friendship between Bradley and Monsieur Claire's array of fine, bespoke suits and accoutrements. Bradley personalized those suits as much as they personalized him.

He *made* those suits. Brought them alive. He was, in effect, doing those suits a favor.

And if the Frenchman ever turned up at the last minute (which had only ever happened once and he still gave a couple days' notice), thank God for twenty-hour dry cleaning in New York City! And even then, the polite Frenchman, ever respectful of Bradley, Monsieur Claire took a hotel for the two nights he was in the city, because it wasn't fair, he'd said, to spring his unannounced arrival on Bradley at such short notice. The only thing Monsieur Claire requested was to spend an hour or two in the conservatory on the roof terrace, where he fussed over a few plants, made some suggestions about planting this and that, and then left, not returning for one whole full year.

However, Bradley was careful. He concocted his own rules: no woman was allowed to leave as much as a toothbrush in the apartment. He kept the place spic and span at all times. He couldn't resist the temptation though—once he understood the power of his new wardrobe and stunning apartment. He suddenly became a catch. The only problem was… the women he attracted demanded maintenance. Expensive gifts, lunches, weekends away. He found this out through many months of trial and error. They were looking for a rich husband, most of them. Even the Ashtanga yoga lot. So the whole experiment had turned sour.

The money-magnet thing was a bore in the end.

But by this time, he had grown accustomed to his chic suits, and above all, the glorious apartment that was as good as his. And Bradley, while not in the "Wall Street" money league, made a pretty good salary. He'd managed to save enough to buy his dream home—a simple one—in Hawaii, and retire.

And once he got his place in Hawaii... Maui probably, or Kauai, he wasn't sure yet... he'd start afresh and leave behind his vices. Just because he'd taken a bite out of the Big Apple didn't mean he had to eat the whole fruit.

"I promise you," Delilah Scott went on. "You won't regret meeting Sara."

Bradley wrenched himself away from his ruminations about Monsieur Claire and the suits and his luck and Hawaii, and focused his attention back to Delilah Scott, an ex-girlfriend of his father's, from before his dad got married to his mother. Since Bradley had been in New York, Delilah had acted as a sounding board for him, and he enjoyed their chats. His mother had no clue Bradley was seeing his father's ex; she would have had a hissy fit, but Delilah did mean a lot to his dad. He couldn't face disappointing Delilah by not meeting Sara.

"Even if you don't fall for her romantically," Delilah said, "she'll be a lovely friend to have and I'm sure you can enjoy going out to movie every once in a while or a nice dinner. I just want her to get out of her apartment and have some fun. I babysit her dog, you see. Sara's such a delightful, lovely girl and she deserves some attention. Some male attention would do her good."

"Okay," Bradley agreed, trying to hide his sigh. "I'll check her out, if you insist. But no promises."

When he did spot Sara in the park a week or two later, he ate his skeptical words. Gobbled them up, in fact. She was gorgeous.

CHAPTER THIRTY-SEVEN

Mrs. Scott

Now

Yes, I admit it. The reason Sara and Bradley met was because of me. Jack had not filled me in with Sara's whole backstory, you see. He had left some very important factors out of the equation, so I had no idea what either of those two were getting into. If I had known what would happen, I would've kept my big mouth closed and not meddled in other people's lives!

CHAPTER THIRTY-EIGHT

The Watcher

One month earlier. Mid July.

It made me laugh that Bradley was slinking around, skulking, thinking nobody knew what he was up to, getting into that car.

Sneaking.

Skulking.

Shifty eyes looking this way and that, no inkling that someone was watching.

What a dunce.

Well *I* was watching.

CHAPTER THIRTY-NINE

Bradley

"It's a stick shift?" Bradley asked, looking at the gears. He needed to make some kind of conversation with Cecelia. The atmosphere was charged. Fizzling, sensual, sexual energy dancing between them.

Every time Cecelia changed gear she brushed his knee, because his knee was purposefully spread in her direction. The heat between his legs was too much, he needed space. She changed down to second, up to third, and fourth, and then to fifth, the car heading downtown, her hand brushing against his thigh, against the soft wool of his suit, yet still he could feel the heat from her fingertips emanating through the fabric.

The next thing that came out of his mouth was, "Who drives a stick shift these days?"

"I learned to drive with gears. I prefer them to automatics, feels like I'm more in control," she said coolly, flashing him a knowing glance.

He had her pegged. She was the type who liked to be on top, he bet. He'd see about that.

"So why Virginia Beach?" he asked.

"I just felt like a road trip, you know, instead of flying. It's been a while. I considered staying at a pretty little town en route, Onancock—very cute, very quaint—but my fans want to see beaches, so I'm partnering with The Cavalier Hotel. You know, free night, free everything, so I'll post a picture on my Instagram. They pay me too, of course."

"Will you do bikini shots on the beach?" He pictured that neon pink bikini, his favorite so far, hiked up the crack of her ass. He wondered what her tan line would look like naked. Breasts like two vanilla ice cream cones. He caught himself licking his lips again.

"Maybe. Maybe not. I'll go with the flow, see how the mood takes me. I may still pass by Onancock and check it out. Have you heard of Onancock?"

Was she kidding him? Did this town even exist? Or did she just like the way the *cock* part of it rolled off her tongue?

"You do very well with this Instagram stuff?" he asked, ignoring what she'd just said.

"Oh, yeah, I make pretty good money and get everything for free. Clothing, you know, stuff like that. Jewelry too." And then she said something that made his blood run cold. "You like giving jewelry to women, don't you, Bradley?" She flicked her eyes at him then back to the road.

An ambulance passed. The siren loud, brazen, slicing into his thoughts.

He arranged his answer in his head. Her question had popped out from nowhere. *Did she know?* "I gave Sara an emerald ring. Is that what you're talking about?"

Cecelia's eyes were glued to the road. "Actually, I was thinking of that beautiful charm bracelet Sara found in your bathroom."

He shifted his knee away from her. "I don't know what you're talking about."

"Yes you do, Bradley. Because it was there one moment and gone the next. You don't have a cleaner so…"

Bradley said nothing.

"A charm bracelet. Gold," she reminded him. "She told me there was a tennis racket, a dog, oh, what else… you know, one of those pretty, girly, charm bracelets but expensive looking. Tiffany quality. She found it in your bathroom. Level with me. Do you have another girlfriend?"

He scoffed. "Course not."

"But you're here with me now so what does that say about you?" She threw him a sidewards glance.

He couldn't answer. Maybe he'd got it all wrong. Maybe Cecelia *did* just want to talk. Maybe all of it was in his head. This… this fantasy of his that she wanted sex with him. Had it all been his doing at that dinner when he'd kissed Cecelia outside the ladies' room? Had he forced himself on her? They'd drunk so much wine.

"Tell me about your family," he said, swiveling the conversation round to safer ground. He wondered if her story was anything like his.

"Why haven't you made love to my sister yet?"

"She tell you that?"

"You're not attracted to her?" She gave him that flash of a look again that gave him so many conflicting messages: *I'm available, I want you. You're not good enough for my sister but good enough for me. Mess with me and you mess with her.*

His head was spinning. "Of course I'm attracted to Sara, she's gorgeous," he shot out.

"As gorgeous as me?" Cecelia laughed. That cackle again.

She irritated the hell out of Bradley. "Actually," he replied, his jaw raised, "she's *more* beautiful than you."

Cecelia made a right and slammed her hand on the horn, missing the fender of another car by inches. "Ooh, I like that. Seems I hit a nerve."

"It's none of your business what's going on between us," he snapped.

She laughed. A heady, throaty, side-splitting laugh. He wanted to smack her. Bend her over and smack her. He was sick of this cat and mouse game. He couldn't believe he'd gotten into the car in the first place. He'd do what he had to do when they got to the motel then pretend this never happened. *Get this woman out of your life,* a voice pattered in his head.

"Our parents ignored us pretty much when we were growing up," Cecelia suddenly offered.

An olive branch.

He shifted in the seat and cracked the window a little. Traffic choking the street. He was trapped in this car. He considered getting out and walking but something compelled him to stay. *Desire to do what he had to do.* "Oh, I didn't realize that," he said. "Sara never told me. I thought you had a great relationship with your mom and dad."

"No. They were too busy saving the world to remember we existed."

"That sucks." So Sara's parents weren't as perfect as she'd made out? She always described her childhood as idyllic, magical.

Cecelia cranked the car into second gear and jerked forward only to slow down to first again.

Why the hell did she borrow this piece-of-shit car and not rent something decent for her trip? Bradley couldn't fathom. He thought Cecelia had money.

"We didn't care about their shitty attitudes," she said. "We had each other."

"Everybody cares what their parents think even if they pretend they don't."

"No," she said emphatically. "We didn't care. The two of us were one happy family. We didn't need them."

"And then you spent time in Switzerland? After Africa?" Bradley asked.

"I hated that place."

"Africa?"

"No. Switzerland. Africa was my heart and soul. Especially Botswana and Kenya. It was Switzerland I hated."

"I've heard Switzerland's beautiful."

Cecelia made a face, her lips turning down at the corners, her gaze fixed ahead of her. "I loathed that country with all my heart. Everything that was wrong with my father was wrong with that place. Beautiful, yes. But cold, clinical, heartless."

"Heartless? I find that so hard to believe. With the job he chose? Giving up his life to help others when he could've been making a fortune as a private doctor somewhere else? Living in mud huts, with no electricity, going into war zones, places riddled with diseases, risking his life for others?" Bradley was aware he might be needling Cecelia. Poking a reaction out of her gave him a strange thrill.

"It was all about his ego," she said. "The job made him feel like a good person and massaged his ego on a daily basis. He felt like a big cheese."

Bradley chuckled. "I haven't heard that expression in a long time. *Big cheese.*"

There was something so childish about Cecelia, as if her development had been arrested at the age of fifteen. She had a cattiness about her. A schoolgirl spite mixed up with her naiveté.

"But you must've been very sad when your parents died. It was around ten years ago, right?"

Cecelia cocked a shoulder like she was shrugging something off. "Not so sad."

Bradley had gleaned more about Cecelia in a couple of hours than he had with Sara over the last few months.

"It was Sierra Leone, wasn't it, where the accident happened?" he pushed on.

She nodded.

"And you were high while driving?"

"Is that what Sara told you?"

"Yes."

"Well, it's not true. She's making it sound better than it really was."

Better? What did she do? "So what actually happened?"

"Oh, I don't think I'm going to share that with you."

Everything about Cecelia made Bradley's hackles rise. The hair on the nape of his neck... rise. Other parts of his body... rise. Like there was no gravity when she was near him.

He needed to put an end to this.

An end to Cecelia.

They arrived at the motel and parked. He considered, for a New-York-minute, to leave, walk to the subway and go home. But something deep inside him, an imperative, instinctive force, propelled him on. It was a Saturday; he had time on his hands.

"I really don't know why I'm here," he told her, getting out of the car.

She slammed the door shut and popped the trunk. Strutted over in her platform heels, lifted out her suitcase and laid it on the ground.

"Do you need help with your case?" Bradley offered, embarrassed he was a little late in the chivalry department. Sara brought out his good manners but Cecelia brought out the beast in him.

The motel wasn't seedy; it appeared quite upmarket, but still, the idea of a motel at all, an anomaly in Manhattan, spoke of elicit, clandestine sleaziness.

He considered again turning right around, leaving his impure thoughts right there in the parking lot with the cigarette stubs and mashed chewing gum that speckled the asphalt. But this irresistible pull, a lure he couldn't even put a name to made him follow Cecelia to the reception, several steps behind her... he didn't want to be seen, his guilt her shadow. He waited while she collected the room key.

In the bedroom there were two beds, both queens. A nondescript beige bathroom. The place could've been anywhere in the world. No character at all. Bradley suddenly felt sorry for Cecelia that she was spending the night in this faceless, sorry place. There was something rejected in the way she held her head. A loneliness. Her sister had spurned her. Cecelia was a one-woman show.

Setting down his small suitcase in a corner, Bradley said, "Do you mind if I ask you a question?"

She kicked off her shoes and one landed on one of the beds. Beige bedspread. Bland and beige. "Depends what it is."

He cleared his throat. "Do you have feelings for me?"

"What do you mean by 'feelings'?" Her voice was a bored, I-don't-give-a-shit voice. He wanted to break through to her, break her down to her lowest common denominator. Crunch her numbers into something, someone he could compute.

She was an enigma to him.

He felt his jaw twitch. "You *know* what I mean."

"You belong to my sister," she answered. "Why do you ask? Do you have feelings for *me*?"

His eyes were unblinking. "No."

A flippant smirk played on her lips "I think you do, Bradley. How can you not?"

Arrogant much?

"How can you not have feelings for me when I'm identical to Sara and you profess to be in love with her?"

"You keep going on about how identical you are, but you're a universe apart."

An unexpected tear slipped from the corner of her eye. He'd struck at her cold heart. Hurt her by what he'd said. Finally pierced her carapace. Half of him rejoiced, the other half wanted to hold her in his arms. He strode toward her, focusing on that tear, telling himself she needed him, how they needed each other. He cupped her head with his hands and kissed the tear, letting its saltiness linger on his lips before he licked it into his mouth. Tasting her. Relishing her. He needed to taste *all* of her, down to her toes, each inch of her skin. The ins and the outs of her. Especially the ins.

"Let's stop playing games," he rumbled, before he tore off his jacket and pushed her backwards, down onto the bed, where she crashed with a comfortable thump.

Unsurprised, she lay there, unmoving, as if resigning herself to what would happen next, her expression not giving anything away.

But he knew Cecelia wanted this.

He straddled her, his powerful knees either side of her torso. And yes, it did give him that thrill of manly dominance, her slim frame so helpless, just lying there hopelessly beneath him, her luscious, shiny hair spread like an angel's. Hair that he would muss up, breathe into, wrap around her throat if he so pleased.

His hands were on hers now, pinning her down, his power thick and visceral, his breathing guttural, his inhale, his exhale, his mouth finding hers; a blossoming rosebud he parted open with his hungry but teasing tongue.

And she was loving it. She was, oh, yes… she was.

He groaned into her and heard her moan back. He felt his heat and every part of him surge into her, sweet and delicious and *his*. Finally this was happening.

She was his.

All his.

And he could—and would—do with her whatever he fucking wanted.

Cecelia was siphoning out the worst in him. The depraved Dorian Gray-darkness was calling him back into its shroud of temptation. It had reached a point where he had to end this. He needed to put an end to Cecelia and everything she represented.

Before she consumed him whole.

CHAPTER FORTY

Sara

Sundays were my favorite day of the week. I'd always get up early, take Poppy out to do her business and then we'd come back and snuggle in bed, just the two of us. I'd read and Poppy would nestle next to me.

Today was just like any other Sunday: my preferred day for reading something that had nothing to do with work. I might do a crossword, or delve into one of my favorite African authors, which would transport me back home to my childhood: the tastes, the smells, the food, the languages. A world away from my life now.

When I first arrived in New York, it was so alien to me. The clean, tasteless fruits, so perfectly formed but without flavor. The sharp lines and shapes of the cityscape, different from everything I had ever experienced. The sirens, the rush of people, seemingly going nowhere and everywhere at the same time. Hurry, hurry, hurry. Now, I supposed, I was no different from those hurried humans; a bona fide New Yorker. I'd been here eight years. And the strange thing was now that I was here, so settled into my routine with Poppy, I was not ready to leave, not even for beautiful Hawaii.

Nor for Bradley.

Especially not for Bradley. As things stood presently.

My phone buzzed. Speak of the devil.

I was expecting his call. He had been taking me out for brunch on Sundays. I always enjoyed a Bloody Mary and a French omelet, and with the weather so fine Poppy was able to come too since we always sat outside, choosing a restaurant with a terrace. I loved our brunches, but today I ignored the phone, watching it ring, Bradley's name lighting up the screen with a frantic glare.

I didn't want to see him. Not today. I needed space and time to think our relationship through.

Figure out my next step.

CHAPTER FORTY-ONE

Bradley

Yesterday, at that dirty little motel, Bradley had soared so high and relished every second of it. He replayed the scene over in his souped-up mind and he felt drunk with ecstasy.

Laser beams of thrilled emotion sang through his body, making each and every cell of his dance with joy, like a great giant hand was lifting him into the air. Flying high.

All was well in his world... until the phone rang. He grabbed it happily, assuming it was Sara finally returning his string of unanswered calls.

"Bradley?"

"Oh," he said, his tone grave. "Hi, Mom."

"Bradley, why haven't you called me back?"

"Sorry. Been so busy."

"Selfish behavior, and coming from my own son too!"

Bradley's skin prickled. "I've been crazy busy."

"Too busy for your own *mother*?"

"Just, like... insanely busy... at work."

"Like*? Like?* 'Like' insanely busy? Either you are busy or you are not busy, but 'like insanely busy' does not make sense! Why can't you speak proper English? How many times do I need to tell you, Bradley, not to overuse and misuse the word like? Like, like, like. What is wrong with you people?"

"I apologize, Mom. I wasn't thinking."

"That's your problem, you never think!"

"How's Dad?"

"He's very disappointed you didn't make it for his birthday. Very disappointed. But of course your 'like busy' life in New York is so much more important to you than your family, isn't it, son?"

"Hello? Hello? Mom, are you there?"

"Yes, I'm here."

"Hello? I can't hear you. The line must've gone dead. Hello? Hello?" Bradley pressed End, pretending he couldn't hear her tirade, wondering how it was possible to be so happy and then so sad all in the space of five minutes. *The ruinous nature of family*, he thought.

That's just the way it was the world over. Rich or poor, furious with one another or proud, you couldn't escape family. He asked himself if there was something he could do about it.

At least… something about his mother.

CHAPTER FORTY-TWO

Bradley

One week had gone by since what went down at the motel. No word from Sara. Cecelia gone. He regretted it, what he'd done, but there was no bringing her back now.

Sara was the important one in his life. Sara was the one he couldn't lose. Cecelia had been like an appendage: non-essential, un-needed, even for Sara. In fact, no, he had no regrets at all when he thought of it this way.

Sara wasn't returning his calls. He had gone to all the usual places in the park, at all different times of day to make sure he'd find her. Not a trace of her or Poppy.

He'd never felt so alone.

The only person who was repeatedly calling him was Sara's cousin, Robbie. The last person Bradley felt like seeing. Robbie was haranguing him for a job on Wall Street. As if he could help even if he wanted to.

Bradley pulled out his phone from his pocket and looked at his messages again. Nothing new. No voicemails, no calls, except from that little punk Robbie. He went onto Instagram and flipped through Cecelia's photos.

No posts for one whole week.

*

Busy in the kitchen, polishing the work surfaces to a high shine, Bradley finally picked up Robbie's call. He couldn't bear the tension any longer. *Speak to the creep then get him off my back for good.*

"Robbie, how can I help?" Bradley said this in a clipped, businesslike voice, assuming Robbie was calling about a job.

He was wrong.

"I've noticed Cecelia hasn't posted on her Instagram for a week," Robbie said in a smirky, slightly singsong voice. Bradley pictured this loser: his anemic face splattered with freckles that merged into ungainly splotches, almost like one big birthmark, his red-rimmed eyes, his skinny, stooped neck. How this guy was any blood relation to Sara, he couldn't fathom.

"Oh, really?" Bradley answered. "I never go on Instagram, I wouldn't know."

"Oh, puh-lease. Don't think I don't know what you got up to, Bradley. You were *seeing* Cecelia."

Blood rushed into Bradley's ears, making him almost black out. He stopped polishing and leaned against the countertop to support his head rush. "I have no idea what you're talking about."

"I think you do."

"No. I don't."

"I have photos, Bradley. Proof. Proof you were seeing her. Getting into her car. The motel et cetera."

Bradley felt that nervy twitch in his jaw again. The muscle that uncontrollably did its own thing. "You're just trying to get a reaction out of me." Bradley's voice was cool, unperturbed. He was good at this. Good at lying.

"Well, of course I'm trying to get a reaction out of you! I'm sure the NYPD would be very interested in what I know," Robbie squealed. Bradley could picture the jerk's devious little smile.

"Look, you little shit, what are you trying to tell me?"

"I think you and I could come to some kind of arrangement."

"What kind of arrangement?"

"I don't want to talk about it over the phone. Let's meet."

The last thing Bradley wanted to do was meet Robbie or even ever see the creep again. But he had no choice.

People were always pushing him into situations, pushing him into doing things he didn't really want to do, weren't they? Like Jacinda. Making him react in ways that he ended up regretting. Cecelia too.

Bradley forced his tone to be flat, unfazed. "I don't know about meeting up. I'm very busy."

"Oh-so-busy with your *Wall Street* job," Robbie mocked.

"Yes, I work on Wall Street, and?" Bradley snapped back.

"On the street itself, yeah, you lying shmuck, pretending you're some hotshot banker when you're not."

"I work in finance. If you read it a different way, Robbie, I'm sorry."

Robbie scoffed. "I know where you work. I know you're just a dime a dozen accountant. And your fancy-schmancy apartment that doesn't belong to you but a totally different person who happens to be French. I found out everything there is to know about you, Bradley Daniels 'Junior.' I've done my homework."

Bradley said nothing. Watched with fascination as his now-clenched knuckles, curled around the kitchen cloth, turned a pasty shade of white. His chest felt tight, his lungs like they needed more oxygen. He wanted to squeeze the last breath out of this nasty, nasty little weasel, show him who'd have the last laugh. "Have you said anything to Sara?"

"Not yet. But if I'm not reimbursed for my knowledge, I think Sara might be fascinated by what I have to tell her. Along with the NYPD, of course."

"Okay. Where do you want to meet?"

"Why, at your apartment, of course. I've heard it's pretty amazing. The trompe l'oeil in that round dining room? I'd like to see it with my own eyes."

"Be here in an hour then. I'll be waiting."

Bradley would be waiting, all right. Waiting patiently.

His phone buzzed again. Delilah Scott. She hadn't been able to get hold of Sara. She had an emergency with Poppy and needed him to look after the dog until Sara resurfaced. Sara still had no idea that Bradley and Delilah knew each other. He'd have to explain that.

Damn.

CHAPTER FORTY-THREE

Sara

I had been consumed by work and meetings all week, and today was no different. I had left Poppy with Mrs. Scott, as usual. She was heading off for a one-week vacation to Jamaica and so she was, as she told me, "milking every last second with Poppy" she could.

I was riding the subway, on my way back home to collect her from Mrs. Scott's apartment, after an important lunch meeting with a publisher. I'd been avoiding Bradley during this busy week (work, the perfect excuse… I could hardly bring up the Michelin dinner or he'd accuse me of stalking him), but I felt bad that I hadn't been more straightforward with him. We needed to talk things through. I hadn't been honest with him. And he hadn't been honest with me either. I thought we could meet at Le Pain Quotidien in Central Park, the place we first started talking. Somewhere public, somewhere safe, where he couldn't admonish me when I handed him back the engagement ring.

I hadn't ghosted him completely; I'd had the politeness, at least, to answer his calls with a simple text telling him how busy I was with work, which was only a sliver of truth. I had changed my route in the park to a different place every day and never my usual haunts, so I wouldn't bump into him. But I'd needed time to work it all out in my head.

My procrastination was answered for me, though, in the form of a note. I arrived back home, on time, and went straight to Mrs.

Scott's apartment before even opening my own door. There was
a note on her front door:

MISREAD PLANE TIME. HAD TO LEAVE. POPPY
IS WITH BRADLEY. CALLED YOU SEVERAL
TIMES BUT NO ANSWER. XXX

Poppy with Bradley? But how did she even have Bradley's
number? I checked my phone. Three missed calls. A voicemail
message. Infuriating. This kept happening with my phone and I'd
even been on forums about it; others also had the same problem:
our iPhones not ringing sometimes, then a time delay in receiving
missed calls and voicemail message notifications.

I called Bradley instantly.

He picked up on the second ring. "Sara."

"Poppy's with you?"

"And hello to you too, stranger," he said in a cool voice.

"Is Poppy with you?" I screeched, ignoring my bad manners
and his veiled accusation.

"Calm down. Yes, she is. And we're on the roof terrace and
she's absolutely delighted, just like her namesake."

I heaved a sigh of relief. "Thank God."

"She's doing great. I have a water bowl up here. Plenty of shade
under the pergola. The roof garden's totally safe."

"I had no idea Mrs. Scott even had your number."

He hesitated. "Well, actually, yes. We know each other very well."

"You do? Since when?"

"Since… look, we need to talk, Sara. I've been phoning you
all week."

"I know, I'm sorry. Can we meet in the park?"

"I think the least you could do is make the effort to come pick
up Poppy at my apartment. She's tired. A walk to the park would
be too much for her. Besides, she's so happy here."

"Okay, sure. I'll be right over."

"Good."

I raced to the street. It was splashing down with rain—a sudden summer downpour—so I decided to take a cab instead of walking. I did not like it one bit that I would be alone with Bradley in his apartment and cursed Mrs. Scott for taking Poppy there in the first place.

Robbie called while I was waiting under the awning of my building for a taxi, my eagle eyes trying to spot an elusive free cab. Uber was telling me it would be a fifteen-minute wait. Too long.

"Robbie, hi."

"I'm on my way to Bradley's," Robbie announced.

"What are you doing, Robbie? Begging for a job again?" I was pretty sure this could only mean bad news.

"I know stuff about Bradley you don't," he said, in a teenage taunt.

"What are you planning, Robbie? Leave the man in peace."

"He's either really dumb or really clever. I'm betting on really dumb."

"Look, could you please just hold off seeing him, because I'm on my way there right now myself. And I'd rather you weren't in the way."

"I'm inside his building as we speak," Robbie breathed into the phone. "Why don't you just cut your losses while you can?"

"Cut my losses?"

"Thought I'd make a deal with Bradley."

"What are you talking about?"

"I've noticed Cecelia hasn't posted for a week on her Instagram page, and I was wondering where she was," he said. "She's, like, disappeared."

My heart thumped nervously, all the more so because there were no free cabs. Rain in New York City… "Robbie," I warned, "what the hell game are you playing?" As I was fumbling around to check I'd brought a fold-up umbrella, Robbie and I got cut off. I called back; it went straight to voicemail.

I pressed Bradley's number, but he didn't pick up. I dictated a text, warning him:

> *Do not under any circumstances let Robbie into your apartment.*

Still no reply from either Robbie or Bradley. Finally, ten minutes later, just as I was about to go by foot, a cab pulled up, by which time, I realized, I should have simply walked to Bradley's. Then the taxi got blocked in a traffic jam on Park. Roadworks. I contemplated getting out and walking… or rather running in the rain.

Robbie was capable of anything. There was no telling what he might do.

CHAPTER FORTY-FOUR

Sara

I ended up getting so frustrated in the cab I got out and walked to Bradley's. By the time I arrived I was soaking wet and panting. He greeted me at the door, Poppy in his arms, a big grin on his face. The perfect "dad" as if he were welcoming me home from work with a hot dinner in the oven. If I didn't have all these reservations about him, knowing what he'd gotten up to at that Michelin-starred restaurant and everything that followed, I would have been delighted.

"Poppy! Sweetie!" I kissed my dog hello. Bradley bent down to kiss my cheek, but I moved away. "Where's Robbie?" I asked.

"Sara, you're drenched. Let me get you a towel to dry your hair. Better, there's a hairdryer in the bathroom. Take off your shoes, you're soaked."

"I'm fine," I said, making puddles on the floor. "I need to get going, I just came by to pick up Poppy. Is her wheelchair around?" I moved forward to take Poppy from him, but he stepped back.

"Is Robbie here?" I asked again.

"Robbie?"

"Yeah, Robbie. He's here, right?"

Bradley shook his head in surprise. "No."

"How weird, Robbie said he was coming, he was right outside your building. I even sent you a text."

"Haven't looked at my phone, I've been playing with Poppy." Poppy licked his face at hearing her name.

I wouldn't have thought much of this, just that Bradley must have been on the roof terrace and didn't hear Robbie arrive, but the look in his eyes was shifty, evasive. I came forward again to take Poppy from him. Again, he stepped back.

"Haven't seen Robbie. I know nothing about his plans," he said, turning his back to me.

"Look, sorry to sound rushed but we need to get going. I've got a deadline, I can't hang out right now."

Then I wondered; had Robbie been fooling around with me? Just his style to tease and taunt. Of course he hadn't arranged to meet Bradley. I'd been gullible to believe him. I'd call Robbie and find out what the hell was going on.

Bradley, still holding Poppy, finally swiveled around to face me. That stone-eyed look was making me nervous.

"Her wheelchair?" I said. "Can you get it, please?"

Bradley didn't move. "It's on the roof terrace. Like I said, we were playing ball." Then he smiled. "Come on up."

"No, that's okay, I'll wait down here while you go get it."

"Please yourself," he said, handing me Poppy, sad to part with her, making a kissy face. "But we need to talk."

"Sure," I answered, humoring him.

He left to go upstairs. Poppy, wriggling with excitement, was too heavy for me to hold for long. I was bursting for a pee, so I laid her down on the floor outside the bathroom and went in quickly. It was one of those pees where you want it to be fast but it streams on and on. I realized I hadn't been to the bathroom pretty much all day and when I got home I was in such a tizzy about Poppy and Mrs. Scott's note and then catching a taxi, I hadn't even gone then.

Finally, I finished. I pulled up my jeans, washed my hands, and when I turned to dry them my heart missed a beat. Robbie's Lakers baseball cap, unmistakable, was sitting atop the laundry basket. *Robbie is still here*, I thought, so why was Bradley lying?

Remembering when I found the charm bracelet, I opened the drawer where it had been. Not there. I gingerly lifted the lid of the linen basket. Tossed on top was a pair of blue platform shoes. Cece's old shoes from way-back-when. I rummaged around. The eerie stocking was still there but buried.

Items of Bradley's women. Little trophies.

Suspicious, I flicked through Jacinda's Instagram page, this time studying each and every photo. Mostly yoga shots, but scrolling nearly all the way to the beginning, there was a photo of her in Australia on the beach, and there it was: the charm bracelet on her wrist, glinting in the sun.

A chill ran down my spine.

"Sara? Are you in there?" Bradley's voice boomed through the door.

"Yeah, just drying my hair, I'll be right out." I tussled the towel on my wet hair and when I came out of the bathroom, my heart beating wildly, Bradley was standing there, Poppy in his arms again.

I tried to stay calm. Like a fool, I'd missed my opportunity to make a run for it while he was getting her wheels.

"Did you bring her wheelchair down?"

"No, it's still up on the terrace."

I swallowed. "I thought you were going to bring it down?"

"Why? Poppy's having such a nice time here, I thought we could all go up and have a drink. Have a talk, how about that?"

"She's tired," I protested. "We really need to get home. Never mind about the wheelchair, just give her to me and we'll go. I can pick it up another day."

Poppy woofed and licked Bradley's face again.

"See? She's not at all tired, are you, Poppy? Would you like to play with Daddy again?"

"Please, Bradley."

"Sunshine, why have you been avoiding me all week? Huh? You know we need to have a little talk."

I had the emerald engagement ring in my pocket to return to Bradley, but I was scared of angering him. If I gave it back now that could really set him off. I'd take Poppy the second I got a chance, do it when I could meet Bradley in public in the park, take Jack with me, for backup. I wouldn't give Bradley the ring now; it was too risky.

He started walking off toward the kitchen, Poppy still in his arms. "Come on," he cajoled. "I'll fix you a drink. Make some cocktails. How about a margarita like we did your first time here on the roof terrace when I made the guacamole? Wasn't that a special evening?"

"Yes," I said, whisper-quiet. "It was lovely." But I stood there, not moving. My heart hammering, not fathoming what to do. There was no way I was leaving Poppy alone with Bradley. I was not about to make a run for it without her with me. He knew that. I could feel the bulk of my phone in my back pocket, but his whip-smart eyes were on me. I should've called the police when I was in the bathroom, but how the hell was I to know he was going to hold Poppy, basically, for ransom?

"Come on, sunshine, what are you waiting for? Let's go upstairs." He pulled me by the hand. I couldn't make that call.

"Where's Robbie?" I asked for the third time.

"I told you, I don't know."

If I let him know I knew, I'd be done for. I had to play it cool.

He led me to the kitchen. *If I could just get my hands on Poppy and make a dash for it.* But Bradley, much stronger than I was, held her in one muscular arm while fixing drinks with the other, all the while his eyes never straying for more than a few seconds from my face. I could see he didn't trust me. Poppy wasn't a big dog, but she wasn't small either. I wasn't able to lift her for longer than a few minutes. But it was no problem for Bradley with his worked-out physique.

"Put Poppy down," I commanded.

He shook his head in a *don't-be-silly* way, a cool eyebrow raised. "Why are you playing games with me, Sara? I know what's going through your mind."

"Do you?"

"You look scared of me, why is that, I wonder?" He winked at me and flashed a grin. I couldn't deny how handsome he was, despite myself, despite my precarious situation. *American Psycho* came to mind again. This time for real.

"I'm not scared," I lied, and gave him a feeble smile.

"Because you know what I'm capable of, don't you?"

"What do you mean by that?" I asked ingeniously.

"I think you know exactly what I'm talking about."

He was striding around the grand marble kitchen gathering ingredients for the margaritas. Glasses. Limes from the fridge. "I'm not giving Poppy back to you, if that's what you're hoping for, which of course it is."

I sat in the kitchen on one of the stools, my elbows planted on the marble island, watching him, waiting. Poppy was delighted at being carried around like a baby and was licking and nuzzling his face. If only she knew. Perhaps it was better she didn't.

He pulled out a glass jar of foie gras from the fridge and set it on the island, opened it awkwardly, because holding a dog and doing things at the same time wasn't easy, but Bradley was not going to let Poppy out of his arms. He dipped his finger into the foie gras and offered it to Poppy, who lapped at it, voraciously, absolutely thrilled.

"Sometimes I have a visitor," he told me. "His name is Monsieur Claire. Vincent Claire, a client of mine from France. He brings foie gras as a gift. I know it's not to your taste, Sara. It's very cruel what they do to geese to produce this. They force feed them until their livers burst, ram tubes down their throats. But you have to admit, it is delicious. A total delicacy. You see how Poppy's enjoying her little treat? Now, if you could help me by squeezing these limes, that would be wonderful."

He nodded toward a pile of limes on the countertop. "And in the cabinet over there you'll find the Cointreau and the tequila, and in the other cupboard over there you'll find the sea salt." His voice was authoritative but friendly, as if we were a couple and I was the dutiful wife. All the while holding Poppy and feeding her the foie gras.

Turning my back to him, while he was distracted, I silently pulled my phone from my pocket and, hunched over, was about to quietly tap out nine-one-one. But Bradley had been watching me from his peripheral vision and snatched the phone clean from my hands without even looking at me. It was now in the back pocket of his jeans. Just like that. And when he turned and caught my gaze, there was no anger in his eyes, only an expression of pure adoration.

The man is in love with me.

"We'll all go upstairs onto the terrace and have a delicious cocktail. And then you know what's going to happen after that, don't you, honey?"

"No," I said in a very small voice.

"I think you do. I think you know. I think you have a very good idea of what I'm going to do with you."

CHAPTER FORTY-FIVE

Sara

Once on the terrace, the door from the roof garden to the apartment clicked shut. I tried to push it open but couldn't.

"Oops," he said, "the door just locked itself, and I can't remember the combination to open it." It had a keypad.

"That's so dangerous," I said, my heart rate accelerating.

"The opposite actually. It's in case of fire. An extra safety precaution so the pressure, if there's a fire in the apartment, won't make the door burst open. The old owner, the HookedUp guy I told you about? He had it designed that way so, in case of emergency, a helicopter could land on the roof. You know, after 9/11, I guess he was pretty paranoid."

There was no escape for me now. Bradley was lying about the combination, of course he was.

He set Poppy up in her wheelchair. There was even a little paddling pool for her at the other end of the garden they'd been playing in, earlier, wheels off. "She was having such fun today. It was hot up here at noon," he told me.

Some of the trees provided shade on the terrace and there was a pergola with twisted wisteria, the flowers not in bloom, but the leaves also providing plenty of shade. I looked at the view over to Central Park, gazing in the direction of the *Alice in Wonderland* statue and cursed the day I ever set eyes on Bradley. Sidling closer to the edge, I looked down. Way too far to jump, the trees too far away to spring onto. But even if I could do that, what about Poppy? My only alternative was to stay calm, but I had no idea what screwed-up thoughts were going on in his serial-killer mind. Cassandra, Jacinda, Robbie, and now me. The blue shoes. *The one that got away.* Did he strangle each person with that silk stocking? And those black gloves I remembered seeing last time. But then Cassandra died of cancer, didn't she? I wondered what Bradley had done with Robbie's body. He hadn't had much time before my arrival. Where had Bradley put him? Somewhere in the apartment. In a closet maybe? It was a difficult balance. I needed to keep Bradley talking, but I didn't want to press his buttons and make things worse. If he knew I knew…

My mind was doing acrobatics… maybe I was crazy? Maybe I was hypothesizing, letting my imagination go off on some wild tangent? Bradley was not that person! If he were, then there's no way I would have dated him. I would have sensed something. *No, he may have women issues, may be a lying, two-timing bastard, but he is not a murderer.*

He had spread out the tartan blanket on the lawn, under the shade of the pergola. The same wool blanket he had used for the picnic in the park at Cherry Hill. Getting everything up the stairs had been quite a mission. The drinks—the jug of margarita—was beside us on a low table. All the while, he had had Poppy canoodled in his arms, so what could I do? I knew what some people would think… *But it's only a dog. Leave, make a run for it, never mind the dog, get the hell out of there, it's your life!*

But I am not one of those *it's-only-an-animal* kind of people. Poppy was my *child.* How would you feel if your child had been abducted? Would you make a run for it and leave your child with the crazy person? No, I didn't think so. Besides, a little voice was telling me everything would be fine if I just stayed cool. But with the roof door firmly locked…

"So how do you and Mrs. Scott know each other?" I asked.

"Delilah Scott's an ex-girlfriend of my father's. Before her accident they were dating. I guess you know she was parasailing on vacation and had a nasty crash? Mostly paralyzed from the waist down, poor thing. I looked Delilah up when I first came to New York and we've stayed in touch ever since. Thing is, my mother doesn't know, so I guess I've been in the habit of keeping Delilah a secret. Plus, I have a confession to make."

He recounted the story of how Delilah Scott had told him to find me in the park; how she had recommended that he date me. Shocked was an understatement to how I felt. I'd been deceived too. I had trusted her implicitly. *Thank you so much, Mrs. Scott, for landing me in this shit.* I guessed she didn't know Bradley was a psycho… or was she in on it too? Some kind of groomer for him? Procuring women for his murder habit? How could I get the hell out of there? But I knew if I made any sudden movements, I might end up dead. The man was strong. In that moment it was as if everything was suspended in the air. All I could think of was: *it's not about me but my dog…* what happens if Poppy ends up with no parent? Worse, what happens if Bradley does something to her?

No, that was a crazy idea.

Each and every time my mind pattered on in fear, conjuring up images of dead bodies and Bradley strangling his victims with that stocking, reason would kick in and tell me I was being ridiculous, that just because he was a bit odd it did not make him a killer, and there was some kind of explanation for everything.

But he then went on to tell me about Monsieur Claire, the real owner of this apartment. And my mind jumped back to thinking the worst again.

"But you told me you owned this place," I said, baffled, trying to recall our conversation when I first came here that time for dinner.

"No, I didn't, actually. It was what you *assumed*. I just told you I had contacts, which is true."

"Lie by omission," I pointed out.

"Well, we all know about lies by omission, don't we, Sara? Are we really going to pull the lying card now? I seem to remember the first lie by omission you laid on me was when you pretended I was off to meet your family for dinner and, in fact, I met Jenny and your loser cousin Robbie."

What he said was true, I couldn't deny it. "Speaking of Robbie," I said, my voice trembling. "Where is he? I know for a fact he was on his way here. I know for a fact he came to this apartment." Earlier, I had made up my mind to not mention Robbie, because it would let Bradley know I knew, but something even worse slipped out of my mouth. "I saw his baseball cap in your bathroom." *Oh God why had I blabbed that?*

Bradley's lips tilted into a sardonic smile. "I dealt with Robbie," he said. "Don't worry."

Don't worry? "You *dealt* with him?"

"He got his comeuppance. Or, at least, he will."

"He's still alive? Where is he?"

Bradley burst out laughing. So hard, he was rolling around on the rug, hugging his stomach. "You think I killed him? Oh, Sara, you are hilarious."

But my eyes were smarting, tears rolling down my cheeks.

"Oh, sunshine, you're really scared for real, aren't you?" He sat up and brushed my tears away, then licked his fingers like my tears tasted delicious. He was enjoying this, the sick bastard. Enjoying my pain.

"Am I next?" I whimpered. "All I ask is, please don't harm Poppy."

"Hey, Popps, come here. Come here, Poppy, Daddy wants to give you a big cuddle."

Poppy raced over, her wheels trundling behind her, oblivious to what was going on. Bradley kissed her nose and her eyes and her ears, and petted her head, holding it between his great palms.

He made a smacking sound with his lips. I could hardly watch. Sitting on the blanket, I curled my arms around my legs, tucking my head into my knees. "Did you bring the stocking up here?" I mumbled. "I bet it's in your pocket."

"Stocking? What are you talking about?"

"The old-fashioned silk stocking in the laundry hamper, in the bathroom. Is that what you use to strangle everyone with?"

Bradley couldn't speak he was so convulsed with laughter. Poppy let out a delighted yap, happy he was happy.

"Is that how you killed Jacinda?" my voice croaked out. *I might as well lay it all out on the table, pile on all my chips, because I am done for. Maybe he'll have pity on me, and spare me?*

Bradley's expression suddenly turned poker-straight. Deadpan. His eyes like stones, the brown of his irises turning a dull black. He stared at me. "No, I didn't strangle Jacinda. I chopped her up into little pieces." And then he roared with laughter again, still holding my gaze. "I distributed the different parts of her body all over New York City. You know, an arm here, a leg there."

He was kidding, he had to be. "What about Cassandra?" my voice said. My mind was elsewhere: with the garbage trucks and their sordid contents.

"Okay, now this is where I need to get honest with you, sunshine. I felt terrible really, about that ring. Which I notice you're not wearing, by the way. And haven't been wearing all week, right?"

I nodded, tears streaming down my face. "I was going to give it back to you." I choked out my words, my voice barely audible.

"You know I did wrong by you. Because that emerald ring belonged to Cassandra. At least, I bought it for her, so when she died, my logical mind told me that she, being too stubborn to even *try* to live, and actually being dead too, really wouldn't care if I took the ring back. I had intended to sell it. But then, well… I changed my mind. I think it was your twin's fault, you know, your *twin*? She kind of pressured me into putting a ring on your finger and… we know what happened to Cecelia, don't we?" He started laughing again.

I pictured the blue platform shoes in the laundry hamper.

"But I agree," he went on. "It's not a very nice thing to do really, to give your ex-girlfriend's ring to your new fiancée-to-be. I'm sorry, honey, I shouldn't've done that. It was thoughtless of me. I'll buy you something, just for you."

I took the emerald ring out of my back pocket and handed it to him. Another one of his trophies, but worse, because he'd passed it on to me, it made it feel like warmed-over death. What "trophy" would he take from me? If he was into body parts it could be anything: a tooth, a finger… oh God, it didn't bear thinking about. Yet now he was talking about buying me a new ring? The guy was really warped. I bent down and drew Poppy to me, our heads touching, my tears spilling on her fur. I breathed in her Poppy smell warmed by the sun… there was still good in this world.

"Don't worry, sunshine, Poppy's safe with her daddy. Daddy would never harm little Poppy, would he, baby?"

After coochy-cooing with Poppy for some minutes, he turned to me. "I think she's had her wheels on for long enough now and needs to rest." And then he said, in his baby-voice again, "Little Poppy needs to rest, doesn't she? She can come and snuggle next to Daddy."

He took Poppy's wheels off—he had it mastered—and settled her down on the rug. Lying back on his elbows, gazing at the bright blue sky, a few clouds scudding past, he remarked, "Wow, New York really is *beautiful* in the summer, isn't it? So many people leave the city in the summertime, but they're fools. I always think New York City in the summer is just perfect."

I didn't reply. The only thing going through my head was getting off this roof terrace with Poppy, both of us in one piece.

"Okay, okay," he went on, "it's true, there's a bit of a garbage smell here and there and it can get unbearably hot, and, oh, God, in the subway it's awful—and I have to take the subway to work, a taxi would take forever—but otherwise, this city's just great, isn't it? But now I've been told I've got to leave this apartment soon, because Monsieur Claire wants to sell—well, I'll miss New York, that's all I'm saying. But that doesn't mean… oh, Sara, aren't we just the perfect family, you, me, and Poppy?"

He was still blinking at the sky, all dreamily. "I think we should have kids, don't you, honey? What would you prefer, a boy or a girl? Maybe both. I think one of each would be perfect, what do you think, what do you say, sunshine?" He flicked his eyes to me then back at the sky, not waiting for an answer, almost as if what I thought about all this was incidental.

"Do you think it's better to have the boy first and then the girl?" he droned on. "Or the girl and then the boy? If the boy comes first, he might bully his little sister, which would be terrible, being stronger and all. I think it's always better if the girl's a little bit older, what do you think?"

I needed to humor him, lull him into a hopeful sense of security so maybe he'd unlock the roof terrace door. There were a couple of landlines downstairs, I could call 911. Even if I didn't talk, they'd have my location. If I could just whisper "help" and hang up the phone, that would be enough. "I think," I said cautiously, my voice wispy, "it doesn't really matter as long as the child's healthy and happy. And it's up to the parents to make sure no bullying goes on between siblings."

"Or maybe you'll have twins, that's possible isn't it, or does it jump generations? Were you and Cecelia natural twins, or was your mom taking Clomid, you know, one of those fertility drugs?"

"Natural." I sniffed. "How do you know about Clomid?"

"Cassandra and I were trying, you know, before…"

Then something scary dawned on me. "You just said '*were* you and Cecelia natural twins,' not '*are* you and Cecelia natural twins.'"

"Did I?" he said.

That's when I suspected he knew what I'd done.

CHAPTER FORTY-SIX

Sara

Now

"Do you have any idea why we brought you in here for questioning?" the detective asked me. The nice detective, this time. The Bronx guy, Detective Elba.

"I can guess," I said enigmatically. I knew this was all about Cecelia.

"We'd like to know more about Bradley Daniels, who you and your twin were, or still are, both dating," he said, folding his hands together behind his back.

My lips were sealed.

The female detective zoomed in on me at that point. Her eye contact was unwavering. She'd no doubt been trained to read my facial expressions for clues as to whether I was lying or not. "When did you last see him?" she asked, drilling her gaze into me.

I said nothing. My nerves had made my mouth go dry.

She started talking about video surveillance footage they had of Bradley and Cecelia entering the motel. My head was buzzing with my own fearful thoughts mixed with the drone of her voice. She leaned in closer, saying, "Thing is, three hours later, Cecelia, your sister, left that very same motel, and Bradley Daniels wasn't with her, so we were hoping you could shed some light on this. Because nobody has heard of her, or from her, since. She stopped posting on her Instagram page. You think that's normal, with nearly a million followers, to suddenly stop posting?"

This is the moment, I thought. *The moment they're going to arrest me for murder.*

She prattled on, "We think something happened to her. We're not assuming this is a story about a woman who simply got fed up and needed a break. No, a person who posts consistently over a period of several years"—she looked at her file—"six years, every single day, come rain or shine… well, in her case always shine, is unlikely to just opt out. You know anything about that?"

I kept my mouth shut.

The detective went on, "Your sister is *missing*, Miss Keller. Does that not bother you?"

Was it just my imagination or did the way she said Keller sound like "*killer*"? I could no longer listen to this. "Look, this is so not what you think."

"What do we think?"

"That I killed my sister."

"*Killed* her? Who said anything about her being dead?" The detective's lips lit up into a tiny *"Ha! caught-ya!"* smile. They had me on tape. Their evidence against me. I was really screwed now.

"I need an attorney, please."

CHAPTER FORTY-SEVEN

Sara

A week earlier

"I'm sorry," Bradley said, absentmindedly stroking Poppy, who was stretched out sleeping, her little snores the only calm in the midst of this emotional storm. He took a long gulp of his margarita.

"Sorry for what, exactly?" I was curious. There were *lots* of things he needed to be sorry for, but I wondered what exactly he was referring to.

He frowned. "You know what I'm talking about."

"Do I?"

"Yes, you do. I know who you are, Sara. I know about Cecelia."

I looked down at my chewed cuticles. My whole world felt as if it had tumbled in on itself. I had been waiting for this pivotal moment, fearing the worst, but I hadn't prepared myself for the consequences. Bradley was right in the middle of this mess, had been the catalyst, and now what would happen? Would he put an end to it all? "What do you know?" I said. My voice had lost all strength; a numbness spread through my body, reaching the tips of my fingers. I studied them, too afraid to look up. He didn't reply, so I repeated my question, a little louder this time. "What do you know?"

"That you and Cecelia are the same person." There was no anger in his tone. No accusation, just a statement of a simple fact. He waited for me to respond.

I said nothing. How was I supposed to react? My heart plummeted to a place no heart belongs. It was as if my body was separated from my mind, my soul somewhere in a void, looking on helplessly, remembering.

Remembering why.

He carried on, his voice low and soft. "It was after we had sex. She… or rather, *you*, were lying in bed quietly, your gorgeous hair spread out. So beautiful. You thought I was asleep, but I had one eye open. You were waiting for your moment to escape me. You turned on your side, and your back was white, the flesh pale, but the rest of you sun-kissed. At first I thought, *Oh, Cecelia isn't naturally brown, she uses fake tan on her legs and arms and couldn't reach her back.* But the sheets and pillowcase were streaked a bronzy color, and I thought, no, fake tan doesn't stain like that; it was, in fact, body makeup. Body makeup that could be applied and washed off again so you could switch back and forth between the two identities. It seemed crazy though. *Would she really go that far?* I asked myself. But then I noticed 'Cecelia's' hand, or rather, *your* hand—your left hand—was splayed out over the sheet. There was a slight indentation on your finger like you'd been wearing a too-tight ring. It was swollen, like you'd battled with the ring to yank it off your finger. And that's when I really got it, when I was onto you. Your white back, the bronze body makeup, the mark on your ring finger from the engagement ring you'd taken off… it all slotted into place. You, Sara, were pretending to be Cecelia."

I breathed in, breathed out, waited for Bradley to go on, which he did.

"Was it just this one time, I asked myself? Or each and every time I'd met up with Cecelia? I had no way of knowing. I was about to confront you, see if that beauty spot was real, and that's when you got out of the bed, tiptoed off, noiselessly. I lay there like a stone, so shaken I didn't know what to do, what to say, wondering if I was bat-shit crazy imagining stuff. I couldn't be a hundred percent sure of anything anymore. Because certain things didn't make sense. Why would you, Sara, eat hamburgers when you don't eat meat? By this time, I was so confused and so screwed up with you both in my life: Sara, and Cecelia, or maybe just Sara being two people, I couldn't think straight anymore. Couldn't figure out what was real and what was false, or if I was going nuts."

I sat there silently, saying nothing, denying nothing. Bradley talked on, hardly stopping for breath. "It was Robbie who confirmed it when he came here, earlier today. Told me you led a double life, that it was you who ran Cecelia's Instagram page, used Photoshop to manipulate the images with ocean backdrops and even tweaking your own body with filters and stuff. That Cecelia died a long time ago, along with your parents in Africa. That she wasn't real, she didn't exist. Or she did once but hasn't for ten years. And even now I know nothing for sure, but what I do know for sure is that I loved a woman named Sara and got reeled in by her twin sister, Cecelia, and kind of fell for her too, and now… well, the beauty of it is that I don't have to choose. Because you're one and the same person."

CHAPTER FORTY-EIGHT

Sara

Being Cecelia had started off incidentally; I had never planned it.

Six years ago, four years after the loss of Cece and my parents, I went to Thailand on vacation. Thailand had always been Cece's dream. This trip was a homage to her. I went to a small island called Ko Phangan, famous for its full moon beach parties, though I stayed in the quieter, northwest part of the island, in a lush jungle setting, not far from the azure-blue sea, warm and wonderful. It was all about palm-leafed bungalows: a backpacker haven, although quite a few tourists came over from the more commercial hotspot of Koh Samui, only ten or so miles away.

I remember looking in the mirror and being stunned as I no longer saw myself, but Cece. Tan, my eyes shining: chips of ice blue they were, my skin a deep caramel brown from so much sun. I'd never felt so happy, not since my family was alive. It was just what the doctor had ordered to pull me away from my misery.

I hung out with this guy from Paris who was a photographer and he took a bunch of awesome photos of me on the beach, in the sea, splashing, playing and throwing my hair so it made an arc of water. When I saw the pictures, all I could see was my sister. He sent them to me via email and told me they were mine to do what I wanted with. He suggested that I start an Instagram page. I asked, "What for?" And he told me *that's what everybody's doing.* There was no way I wanted to put myself out in public like that. I was far too shy, but then I got thinking… as far as I was concerned I was looking at photos of my sister. And then I came up with the idea of making it Cecelia's Instagram page instead of my own. It was a way for me to imagine how her life would be now; what she would be doing, and I knew this was the kind of life she would be leading. Free. Wild. Traveling. It was always what she dreamed of doing. She talked about taking a couple of years off backpacking, visiting Southeast Asia and Australia, and New Zealand, working along the way, as a waitress or bartender or a sheep shearer, or whatever. That was her dream. Of course, her dream died along with her. This was what her vision board had been all about before the dreaded rape. Before her confidence was smashed.

Before. Before.

Before her life was ruined by that monster in a respectable white coat when she was sixteen.

Our deflowering, losing our V-cards, was meant to be fun, meant to be special: the two of us losing our virginity at the same time. We had even discussed doing it the same night, dressing up in identical outfits and tricking a man of choice into sleeping with us. So we could share that life-changing experience, forever and ever till death do us part.

It was Cece's idea, this madcap scheme, to do it on our eighteenth birthday. She said, "We can pick the most gorgeous man, whoever we choose. Maybe even a movie star."

Ever since my mother had met Angelina Jolie, who'd come to one of the refugee camps where Mom was working, Cece was convinced that meeting celebrities was a given. That it was written in the stars for us.

"But we might not love the man," I said, worried.

"That's the whole point! We don't want to *love* him! Just find him sexy and nice. If you love someone, you give them your power. Do you want some man holding his power over you for the rest of your life, him knowing he has taken your virginity?

No! We won't even tell him. It'll be a secret. Don't ever give them your power."

I didn't quite get what she was telling me, but I nodded anyway.

"We'll plan a dinner," she said, eyes wide. "Buy the most beautiful dresses, the same *exact* dresses. Everything will be the same, he won't have a clue."

I tried to wrap my head around the logistics of it. "But it's impossible," I told her, "because whoever's first in bed will be the first to lose their virginity, so it can't be at the same time."

"So what? The main thing is that we do it the same night. We'll take it in turns."

"So who gets to have dinner?" I asked, thinking of the sumptuous meal with this phantom man who would lavish his money on us. "Will he take one of us or both of us to dinner?" The delicious dinner was more important in my mind. I wondered if I could leave the virginity-losing part up to Cece and back out at the last minute, but then I knew she'd never let me get away with that.

"You have the hors d'oeuvres," she said, "then you go to the ladies' room. Then I have the main course, then I go to the ladies' room… you get the idea?"

"That's not fair," I pointed out. "I want to have a main course."

She laughed. "Okay, fine, we can do it the other way around. I'll start and then you continue, and then I'll have dessert."

"What happens," I hypothesized, "if during the dinner we decide he's a jerk and I don't want to carry on with it. Or vice versa."

"Then, when we cross paths, to and from the ladies' room, we can make a sign to each other."

"That means we won't be able to do it on our eighteenth birthday," I reasoned.

"It doesn't matter. The point is we have to do this together, both of us. We can't have one of us being a virgin and the other one not."

"What if one of us gets a serious boyfriend before we're eighteen?" I asked.

So far, neither of us had had a steady relationship. We hung out with various guys, but no one special had snagged our attention to the point of being exclusive.

We were sitting cross-legged on our beds, trying on different outfits and makeup. It was amazing how, with different colors or outfits we could change ourselves to look unique, different from each other. And likewise: if we wore the exact same thing and the same colors, nobody could tell us apart. Not even our parents. Except, of course, for Cece's mole.

"No worries," Cece said, "we have lots of time. We're still only fifteen. I have no intention of going all the way with a boy. I know what they're like. They can look but they can't touch! If they get their way, they change personality. If you want to keep your power you have to make them *wait,* you have to make him *long* for you. Never give them what they want," she advised.

"But what if you want to?" I asked. "What happens if you want it just as much as the boy?"

"Then you kiss and you do other things, but you don't let them put it in."

I noted Cece seemed to know everything when it came to the opposite sex. I trusted her implicitly.

"Blue is your color," she told me. "Red's mine. I look good with a tan, you look good pale. Isn't that strange?"

Cece was cutting out a model in a woman's magazine, carefully guiding the scissors around the contours of a red dress. She was making a collage of how her life was going to be. Beaches, exotic places, palm trees. "Creative visualization," she told me, "is the way to go."

I didn't have a collage because I had no idea what I wanted. Not yet anyway.

And here I was, all these years later, in New York, still not really knowing what I wanted, just knowing what I didn't want. Cece's creative visualization had been trampled on, torn to pieces and trashed by that man in the white coat.

Cece's Instagram page was my way of putting things right in this unfair world. Visualization, if you like, on her behalf.

I put up the first fifteen photos, with all the relevant hashtags, and my account went wild. Girls in bikinis sell, don't they? It was strange; I could be objective. It was as if the photos were not of me at all, but someone else.

My sister.

I got so many likes, so many followers, mostly (strangely) from women, not men. People would say how great these pictures were, as it gave them hope. Maybe it was a way for them to envisage what their vacation would be like if they took the plunge and went somewhere exotic like Thailand.

I hadn't thought ahead: where this account was going. But it seemed that all my followers assumed I was living in Thailand, where my home was, full-time. I was this beautiful girl living in Thailand having the kind of life they all wished they had. But nobody was resentful or jealous. Quite the opposite. It was all so positive, so girl-power. They didn't want me to come back to New York, I could tell by the comments. They wanted to sit at their desks at work, looking out the window at the rain or the gray skies and fantasize about what their life would be like if they could be me. Yeah, I got a few mean comments here and there: some trolls bitching about their lives and how sickening it was to see me doing nothing all day except sipping cocktails and swimming in the sea, but mostly everybody was very positive.

When I got back to New York, there was a hiatus when I didn't post any more photos. My followers—or rather Cece's, because that's the way I saw it—were clamoring for more posts.

So I dug into other photos: the ones the Parisian photographer had done. There were hundreds. Then companies started asking me to partner with them, for me to sponsor their products. It was crazy. With my Photoshop skills I was able to add a piece of jewelry on my body or put a drink in my hands or change a bikini over. It took a lot of work, but then that's what I do. It's my skillset. I know how to make it look real. So, unwittingly, I had started something and I just couldn't stop.

Cece came alive.

And I didn't stop there. It occurred to me, while I was in Thailand, that I was still two people. I had Cece's passport; it hadn't expired yet. It had eight months to go before it needed to be renewed. There was nothing that could tell us apart except for Cece's mole on her cheekbone. Other than that we were one and the same.

Or rather, we were now two.

I opened up bank accounts in Cece's name. I was making extra money, although in my head it was Cece's money. It was like a parent saving for her child's college education or something. Completely crazy, but there I was storing away this money in a savings account, with the earnings from Instagram. I had even set up a brokerage account and bought some stocks and shares, also in Cece's name.

The imaginary conversations between us started. I missed my sister so much, and now she was alive with her own Instagram page, her own bank accounts, we'd chat every night. We had so much to discuss! I would ask, wait a beat while I listened to what I heard her say in my head.

It was easy: every time I looked in the mirror I was seeing her, not me. That's what happens when you are mirror twins. You never really know what you look like, but you do know what your sister looks like.

When I looked in the mirror, Cece was staring back at me.

I was her and she was me.

Filters and Photoshop tricks were getting more and more sophisticated, so it was easy for me to airbrush out any cellulite or unflattering skin tone. Cece was a sun-bunny. With Photoshop I could make anything come true. Give myself a nice round butt, for starters.

When I had run out of photos from Thailand, I started to pose back in New York, using a green screen as backdrop, which I set up in my apartment. I had it affixed to the wall and would roll it down when I needed it, using a tripod and a timer on my camera. I'd do poses, then I'd superimpose the background afterward. Even amateurs can do this these days, but with my skills I was able to make it all look so realistic and carry on where I had left off in Thailand. By now, it had turned into a little business. How could I pass up this opportunity to make money? The more I did this, the more Cece became an integral part of my life once more. It made me feel like she was still with me. I imagined what she would say, the advice she might give me, the things she'd find funny or outrageous. The scathing, cutting remarks, the eye-roll, the banter. I was able to live through her, and she through me. It gave me strength, made me feel I was not alone.

And Cece wanted—no, needed—to be heard.

Sometimes the silent voices are the loudest of all.

CHAPTER FORTY-NINE

Sara

I reflected on that day in the motel last week with Bradley. The culmination of it all, the finale.

Driving to the motel, there was a car in front of us, with a bumper sticker that read:

BE THE PERSON YOUR DOG THINKS YOU ARE

Not even Poppy knew this persona I had created. I had veered way off course, was doing things alien to me, Sara. I had allowed myself to spin out of control.

That day would be Cecelia's swan song, I decided, at least the "Cecelia" I had created.

Being this mishmash Cecelia—a person who wasn't even like my sister anyway—was stripping me of my own identity. My God, I was even eating meat! It was as if I was giving myself permission to do anything at all, to be a bad girl.

That day in the motel, after everything happened, Bradley had dozed off and was sleeping—or so I'd thought—when I slipped out of the room, late afternoon.

Before I left, I gazed at him for a couple of minutes, watching him sleep; not quite the face of the same Bradley I had met in the park, four months before, but almost. This was the face of a man sated by sex.

I saw, I conquered, I came. Is that how he felt?

Everything had changed now.

It had been quite fun playing "Cecelia" up until Bradley pinned me on the bed and fucked me. He did not make love to me but ravaged me. Raw, forceful. It wasn't rape; it was consensual, but only just. There's a fine line between wanting something and allowing it, and I guess if I had yelled at him to stop, he would have. But I didn't even think of yelling. So yes, it was consensual, maybe even sensual, in a strange, twisted way. I went with the moment, letting myself succumb to his passion and my warped need to go through with what I'd started. What began as acquiescence turned into something visceral, bordering on erotic.

I did feel our passion for a while, I truly did. But I understood that Bradley had a problem. He was two people, even more so than I was. He had a madonna/whore complex and a strange relationship with women. As Sara, he respected me, revered me. As Cecelia, he hated me but was also obsessed. And I had played him. I had invited all of it. As I lay beneath him, his mouth over mine, his hands pinning my own above my head, he powered into me, growling filthy words, his tongue sliding into my mouth, claiming me, love and hate mingling in a medley of crushed emotions, but on both sides. I felt the drum of his heart against my breast, and when he unclasped one of my hands and set my arm free, I didn't try to escape or push him away. I let him carry on.

I let him. My body welcomed him.

And when he cupped my ass in his hands and brought me closer, I cried out, not with anguish but with desire, despite myself.

I was with him in the moment. Every heated, bruising inch of him, every hot, pounding breath, I was there.

It ended in a crescendo of slaked, impounded lust.

As Cecelia.

That was my last reenactment of my twin.

It was time to reclaim my mental equilibrium. For years my identity had been wrapped up with my sister. It was time to let her go. To free myself, to free her too.

I left her suitcase in the room; I didn't want to make a noise for fear of waking Bradley. In the case were things of hers. Stuff I had kept that I also needed to let go. Some old dresses, jeans, and a couple of pairs of shoes, some cheap jewelry. Why hang onto these any longer? I picked out a pair of sneakers from the case, some clean jeans and a T-shirt and left everything behind, including some high, blue, platform shoes I'd been wearing.

I was back to being myself, back to being Sara. I had taken off all my makeup, the false eyelashes, rubbed off the beauty spot with cold cream. I didn't have a shower; I did that later when I got home. I smelled of lust and lies and deceit.

I had a feeling, at that point, that Bradley might be onto me. He would have been a fool not to twig that I was two people in one.

And now, after what he'd told me, I knew for sure.

The car I drove that day belonged to a friend. I had borrowed it that morning to move some stuff out of my apartment and take to Goodwill: namely the huge green screen I'd used as a backdrop for all the Insta photos. Meanwhile, Mrs. Scott was babysitting Poppy.

If Bradley had *not* caught onto my game, for some reason, and was confused as to why Cecelia's suitcase was still in the motel room, it served him right. But then it dawned on me he probably wouldn't care. He had treated "her" so badly, perhaps he didn't give a damn if he never saw her again. So, as far as he was concerned, she must have left on her road trip.

It was such a relief when I picked up Poppy from Mrs. Scott's that evening, and woke up in bed with my dog the following Sunday morning. We didn't need to think about a third-party in our lives because we had each other and it was perfect.

It was over with Bradley.

At least, that's what I thought.

Until his unbeknownst-to-me-friend Mrs. Scott left Poppy at his apartment, a week later, when she nearly missed her flight and I had no choice but to collect my unsuspecting dog.

And here I now was.

Trapped.

CHAPTER FIFTY

Sara

"So, tell me," Bradley said, his legs stretched out on the tartan rug, under the shade of the pergola and the maple tree on his roof terrace, "how did Cecelia die?"

"I'm not ready to discuss it," I said.

"Why was it that 'Cecelia' was so happy to talk to me about things… so open and honest, but you aren't?"

"Because she was an open and honest kind of person," I reasoned.

"And you're a closed and dishonest kind of person?"

"It's too hot up here on this roof terrace, this is crazy, holding me hostage, Bradley. Can we go downstairs, please? It's too hot for Poppy up here."

Poppy was fast asleep on the rug, also in the shade.

I thought of the blue shoes in Bradley's laundry hamper. *The one that got away.* The one who slipped from his grasp, just in time. Just because he hadn't killed Cecelia, i.e., me (yet) didn't let him off the hook. Why was he locking me up here? What had he done with Robbie?

"I need to know about Jacinda," I said.

"Jacinda?"

"Yes, Jacinda, the yoga instructor. The one that disappeared, the one that's no longer posting on Instagram. The one you had an affair with." *The one whose bracelet you kept.*

"You're pretty obsessed about Instagram, aren't you? People have lives outside Instagram, you know. Why did you stop posting last week?"

"People will think you've killed her," I said coolly, as if the idea had just occurred to me. Maybe that was why I left her suitcase with Bradley. Was I, subconsciously, trying to set him up? Punishment for him fooling around with my "sister"?

"Is that so?" he said with a smile. "I don't think so."

"You've got Jacinda's bracelet," I said. "I saw it on her Instagram post. One of your trophies. Just like the emerald ring that belonged to Cassandra. That was pretty sick, you passing off one of your 'serial killer' trophies on to me."

"Come on, honey, this is no longer funny, this silly joke you're playing."

I shook my head. "It's no joke."

"Yes it is, let's stop playing this game. You playing Cecelia was one thing, but this? Accusing me of killing people? It's nuts."

"Where's Robbie?"

"He's not here. Like I said, I dealt with him."

"What did he want?"

"To blackmail me. I gave him what he needed and he left."

"Prove it."

"Okay," Bradley said. "We'll go downstairs and you'll hold my hand and we'll look in every single cupboard and in every single closet, would that make you happy?"

"Yes," I said. I *had* been planning on grabbing my phone from his pocket to call the cops. Or better, the landline. There were several. But now, knowing what he knew, I wasn't sure it was such a great idea. Did I really want the authorities on my tail?

Jack had kept my secret. Robbie too, up until today that was. God forbid if he should blab to anyone else.

When Jack and I were hanging out, soon after we first met, Jack caught me in the act one day, as Cecelia. I thought I had locked my apartment door, but it was unlatched and he came in with a couple of coffees. There I was, in a bikini, in the middle of winter with the green screen behind me, posing away. There was a pile of other bikinis—all the latest models—and brightly colored swimsuits: thousands of dollars-worth, most of them sponsors' products. Jack wondered what the hell I was doing and asked me straight out if I had some kind of Instagram page, or if I was moonlighting as a model. He wasn't stupid.

I had to admit what I was up to. He found it kind of fun until he realized it wasn't fun anymore. Because then he saw my Insta account with his own eyes. He knew all about Cecelia: my dead twin sister. I had to tell him the truth. He told me he felt sorry for me, that I was a sad, lonely person. The last thing I had asked for was pity or sympathy.

In my "real" life, my day-to-day life, I was a shy, quiet person. And now I was in a situation where I was leading a double life, playing two roles. I had no choice if I wanted to keep the Instagram account going. There was no way I was going to stop. It was like I had thrown a ball down a hill and was trying to chase it, or a piece of paper fluttering in the wind that I couldn't catch up with. It was out of my control.

I saw it like this: some people play video games and lose themselves in another character. An avatar of sorts. What was the big deal? Why not play another person part-time? Especially when that person was my other half. I had a right to give Cece another lease of life through social media. It made total sense to me.

Understanding that Cecelia was now a part of me and my everyday life, Jack warned me to be careful. I was a woman breaking the law. The minute I opened bank accounts in Cecelia's name, that was straight-up fraud. I knew I could be arrested and put in jail for such a crime. Jack swore himself to secrecy though, and promised he wouldn't tell a soul about my double act.

I just couldn't break away from what I had started.

And then I took it a step further. I wanted to know what it was like to *be* Cecelia, to live in her shoes, to sense those eyes on you as you walked down the street, to feel men stare at you. Don't get me wrong, I was delighted not to have wolf whistles and attract lots of attention on a daily basis—it's just not my style. But I thought... *just one day, what's the harm?*

To know what it felt like to be her for just one day.

I remember an art school friend of mine—a gay guy from London—saying the same thing. He wanted to know what it was like to be a woman, for just for one day. He was perfectly happy being gay and he wasn't trans or anything, but he was curious. One night, he stepped out into Soho in the West End, dressed in a woman's wig, makeup, and heels, and a sexy dress that flashed off his rather nice legs. He told me it was a nightmare. Admittedly he was walking around in the red-light district, but still, he said he couldn't believe how many men grabbed his ass, how many men thought they could get away with harassing him and manhandling him. He said it was such a wake-up call and understood what it was to be a woman.

He never dressed up as a woman again.

Well, here I was wanting to know *for just one day* what it was like to be Cecelia. I had not lied, not in my mind anyway. All I was doing was bringing her close to me again, keeping her alive by giving her a new life through Instagram. She was happy, making money, popular with everybody. They loved her, and it gave me such a thrill because I loved her too and I missed her desperately. Yes, I was still angry with her, yes, I still found it hard to forgive her for what she had done, but it didn't mean I loved her any the less.

She was my other half. She was one half of my soul. My everything. My life had stopped after she died, and now I was breathing again. Because *she* was breathing again.

One evening, dressed up in heels and a miniskirt and lots of makeup, I came out of the elevator, and there was Mrs. Scott

with Jack. I was mortified. I shouldn't have been, but I was. Jack
knew my secret. I looked like me, Sara, wearing makeup, *and
why shouldn't I wear lots of makeup or a sexy skirt, why shouldn't I?*
I thought. But I did feel deceitful because I knew all the things
I had done, not least opening a bank account in Cecelia's name.
What was weird was that I was all dressed up in the middle of
the day, not even evening, so I literally looked like a call girl, or at
least that's what I assumed Mrs. Scott would think. I'm sure she
didn't; it was my own paranoia. This was pre-Poppy, obviously. I
didn't know Mrs. Scott so well back then. But before I could say
anything or make excuses, Jack said, "Hey, Mom, this is Cecelia,
Sara's identical twin sister."

The decision had been made for me, just like that. I wasn't
sure if this was tongue-in-cheek on his part, but anyway, once
he'd said it, I couldn't retract. I didn't know how to react or what
to do, so I just said shyly, "Hi, Mrs. Scott." I couldn't even bring
myself to say *nice to meet you* because that was a big fat lie, because
I wasn't meeting her, I already knew her. To cover myself, I just
smiled and then looked down at the floor.

Apart from the Instagram posts, I abandoned dressing up as
Cecelia ever again.

Until Bradley came along.

CHAPTER FIFTY-ONE

Sara

Cecelia was "unleashed" for the second time in the flesh after Bradley spotted that photo of us at my aunt's. But it was his messages to her Instagram account that really got the ball rolling. I should have ignored them, but the game was on. How could I not play?

Because Cecelia already existed privately for me. I had never been able to accept her death. By accepting her death, I too—and I still believe this—would have died. At least my psyche, my soul, my other half.

Creating Cecelia for Instagram was my homage to her. The *what-should-have-been*. The life she *should* have led. The success she deserved. The adoration that was fitting for her. All snatched away by the man in the white coat. All I was doing was giving her back her dignity, her sexuality in a beautiful form. Tastefully sexy pictures of her on the beach. That was who she was, who she should have been. By creating that, I was able to erase, not only her death, but the drug-ravaged eighteen-year-old she became.

But being Cecelia, as *I* became for Bradley, was an even newer creation. It started as a test. Was he good enough for me, for Sara? My sister had always been protective of me. Guarding me against any bullies in the playground, she had my back. So "Cecelia" had questions for Bradley that first time they met. *I need to know if your intentions with my sister are honorable.*

But then (and it really *did* happen by accident) "Cecelia" got a little flirtatious and I just knew Bradley wouldn't be able to resist. Fascinated and appalled at the same time, there was no stopping me by this point.

Would he cheat on me with my sexy sister? I had to find out for sure.

What I was doing was, some might think, a little crazy, but my compulsion grew strong. Like an itch you just have to scratch, but every time you dig your fingers into your flesh, it gets worse, till finally you've created a wound that then becomes a scar. A wound that wasn't even there in the first place.

I assumed he'd catch me out instantly and say, "Are you kidding me, Sara?" But he didn't, and Cecelia's "becoming" was unstoppable.

It's amazing what makeup can do. There's a famous model who apparently said, "Even *I* don't look like me when I wake up in the morning."

And I *didn't* look like me anymore. Not when I became Cece. In less than twenty minutes, she was my living, breathing twin. False eyelashes and nails. Eyedrops from France that made the whites of my eyes whiter and the blue more intense. Copper-colored eyeshadow: the complimentary color of orange against my blue eyes made the blue pop. The beauty spot; a brown eyeliner always comes in handy. Penciling my brows defined my eyes all the more. Short dresses, and bronze powder with gold highlights for my skin gave my arms and legs a sun-kissed glow that Cecelia was so famous for. I used extra-large makeup brushes to dust my skin. No fake tan, obviously, because I, Sara, was pretty pale, so body makeup was the way to go. Heels to elongate my legs.

Cleavage.

Bradley never saw me, Sara, with a low-cut top. But "Cecelia" looked great in that style. And lowering my voice a notch also did wonders, not to mention my teenage-surly attitude, eye-rolls and snappy, acidic comments. Because, in my memory of my sister (and that's all I had... my memory), that's the way she had been: confident, cocky, assured. In her teenage years, before that dreaded party, before that monster Dr. Atkinson got his hands on her and ruined her life, she strutted, she swayed, she swaggered. She showed off.

But I had done my twin wrong. I used her to get to Bradley, to appease my curiosity. It was a disservice to Cecelia to play with the memory of her persona.

That's why I had to put an end to it all.

That's when I stopped posting on Instagram.

CHAPTER FIFTY-TWO

Sara

"Come on, baby, let's go downstairs where it's cooler." Bradley kissed Poppy. Poppy, all dozy, responded by licking him on the lips. He scooped her up from the tartan blanket into his loving arms.

"I want to see the trash bins outside the elevator, too," I demanded, still suspicious about what he'd done with Robbie. Robbie loved that baseball cap. There was no way he would have left it behind. Was I being crazy? Overly suspicious? Maybe, maybe this was all in my head.

Bradley laughed. "You've been watching too many true crime shows."

The code to the rooftop door turned out to be something so obvious, I kicked myself: Bradley's birthdate. Coming from someone who worked with digits all day long that was pretty lame, but worse, the fact I hadn't thought of it myself told me how the summer heat was doing things to my brain.

This time, hoping against hope, I brought Poppy's wheelchair down.

Bradley led me around the apartment, laid Poppy down on the couch in the library, and she carried on with her nap. He opened every single closet door all around the apartment, while I watched.

"The panic room," I said. "You told me there was a panic room off the library, behind the bookshelf. I need to see it for myself."

"Okay," he said, amused. "Close your eyes, don't peep, I don't want you seeing which book is the one that opens the door. In fact, I'm going to cover your eyes and make a blindfold so you can't cheat."

"Don't be silly, I'll shut my eyes," I promised, pretending to shut them.

"You can't see?" He tried to shield the secret book by looming over it with his torso, but I saw him pull out *Robinson Crusoe*.

For a moment I freaked, wondering what he'd do. Shove me into the soundproofed panic room where nobody would hear me scream, dumping me there with Robbie's corpse and the bones of Jacinda?

"Can you see?" he asked again.

"No, I promise," I lied, peeping through my fingers.

We walked toward the bookcase, me holding his hand but dragging behind him. He left me to stand alone. Blood thundered in my ears; the sound of my fear, the beat of my heart sending extra oxygen to my brain, in case I needed to make a run for it. A rumble of the door opening. To my relief, he didn't give me a sudden push, but permission to open my eyes. I followed him, step by little step and peered into the panic room, grabbing a lampshade from the edge of the bookshelf to use as a weapon, to smash him over the head if need be, but it was plugged in and sent an ornament crashing to the floor. Amazingly, it didn't break.

Bradley clasped my wrist. "Play fair, Sara," was all he said, taking the lamp away from me and leading me into the tiny room. I regretted my harebrained idea of asking to see this place. It was a small dark room without windows, with a desk and a chair and nothing else. My eyes spotted a red button by the desk. I supposed it was hooked up to the NYPD, and just as I was contemplating running toward it, Bradley clasped my other wrist in an equally firm hold.

"No you don't, smart-ass."

"If you're so innocent why won't you let me call the cops?" I said.

"You really want them sniffing around you, after what you've done?" He wasn't stupid.

"I don't understand, where's Robbie?"

"He left of his own accord, his own free will."

"Why didn't you say that earlier?"

"Because I was amused by you being so suspicious, I thought I'd play along."

I glowered at him.

"Why won't you believe me?" he said.

"Why did he leave his baseball cap behind?"

"I have no idea."

"It's a bit of a coincidence. It was left in the bathroom along with everything else. And where the charm bracelet was before you obviously moved it."

"The charm bracelet was in the bathroom, true. Then I gave it back to Jacinda."

"Bullshit. It was one of your trophies."

He laughed. "Your imagination is quite something, you know that?"

"You got rid of her somehow."

Bradley chortled again. "You are so crazy it makes me crazy. But then of course that's why I like you, because you're a little bit wacky in the head. I knew that the second I met you, and I fell in love at first sight. You certainly are different from any other woman I've dated before."

"Great," I said. "A serial killer's in love with me."

"You're a hoot, really, Sara."

"How did you do it? With that freaky stocking I saw in the laundry hamper?"

"Stocking?"

"That old-fashioned silk stocking."

He laughed again. "I use that for cleaning."

"Bull."

"I stretch it over the nozzle of the vacuum cleaner so I can vacuum delicate things safely, without them getting sucked up."

I narrowed my eyes at him skeptically.

"You didn't know about that tip? If your place wasn't such a pigsty and you took care of your apartment, perhaps you could benefit from that cleaning tip yourself."

My mind was wavering, not sure whether he was lying or telling the truth. "What the hell was that, giving me your ex-girlfriend's emerald ring?" I fired out, confused.

"It was wrong. I'm sorry. I just didn't want that beautiful ring to go to waste. That ring was bought with love, with care. It *meant* something at the time."

I didn't reply. Was this all bullshit? I searched his eyes.

Taking me by the shoulder, he said, "Sara, you and I make a great team, we're both oddball human beings. What do you say we put all this behind us and start afresh?"

I made a face as if I were considering it, as if I thought what he was saying was normal, even a good idea. Maybe there was some explanation. But it struck me as a little bit too coincidental that he had two pieces of jewelry from two dead women, at least one dead woman for sure, and the other one missing. These bits of jewelry were his trophies, I couldn't shake that idea off. I felt his eyes on me now, raking over me, perceiving me in a new light. Not as Sara the sweet perfect girl whom he could introduce to his parents, the girl he was proud of, but the slut "Cecelia" in that motel room, on her back, being fucked by him in a crude, unforgiving way, and her allowing it. Relishing it. I would now forever be that person etched in his mind. He smiled just a little and suddenly his smile looked lascivious and sexual. I could almost hear my heart pattering behind my rib cage, but my reason was yelling at me to get the hell out of that apartment.

"Listen, I have to go," I said. "Poppy's got an appointment with a hydrotherapist."

"At"—and he looked at his watch, yet his watch was no longer there—"what time is it now? It must be like, six forty-five p.m.?"

"It was a last-minute booking."

"Don't lie to me, Sara, please just stop with the lies, okay?"

"She does, I promise."

"No, no. I'm not letting you guys get away that easily. We need to talk this through, we need to discuss our relationship. I spent a whole week calling you, calling and calling, trying to find you in the park and you just ignored my calls, ignored me, made me feel like a piece of trash. How do you think that made me feel? I needed to talk to you!"

For the first time, ever, I was seeing Bradley's rage. Real fury, his face beet-red, the veins in his neck rivulets of blue.

My hands were trembling, my whole body, trembling. "I'm so sorry. I didn't know how to handle the situation." My eyes veered to the fire escape. If I had just been on my own I would've dashed to the window, opened it up and scrambled out, I wouldn't have cared about the height. But I couldn't do that. I couldn't leave Poppy there, alone with "Daddy."

CHAPTER FIFTY-THREE

Bradley

Leading Sara into the panic room, so many emotions spiraled through Bradley's mind. It was as if his whole life was flashing before him because everything that had happened so far defined the man he was. It pained him that Sara was genuinely frightened of him, but he supposed it made sense after everything that had gone down recently.

How could he explain to her about his childhood, his mother, and the gamut of feelings he harbored toward women? Everybody spoke about women being abused; nobody talked about little boys, about innocent little boys… what some fucked-up mothers did to their sons and how it scarred them for life. He would never really have a healthy relationship with females. Sex for him would forever be a dirty thing. And the humiliation of loving that dirtiness dug deep into his soul. The shame of it, the penetrating shame of it all. And the worst thing of all was that it felt like yesterday: each and every act that had been thrust upon him.

And then, after being in the motel with Cecelia—who turned out to be Sara, who was no longer his sweet pure Sara but some bizarre hybrid of herself—it was as if the universe was playing a joke on him. The mortification of something that should've been beautiful—their relationship—had been ruined and trashed. The way *he* had been ruined and trashed.

And as he looked at Sara now, the desire to lock her in this room, and keep her there and push aside all the bad things that had taken place—to have her just for himself—was undeniably attractive. Undeniably. When Cecelia/Sara left that suitcase and those blue shoes in the motel room, he assumed she was playing a game, a game they'd pick back up in a couple of days. It delighted him and thrilled him because he had finally found the perfect solution to everything that was *him*.

But then Sara didn't speak to him for one whole week, didn't return his calls. Now he understood that she too was ashamed of how she had behaved with her other half. It was so ironic and tragic that they couldn't just carry on as they were. Both of them with their split personalities, both of them able to use this relationship to their advantage. But Sara was not playing ball. They could have been perfect, the three of them: he and Sara and Poppy. A happy family, maybe with children in the future. And here she was now, sitting high on her white horse, thinking she was better than him, believing that the humiliation she put him through was justified. She'd hardly even said she was sorry.

How dare she! *How dare she!*

And he knew she enjoyed being bad just as much as he did, letting herself be free from her tight little values, from her self-righteous, judging rules about what she should do and shouldn't do in her life, what she should think or believe. Her passion, her abandon, the intricate risks she took leading a double life. *That* was the true Sara! And here she was now *frightened* of him! *She* was the frightening one, *she* was the one who sent shivers down his spine.

He had given her a chance to talk things through, to explain, but she had waited until he'd called her out on it, and then all those insane accusations! *What was he supposed to do?* He had laughed and strung her along, letting her believe that maybe he *was* a crazy person, while she accused him of murdering women.

If only he'd known she would feel this way, he would have killed his mother a long, *long* time ago.

He watched her now, shaking in her shoes, this fascinating, infuriating woman who had won his heart then trampled all over it. He'd stretch things out a little longer... why not, after all she'd put him through?

He hadn't shown Sara Jacinda's text messages to him, proving Jacinda was alive and kicking, teaching yoga down in the Village, privately. Jacinda had abandoned her Instagram page because the IRS was onto her, and Bradley had done all this free work for Jacinda sorting out the mess she was in with immigration; helping her with her accounts and finding her a lawyer. He had also lent her money. She hadn't been able to pay him back at the time so, rather feebly, she gave him her bracelet to hold onto until she found the money. Then she'd been too busy to meet up. He wasn't about to get into all this personal detail with Sara about Jacinda's problems with immigration: it was a private matter. And Sara was accusing him of being a serial killer!

Maybe he should, he deliberated. Maybe he *should* lock Sara in that panic room until she saw some sense. He could look after Poppy just fine without her. Sara could stay in the panic room and he'd bring her meals, a potty for her to do her business, leave her there for a week or two till she saw sense.

And that little shit Robbie, her loser cousin, well, Bradley had sorted him out already. Robbie had tried to blackmail him, told him he'd been spying on him and Cecelia, and that Cecelia had disappeared, and if he didn't cough up twenty grand he'd tell the cops.

When Bradley told Robbie that he was pretty sure that Sara and Cecelia were one and the same person, he knew, from Robbie's expression, he'd guessed right. So Bradley offered him a deal: if Robbie told him the truth, he'd give him his Patek Philippe watch—worth a fortune—in exchange for information. *People will do anything for drugs*, Bradley thought. *Anything at all.* It was obvious, the way Robbie continually scratched his skinny weaselly self, his nervous pinned pupils darting here and there, that he had a major problem.

Bradley served that little shit his comeuppance.

Because the watch was a copy, a fake.

Sara's eyes were bulging with fear. She was shaking. Whatever he told her now, she wouldn't believe him anyway, so what was the point? Defeated, weary, and sad, he simply said, "Why don't you and Poppy just go home?"

She gaped at him as if he'd uttered something crazy. "You're letting me go, just like that?"

"Course I am, what do you take me for? It's been a long day, Poppy needs to have her dinner, doesn't she? Doesn't she have dinner around this time?"

"Yes," she responded in a frail little voice.

"So what are you waiting for? Get on home, Sara!"

He knew he'd lost her. He'd tried everything to make her fall in love with him. And he thought he had a window there. A little glimmer of hope. When she played Cecelia in that bed, he could feel it, he could feel the passion. Sara would forever deny that part of herself now she had unleashed it. She had squashed it out of herself. He wondered if that sensuality would ever return. If she'd only allow her true being to break through.

"Go," he said. "Just go. Get out of here, I'm done."

He didn't mean it though. He wasn't "done."

No, Sara had definitely not seen the last of him.

CHAPTER FIFTY-FOUR

Bradley

Sometimes, Bradley thought, people believe their own lies and convince themselves they're telling the truth. He had to admit, he was guilty of this very thing just as much as anybody else. Truths and lies got mismatched in his head. Sometimes he'd end up talking to himself or having discussions about what was right and what was wrong, and justifying things he had done, things he'd said, not only to himself but to others.

He felt sad letting Sara go like that. He wanted to talk to her some more, work things through, but he knew it was no use. She'd come around shortly, she'd come back to him, and then he'd take appropriate action.

The phone rang. The landline. The only people who called him on the landline were his parents and cold callers. People trying to sell you something or persuade you to vote a certain way. Or maybe it was the police? Calling about Robbie. Maybe Robbie had retaliated, found out the watch was fake and was seeing his threat through? What a hot mess. What Bradley had done was ridiculously risky, and now he regretted it wholeheartedly. Playing with Robbie like that, calling his bluff. The real watch, Monsieur Claire's watch, he'd put in the safe. The one he gave Robbie was a brilliant, detailed copy… almost identical, but not quite. He bought it in Hong Kong when he went there on business one time. Only… a fake watch was illegal. He'd deny he'd bought it.

If anybody asked him, he'd say it was given to him as a gift and he had no idea.

Had that little shit Robbie reported Cecelia missing, after all, in revenge? Because, as far as the world was concerned, Cecelia did exist.

Shit.

"Hello?" Bradley said, his voice cool and even.

"Son, it's Dad."

"Oh, hi, Dad, what a surprise."

They never spoke. Their conversations were always through his mother. It wasn't that he didn't love his father, he just had no respect for him and had long since given up trying to nurture some kind of meaningful relationship. He was a weak man, his dad was, had never been able to stand up for himself, had lost his own identity with his wretched, pitiful marriage. Saw himself through his wife's eyes. Did and behaved the way his wife wanted him to behave. Bradley couldn't help but feel sorry for him. He felt a stab of resentful guilt harboring these feelings, and sad that his father had turned into a shadow of a man, especially since his retirement, but there it was, and there was nothing Bradley could do to change things. His father had made his choice in life; his dad had *chosen* to be a wimp. He was going to say *happy belated birthday, Dad,* but didn't dare because that was shoving it in his face: the fact that Bradley hadn't gone back home to celebrate, and his father would think he didn't care enough.

His father said impatiently, "Is your mom there?"

Just those words gave Bradley an odd chill. He hesitated. "Mommy, no. Why?"

"Are you sure?"

Bradley took a breath. "Why? Isn't she with you, at home?"

"She said she was going to New York to see you."

"Really? She didn't tell me that."

"That's odd."

"Dad, I have no idea where she is."

"But that's ridiculous, she told me she was going to stay with you for a couple of nights."

"No, Dad, I don't know what you're talking about. I haven't heard from her for, like, two weeks."

"But this is crazy."

"When did she leave?"

"Two days ago. She told me she was going to call and she hasn't."

"You tried her cell?'"

"Of course I did."

"Weird, that's not like her. How about calling the credit card company? Checking on her cards to see if she's made any purchases. You have a joint account, right?"

"I did that already. Nothing since the plane fare. Well, some smaller items at the airport, must've been her buying a snack or something. Nothing since she landed at JFK. Not a cab ride, nothing, though I suppose she could have paid in cash, but why hasn't she contacted me?"

"Weird," Bradley said again, his feelings strangely numb. And he wondered if his father truthfully cared or was just going through the motions of pretending to, because that was what was expected. She had treated him so badly over the years, always putting him down, always emasculating him. But then his dad was a man of duty. Catholic to the hilt, it would never have occurred to him to divorce the bitch.

"Shame. I don't know what to suggest," Bradley mused. "I mean, if you're really worried, file a missing persons. They could track her cell phone. It works like a GPS."

"But she might have had it in Airplane mode and not switched it on again after she landed."

"True," Bradley said, inspecting his nails. He'd been gardening; he needed to give them a scrub.

Arianne Richmonde

"It's just not like her to do this."

"Do you think she's having an affair?"

His father was silent at the other end. Bradley had been joking.

"Sorry, Dad, I didn't mean it."

"I'm going to call the police," he said, after a long silence. "If you hear anything, Brad, call me immediately."

"Of course," Bradley said, and hung up the phone.

He went into the bathroom. Scrubbed his nails. Gently, he pulled the silk stocking out of the laundry hamper, always careful to never snag it. It was time to wash it. He'd do it gently, by hand. It had been so very useful, this stocking, and great quality too. Amazingly, after all its usage, it hadn't run.

The stocking had belonged to his mother once.

Ironic, that.

CHAPTER FIFTY-FIVE

Sara

It was the next morning, after I had given Poppy her breakfast, that the detectives were at the door of my apartment building. I came down to the lobby to meet them. They told me they were from the 19th Precinct and asked me to come down to have a "chat." They were both dressed in plain clothes but flashed me their badges.

It was only twelve blocks away, on 67th Street, but the idea of going in, in person, gave me goosebumps. "We can talk right here," I told them.

"We could, but that's not the way we like to do things, Miss Keller. We need you to come down to the interview room if possible."

"The interview room?" They knew my name? How? How did they know anything about me?

"There's nothing to be too concerned about, we just want to ask you some questions."

"Questions? About what?"

"We'd prefer to discuss everything in situ, if you don't mind. It's just protocol."

"It's not convenient," I said. "Am I under arrest?"

The lady detective—a petite blonde—shook her head. "No, no, nothing like that. We just want to have a conversation. A voluntary interview. When can you come down at your convenience?"

I hesitated. "I don't know."

The guy, smiley and friendly—he reminded me of Will Smith—suggested, "In a few hours? Like, eleven o'clock, would that be okay?"

"I'll check… maybe. I just have to make sure the lady who looks after my dog is… no, that's right, she's on vacation. I'll have to ask my aunt if she's free. I have a special-needs dog, I can't leave her alone."

"Well, see you in a bit," the lady detective said, dismissing my "maybe," acting as if we already had a fixed date. "Any problem?"—she gave me a small smile—"call me on this number." She gave me her card.

I took her card and stared at it: Detective Janet Pearce. "Okay, thanks," I said, all confused, my brain a whirlwind of panic.

"Great, thank you for your cooperation."

"You're not going to tell me what this is about?" I asked.

"It's about a missing person."

I hesitated. Tried to look unfazed. My mind was racing as fast as my heart. What could I say? *No, you've got it all wrong… I am Cecelia.*

I had imagined it would be easy: send Cecelia on her way, close down her Instagram account in due course, her bank accounts.

Simple, right?

Evidently not. Because it was no longer just myself and my screwed-up emotions I was dealing with but the fall-out of what I had left in my wake. I had done too good a job of bringing my sister to life, not least with the bank accounts I had created and with all the money I'd earned, tax free, in my sister's name.

I had broken the law.

They don't take fraud lightly in the United States of America.

I had a choice: fess up to my misdemeanors by explaining why she had suddenly disappeared and get done by them for fraud, or end up in jail for a murder I didn't commit. Had someone called the NYPD Crime Stoppers 1-800-TIPS number and grassed on me? Or did they have a direct contact with someone in the force? *Of course*, I thought, *it was Robbie playing games.* He had reported Cecelia as missing!

But then the detective added in a cool voice, "We'd like to talk to you about Bradley Daniels."

"Sure," I said, my mouth agog. A missing person plus Bradley did not necessarily equal Cecelia, or they would have simply asked me just now if I'd seen my sister. Then I was back to thinking about Jacinda again.

Before I could ask them anything else, the two detectives left.

I called Robbie. His phone was going straight to voicemail.

Then I called Jenny to check she could look after Poppy. Luckily, she was free.

Robbie, she told me, hadn't come home last night.

CHAPTER FIFTY-SIX

Sara

In the wake of all this paranoia about Cecelia, I couldn't stop thinking about her death and the effect it had on me afterward, and the repercussions it was having on me now.

After my family's accident, a friend of my parents, a lawyer, helped me with probate and my inheritance. My parents were Swiss citizens, but my sister and I, being born in New York, were automatically given US citizenship so we had US passports right from the beginning. My parents had seen to this. They knew how useful US citizenship was. We would renew our US passports every ten years although usually used our Swiss passports for traveling. You can do that with dual citizenship.

After the accident, my parents' deaths were reported to Swiss authorities, because that's where all their assets were, and I needed their death certificates for probate. Nobody asked for Cecelia's death certificate because she didn't own anything, though I did have one. The lawyer may have reported her death in Switzerland, I really can't remember. He must have, but I did not contact the US embassy because it didn't actually occur to me to do so, since we hadn't been to America since I was six years old. We had either been living in Africa or Switzerland. Often we went to International American schools (when we lived in Nairobi and Lagos, for instance), so were educated, whenever possible, through the American school system with the US curriculum.

Then, a while later, after their deaths, when I was going through their personal things sorting stuff into piles, I found Cece's US passport and hung onto it as a memento. I didn't think any more about it until my trip to Thailand, a few years later.

My parents had always said they wanted to be cremated and their ashes scattered over their favorite place in Africa: the Okavango Delta in Botswana, with its labyrinth of lakes and lagoons, near where we had once lived and they had been at their happiest, and where we had spent time as children, on safari. That's where their hearts were and that's where they had planned to spend their retirement. There was no question of taking their remains and burying them in Switzerland. Once, they had sat me and Cece down and told us that their jobs as medical humanitarians, traveling to conflict countries, were high risk, and that we would return "home" to Zurich to lead normal lives someday soon. I remember Cece asking Mom what would happen if they both died at the same time, and she had explained that the two of us would go and live in New York with her half-sister, Aunty Jenny, who would adopt us.

Cece and I hated Zurich. When we returned to Africa, we knew we were swapping a life of safety for a life of simplicity and danger. It was a choice.

There was irony in their deaths, that with all the dangers they faced with their jobs, their end came in such an unexpected way, and it was their daughter who was responsible, not some bomb or fatal disease or brainwashed child soldier on a rampage.

I scattered their ashes on the Okavango Delta among the rhinoceros, big cats, and elephants, and tried to forget.

Overnight, I was an orphan with no home. I had never really had much of a home anyway, not in the usual sense. We had been such nomads all my life and it was what came naturally to me, and what was normal. Cece and I did fantasize about having a home though. We wanted to live in Lamu where we had been on beach vacations. But Lamu was becoming more and more dangerous after there had been some pirate activity and tourists kidnapped and killed. Once, she looked at a globe and spun it. Her finger landed on Thailand. She started researching southeast Asia, and Thailand became her go-to place, her future dream.

I didn't know what to do with myself after their deaths. I wasn't ready to go and live in New York with my aunt and cousin Robbie. I needed time on my own to assimilate everything that had happened. I didn't want people's sympathy or I would have cracked. I was twenty years old. I wandered like a ghost for two years, working in safari camps as a sort of girl Friday doing anything and everything. Cooking, cleaning, driving people out on safaris. Mixing cocktails for the sundowners. Making beds, setting up tents, whatever needed to be done.

Going out on safari was my savior. Watching the animals, particularly the elephants. Sometimes we would find a murdered elephant parent, the tusks sawn off ruthlessly, feeding the Asian market with their crazy belief that these tusks are aphrodisiacs. It was heartbreaking. I did, at one point, decide I was going to dedicate my life to saving these animals. And I wanted to, but after a while I couldn't bear being in Africa anymore. Too many memories.

Everything reminded me of my family, and I felt more alone than ever. I decided to go somewhere that was the antithesis of my life there, but where? Then I remembered New York. I'd heard how you could lose yourself in the city. I was determined to start afresh, set out in a new direction. Go to a place where no one, apart from my aunt and cousin, knew me, and I could reinvent myself.

It was a shock when I found out I had inherited money. My parents, apart from forking out for our school fees at private, international schools (when they were available, if we lived in a big city) were so frugal and careful with spending that I had never even imagined they owned anything. But they did. A small apartment in Zurich, which they let out to renters on a yearly basis. It brought in quite a generous income every year. It was that rent money they used to supplement their living expenses and which allowed them to carry on leading such simple lives as humanitarians working for MSF, and UNICEF. In Sierra Leone, I had been given some flimsy, unofficial-looking death certificates from the country in question. I needed them because, as the sole inheritor, I had to show them to the bank and the lawyer in order to get my money, to get their apartment put in my name.

I took a plane to Zurich, but instead of selling the apartment, I simply renewed the lease with the people already living there. A banker and his wife, who had been doing a great job looking after it, and who paid the rent like clockwork every month. Zurich is a crazy-expensive city, so the money coming in was more than enough for me to rent a decent apartment on the Upper East side in New York City after things didn't work out at Jenny's, mainly because I couldn't stand living with Robbie.

My parents also had a nest egg of money they had put aside for retirement. I used this to pay for my college education. I didn't want to study too hard. I couldn't concentrate. So I opted for an art degree. I was accepted at Parsons School of Design. Little did I know I'd work harder there than any place I had ever imagined. I never got more than six hours sleep a night. Lunch breaks didn't exist, you grabbed a sandwich. No coffee breaks either. But I loved every minute of it. In fact, hard work was what I needed to distract me from my loneliness and devastating loss.

Losing my parents was bad, but losing Cecelia? It broke me.

Everything boiled down to one thing after Cece died: my internal struggle with myself and my twin identity. Because my twin was part of me, and vice versa. I had to reevaluate my own identity as one person, not two. After Cece passed into the other realm, I believed I would never be whole again. That with her

I had also died, at least, inside. I was locked into a moment in time like a fly in amber.

Psychologically caught. I could not grow as a person because I couldn't trust myself, nor open up to anyone either. So fractured, I was unable to give. The only relationship I was capable of holding together turned out to be, several years later, a relationship with an animal: Poppy.

I could give Poppy unconditional love and she could return it, tenfold. Up until Poppy, my life felt like driving a car in the fog. I could only see as far as my headlights would allow. I had no clue where I was going, nor why. All I could do was hope I didn't drive off a cliff.

Then my dog came along and I was forced to live for another being other than myself. I began to live again, not just exist.

Before the Poppy days, while I was still at college, I started working freelance, a year before I graduated. Work was my only escape from everything I had lost.

A friend of a friend, an author, wanted a book cover designed. Then one of her friends asked me to do covers for her series, and soon I had practically more work than I could manage.

I never did have to send out a résumé or hunt for work. I established myself as one of the busiest book cover designers in New York. Then there were logos and sometimes websites, but only for my top clients, because that was a whole other ball game and far more time consuming. That's when I reached out to other designers and set up a small company. When everything was running beautifully and I had a few employees under my wing, I decided to take a trip to Thailand, for ten days, just to unwind.

When I set off for Thailand I took Cece's passport—still valid—with me, as if I were taking *her* with me. It was all I had. My idea, crazy it was it was, was to swim with her passport out to sea, almost like I was burying her: a sea burial. But once I was there it struck me how crazy that idea was because somebody could find it if it washed up on shore; a US passport is worth a fortune. That was when I found myself at the US Embassy in Thailand renewing her passport, using myself as proof of who she was. It was easy. I just walked in and filled out the forms. No US death certificate had ever been issued for Cecelia. When I went in, I kept expecting them to say, "No this person is dead, this is fraud!" But they didn't. And suddenly Cece was alive again. At least, she had another ten years to go on her new passport, another ten years by my side.

When Cece died it was like a firework exploding in the sky, colors sparkling into a thousand stars, then diminishing into nothing… disappearing into black. Her renewed passport was a new lease of life, a refusal to let her die: she would live on forever.

Always be my star, always be there, bright and beautiful.

This was my way of dealing with my grief, my anger, my sense of betrayal. Cece became my obsession, my new creation.

My work of art.

I didn't use Cece's Swiss passport, because in Switzerland they have records of fingerprints on ID cards, so I didn't dare. I doubted countries cross-checked each other, not unless they were looking into some major fraud or violent crime. I supposed it was possible that it *could* be tracked down somewhere, though, and I was aware I was playing with fire.

Still… playing with fire is what gives a spark.

That's when Cecelia and I re-became one.

CHAPTER FIFTY-SEVEN

Sara

I got Poppy ready and took her to Jenny's, bracing myself for my appointment at the 19th Precinct with the detectives. I knew I had to go through with it and talk to them or it would look too suspicious. I could have said, "I do not agree to this," in which case they might have issued a formal warrant for my arrest. Or I could have said, "Call my attorney" which would have been a red flag. Besides, I didn't even know any attorneys and the cost? I was still paying off Poppy's vet bills.

Which missing person were they referring to, I wondered? "Cecelia?" Robbie? Jacinda? Robbie still wasn't home. I hadn't seen Jenny since that dinner, after she was so weird about Bradley dating—or not dating—Jacinda. Turned out she was right. I gave Jenny the heads-up about Robbie going to Bradley's apartment yesterday and Robbie not answering my calls, and that I was worried about him. Told her also about his baseball cap. Apparently it wasn't the first time he had not come home at night; lately it was quite a regular occurrence. Jenny had called him, too, and sent a slew of texts telling him to get back to her immediately. So far, nothing, but she wasn't worried enough to report him as a missing person.

"He hasn't even been gone twenty-four hours," she reasoned. "He lives a pretty independent life anyway. I can't bother the police about a surly twenty-two-year-old who, quite frankly, shouldn't be living at home anyway at his age, who has decided to stay out all night. I don't want to waste their time. He needs to get his own apartment and a job. I don't know how much more of this I can take."

We were sitting in her kitchen, over a big pot of coffee and toast. Jenny looked tired, her normally clear blue eyes a little bloodshot, as if she needed sleep and had been crying. I felt sorry for her, that she'd been landed with Robbie as her stepson, his only living parent, and that these were the cards she'd been dealt in life. I filled Jenny in on the details: the @sea_celia Insta account I'd started, the bank accounts, how the detectives had mentioned my missing twin, and about the whole Bradley affair with "Cecelia" and Robbie blackmailing Bradley, and Bradley locking us on the roof terrace for hours. She had no idea about any of it but, in true Jenny fashion, she didn't judge me, didn't act shocked. Talking about it out loud made it all seem really crazy. But Jenny knew how badly I had taken my sister's death, knew how psychologically deep the wound was, so I trusted she'd understand why I had done what I'd done. Little did I know it would be her son who had precipitated my run-in with the law.

Jenny topped up my coffee, frowning. "I still don't get why Robbie would do something like that... blackmail Bradley? Really?"

"Bradley said he 'dealt' with him. That makes me nervous, you know. Unless he really did give him money? Robbie must've said something to the police about 'Cecelia' missing... either that, or... search me, I have no clue what they're thinking."

Jenny took a bite of toast and chewed thoughtfully. Swallowing, she said, "So they want to ask you questions about Bradley? I mean, if they think he's guilty of something, why haven't they gone ahead and arrested him?"

"Maybe they already have," I said. "Maybe they're testing me? Maybe they think we're in cahoots and acting as a team. That's what they do, isn't it? Play couples off against each other until one of them breaks? Get one to tattletale on the other. At least on TV, anyway."

Poppy was snuggled down on her dog bed. She didn't come over to Jenny's often, but Jenny still kept Poppy's dog paraphernalia here for the rare occasions I was busy and Mrs. Scott couldn't look after her. I wondered how Mrs. Scott was getting on in Jamaica? Apparently the hotel she was staying at had it well set up for people with special needs and would take those who required assistance down to the beach for swimming in adapted chairs. I had forgotten to ask her if Jack was going with her. I presumed so.

Jenny's phone lit up. "Thank God," she said, reading the text. "A message from Robbie. He spent the night at a friend's apartment in Queens."

"Call him," I urged, suspiciously thinking how a message alone wasn't proof of him being alive. Plus, I wanted to talk to him myself and find out what ridiculous game he was up to. He hadn't returned any of my calls.

Jenny called him and they spoke briefly, before she calmly laid her phone down on the kitchen table.

"He's fine," she said. "He'll be home in a few hours."

"But I need to talk to him."

"Good luck. He just hung up on me."

"Call him back!"

Jenny did. He didn't pick up.

I took out my phone and called Robbie myself. It also went straight to voicemail. I left a message imploring him to call me, letting him know I had a police interview in an hour.

Jenny took a sip of coffee and, with a look of pain in her eyes, said, "Do you think you need an attorney?"

"I don't know. I've thought about it too. I guess it just depends what they're going to ask me. They seemed to want to talk about Bradley."

"The two go hand in hand," Jenny said. "You should probably lawyer-up."

"But that makes me look so guilty, doesn't it?"

"Well, honey, I hate to say it but you *are* guilty."

"I'm not guilty of murdering my *already-died-ten-years-ago* twin sister. I've got nothing to do with her supposed 'disappearance.'"

"Yes, but as far as they're concerned, she exists still. You're in a sticky situation because they could arrest you for fraud. I wish you'd confided in me earlier."

I sighed. "Well, it's too late now. And I haven't got either the time or the money to get a lawyer together. I have a big bill for Poppy's hydrotherapy and I owe a fortune on my credit card."

"I wish I could help, but I owe two months' rent myself."

"Thanks for the thought anyway. I think I'll be okay without an attorney though. Look, if I don't like a particular question, I have the right to plead the Fifth."

If I had a lawyer with me, I rationalized, the detectives would become suspicious, and what might just be a few simple questions about Bradley could turn into a maelstrom of intrigue and legal—or rather, illegal—problems for me. I'd have to fess up, at least to the lawyer… shit, what a mess.

I hadn't told Robbie about the @sea_celia Insta account, of course I hadn't. I would never have been so stupid. But he found it while surfing on Instagram, via the #bikini hashtag. That was when he was younger, when girls in bikinis gave him a thrill, before he moved onto hardcore porn sites. He had taunted me and teased me about it ever since. But I thought I could trust him. Maybe something had snapped in him, and whatever blackmail scheme he had going, he had told the police that Cecelia was "missing" and dropped me right in it. Just his kind of twisted sense of humor. Or maybe just plain revenge for not getting his way with Bradley, if indeed that was the case. Bradley had been so enigmatic, and my focus yesterday was getting myself and Poppy free of his apartment.

"I'm sorry," Jenny said, reaching for my hand, "about this predicament you've gotten yourself into. You're still really cut up about Cece, aren't you?"

I nodded, a lump in my throat.

The worst thing about Cecelia's rape was my parents' attitude toward it. They were cold, detached, especially my father. He was the type of person who would never grieve over something he couldn't change. Cece felt abandoned, although she herself never even verbalized it, except to tell me she hated them. As angry as she became, the more distance grew between her and them. They tried to help her in practical, chin-up sort of ways. That's who they were: practical people. She had been abandoned, and I couldn't save her.

It's ironic how so many doctors have a bad bedside manner, and my parents were exactly like that: practical, *let's-get-it-done*, let's move forward, let's be pragmatic. It was poetic justice that Dr. Atkinson was blown up with a detonated grenade while driving in Afghanistan a year after he had raped my sister. Sadly though, he wasn't the only person to die.

"It was so shocking at the time, wasn't it?" Jenny lamented. "It seemed inconceivable that a doctor could do something like that, let alone somebody whom everybody respected."

"I know."

"At the time, I recall a lot of people thinking Cece was lying, you know, making it up, or exaggerating to get attention. And remember how, just a few years ago, it came out in the headlines all over the world about charity workers paying local prostitutes for sex and even bartering medicines for sex in third world countries, remember? We all realized that it wasn't such an unusual thing, after all, for doctors... hell, doctors working for a global *charity*... to do such unspeakable things to vulnerable women, that people really did behave this way at times. Not just the odd doctor, but it was pretty widespread."

"I know," I said. "It brought it all back."

"I remember seeing it on the news," she went on, "how they said they didn't tolerate 'abuse, harassment or exploitation.' How the use of prostitutes was 'banned by them under its strict code of conduct.' But, you know, if it hadn't been for that brave whistle-blower coming forward, it would have carried on. Apparently it was rife. The whistleblower said how hard it was to challenge anyone because the main perpetrator was pretty senior... taking advantage of his exalted status as a Western aid worker. Such an abuse of power. It made me think of poor Cece, how vulnerable she was too. It's not surprising what happened, she must have been angry as hell, poor lamb."

Jenny was referring to the car crash. Cece, contrary to what I'd told Bradley, had not been high on drugs when she and my parents died in that car crash in Sierra Leone. Cece wasn't driving, she was in the passenger seat, my dad at the wheel. Mom was in the back. Cece had told her she needed to be in the front because she felt car sick. She grabbed the steering wheel when they were going round a hairpin bend, on a hill. They ploughed off a precipice. My mother didn't die straight away; she was in hospital for two days before her body finally gave out. Cece had planned it. She had planned to kill all three of them. Me too, perhaps, although I'll never know for sure. I was meant to be traveling with them but had food poisoning so stayed home. Would she have done what she did if I'd been in that car too? Something I'll never know.

Jenny shrugged. "That's why when I give money to charity, these days, it tends to be for animals and ecology, you know. Stopping the dog meat trade. Protecting wildlife."

I nodded but changed the subject back to the now, because my mind couldn't go back to the horror of my family being wiped out, gone from my life forever. Something I always thought could have been avoided if only they had given Cece the kind of love she needed.

"Has it occurred to you that Robbie's been using drugs?" I said, thinking how Robbie too needed help. "He looks so skinny, so wasted. And what was he doing trying to blackmail Bradley? Money for drugs, I'm betting. He needs to go to rehab."

"Of course it's occurred to me he's using," she replied on a sigh. "I've tried so hard with him. I've really, really tried."

"I know you have, it's not your fault."

"Losing his dad. Not having a father figure in his life."

"I know. It can't have been easy."

"If only I'd met a guy I really liked. A marriage-material man. People are under the impression that dating in New York is like some romantic comedy from the 80s with Meg Ryan, you know? But in this city, all the nice guys are either gay or taken. Only the psychos left for the pickings. Speaking of which, Sara, you'd better let the police know about Bradley locking you on his roof terrace."

"But he let me go," I said. "If he'd wanted to harm me, he would have."

"Count yourself lucky. Don't let there be a next time. Tell the police. I knew that guy was strange." She shook her head. "So you really think it was *Robbie* who reported Cecelia as missing and got those detectives knocking at your door? He wouldn't *do* something like that. It doesn't make sense."

"I guess I'll soon find out. Anyway," I said, getting up. "I need to get going or I'll be late."

Jenny drew me into a huge hug, clasping me close. I felt terrible that I'd second-guessed her motives when it was clear she disliked Bradley.

She had been right all along.

CHAPTER FIFTY-EIGHT

Sara

"Why," Detective Pearce asked me, "do you think you need an attorney? You're free to walk out of this interview any time you choose, Miss Keller. This is voluntary, remember, you came here of your own free will."

Was this a trick? To warm me up? To make me feel confident so I'd spill the beans? These detectives were highly trained. They knew exactly what they were doing: trying to drain information from suspects, to lull people into a false sense of security. I'd already blabbed my mouth off, it was time to shut the hell up.

"When we mentioned your sister was missing, you seemed to think we were accusing you of killing her. Why was that? You're worried your sister might be dead?"

Tears spilled from my eyes. I took a sip of coffee. Then the waterworks started in earnest. Everything descending upon me in one big rush of misery. Not just my own predicament of ending up in jail for fraud, but more the fact that Cece was *dead* and I'd never see her again. The detective handed me a box of Kleenex.

"I need an attorney," I sobbed, grabbing great wads of tissues.

"We just want to know more about Bradley Daniels, that's all," Detective Elba said with a nod, as if to encourage me to open up. "Would you be willing to answer a few questions concerning Bradley without an attorney present?"

"Why don't you just call Bradley in here?" I said, "and ask him whatever you need to know yourself?"

"We would, but he's skipped town and can't be located."

"Oh." I sniffed. "He was around yesterday."

"Yes, we know."

"Where's he gone?" I asked.

"Thought maybe you might know. You got any idea?"

"No, he didn't mention leaving town." As long as we were off the subject of Cecelia, I was safe. I wiped my eyes with a clean tissue.

"Any information you can help us with in connection to another missing person would be useful," the Will Smith look-alike said.

"Jacinda?" I offered.

Detective Pearce sat up straight in her chair. "Who's Jacinda?"

"A yoga teacher Bradley was dating, or may have dated," I told them. "You can find her on Instagram, except she hasn't posted for a long time… what was her handle… damn, I can't remember now… something like: at yoga babe Jacinda, something like that. She kind of went missing."

"Kind of?"

It occurred to me they might suspect me of being Bradley's accomplice. A Bonnie to his Clyde. I said, "My aunt was taking her classes at Studio Zen, midtown. Jacinda was very popular, apparently. Bradley was also doing classes there at some point, I have no idea when exactly. At least a few months ago. Jacinda left very suddenly and nobody knows where she went. Bradley has a bracelet of hers. A charm bracelet. He told me he'd given it back to her, but who knows if he was telling the truth or not."

"We'll look into it, thank you."

"So who else do you think is missing?" I asked tentatively, expecting them to cite Cecelia.

The detectives flicked their eyes at each other again. Detective Pearce nodded as if to gesture to her partner that it was okay to let me in on their police secret. "His mother," Detective Elba said. "Nobody has seen her for several days. Mr. Daniels, Bradley's father, reported her as missing. She was scheduled to stay with her son. Do you know anything about this?"

"No," I told them honestly, relaxing and tensing at the same time. Bradley's mother? This was news. Why had they grilled me for so long about Cecelia if it was his *mother* they were worried about? I wanted to ask but didn't want to bring Cecelia back into the conversation.

"Did Bradley mention her to you by any chance? Or say anything about her that you can remember?"

I shook my head. "No. He rarely talked about his parents, just that he talked to his mom once a week. He never said a word about her coming to stay. She lives in Minneapolis."

"You're sure he didn't mention a visit from her? Talk about the kind of relationship they had?"

"No, he always seemed to change the conversation when I brought up the subject of his parents, but like I said, he told me they talked on the phone and if his mom had her way, she'd call once a day. I got the impression maybe she was a little overpowering? But that was reading between the lines. I mean, I never met her or even talked to her so I have no idea."

They blinked eyes at each other again, so quickly I almost missed the clue.

"His mother is missing? And she was supposed to be coming to stay with him?" I checked.

Detective Elba nodded.

My heart skipped a beat. "Is he some kind of serial killer?"

They didn't answer, they were giving little away.

"Truth is… look," I went on. "I hate to say this but yesterday he really freaked me out. Locked me on his roof terrace. I mean, he let me go, but we were there for an hour or two and I was—"

"He has a roof terrace?" Detective Pearce moved in closer.

"Yes, a big garden on his rooftop. With grass, and trees in huge great planters. It's pretty impressive. You don't feel like you're in a city at all when you're up there, except for the view over Central Park and the skyline, of course."

Detective Pearce's lip twitched a little, like she wanted to smile.

My stomach dipped, imagining unspeakable things. Picturing little Poppy up on the roof alone with him before I came to pick her up. Bradley burying bits of his mother, Jacinda's rotting body working its magic: organic compost for those trees and plants. The black gloves. The stocking. My breath came fast, thinking what a close shave I'd had, that it could have been me. Or Poppy. Or both of us.

"Nobody has seen or heard of Mrs. Daniels since after she stepped off a plane at JFK," Detective Elba said. "We pinged her phone. Found it. But didn't find Mrs. Daniels like we hoped. Did Bradley talk about his mother *maybe* visiting? Any tiny thing you can think of might help."

"I'm sorry but I can't offer you any information about her," I said. "Bradley seemed quite distant from his family."

"But you were dating him."

"Yes."

"And you never met his parents?"

"No. They live in Minnesota."

"And your sister?"

"My sister?" My voice was a squeak.

"Bradley was sleeping with her, you're aware of that?"

I didn't reply, just lowered my eyes so they couldn't read my guilt.

"Look, we have serious concerns about your twin, as well as Linda Daniels. But nobody has reported your sister as missing so… look, Miss Keller, for some reason every time we mention your twin, you go quiet. Is there something you need to share with us? Some kind of information? Maybe Bradley's with her right now? Obviously our main concern is for her safety."

I was about to blurt out, *She's not missing*, but instead, I said, "Thank you. I'm worried too. Please… just find Bradley. The sooner you find him, the faster this will all be over with."

The interview went on for another twenty minutes or so. Most of their questions were about Bradley and his daily habits, questions about his friends, work, and so on. I told them about the emerald ring, again about the charm bracelet, and the freaky silk stocking that he told me he used with the vacuum cleaner. The black gloves. Finally, I was let go, shaken and a wreck.

When I got back to Jenny's, beyond happy to see little Poppy, I held her in my arms as she licked away my tears. Jenny made me a lovely comfort lunch of mac 'n' cheese. Robbie was asleep in his bedroom after an all-nighter smoking bongs with his buddy in Queens and apparently shamed and terrified because he had tried to sell a fake watch to some drug dealer and had been threatened with a gun.

"I've asked Robbie to move out," Jenny told me. "I've given him a month to find an apartment and a job and made him agree to start NA meetings as from tomorrow. I'm done with his behavior."

"Narcotics Anonymous?"

"Yes. He needs to get his shit together."

"Tough love," I said. "I guess you have no choice."

Shoveling another large mouthful of macaroni into my mouth, I almost felt sorry for him, but I didn't feel like talking. I was mentally drained after that interview, the questions, the knowledge that my life had been so on the line with Bradley.

I could have been his next victim.

CHAPTER FIFTY-NINE

Bradley

Bradley had no idea of the mayhem he had caused by going away on a trip for two days after his father had reported his mother missing. The police raided his apartment while he was gone. Dug up half the trees on his roof terrace. Searched his home, even found the panic room. They probably would have arrested him if it hadn't been for the discovery of his mother's body in the East River. Suicide. She had jumped off the Brooklyn Bridge. As far as the authorities were concerned, there was no foul play. Losing his mother was a strange sensation, but he couldn't deny the relief he felt. His father was finally free. In fact, over the last few weeks since the incident, he'd been communicating with Delilah Scott quite a bit, and she had been a real shoulder for his dad to cry on, at least virtually… they were in touch by email and by phone. Thank God for Delilah, Bradley thought. Thank God for the kind people in this world who think of others.

Like Sara with Poppy.

Bradley really had fallen for Sara, and hoped one day she'd forgive him for his lies. He had tried so hard to be somebody else: the dashing man in Monsieur Claire's three-piece suits, but after losing his mother, Bradley, just like his father, felt so emancipated. The years of being bullied and harangued were over. He went home to Minnesota for the first time in many years, for his mother's funeral. It was cathartic to hang out with his brother and sister and his dad. The funeral was beautiful, if you can say that about a funeral, though sad. Of course it was sad, and he did cry for his mom and remembered the good things about her, the positive things, like how she used to read him bedtime stories when he was a little boy and play cards with him.

As for Sara, well, he did still think she was the one for him, but by the way she had treated him with such suspicion, all he could do was bide his time.

Maybe one day she'd be ready. Maybe one day they'd hang out again.

He bought an apartment in Hawaii: a beautiful condominium in Maui. A place that accepted animals, just in case. He carried on working for his company; lots of people were working long-distance these days. He'd fly to New York once every six weeks or so, for meetings. Then go back to his pad by the beach. It was all T-shirts and jeans for him these days. He'd even learned to surf. Of course he gave up the Fifth Avenue apartment and all Monsieur Claire's suits and flashy watches. Strangely, he didn't miss all that at all. It just wasn't him. It wasn't really who he was inside. He'd been kidding himself before.

On his New York visits he would go to Central Park. He spotted Sara and Poppy on a couple of occasions but never had the guts to say hello.

Still, he'd watch Sara from afar.

Waiting for the right moment.

CHAPTER SIXTY

Sara

In the months that followed, I tried to justify to myself how I had played out my life and my twin's life since my family's death and wondered if I could have done things differently.

Cecelia had been dead for ten years, so who was I to decide what sort of person she would be now? Who was I to decide she would have an Instagram account and be an influencer and be the person I had designed her to be?

But I did it from a place of love. Of missing. Fear that if I didn't have Cece with me I would be nothing. But I hadn't given her justice, and the lies between us: her ghost, me, and Bradley, made me create something that was akin to a sort of Frankenstein: a Cecelia that never was and never would be, and never even had been. You should always be able to trust your family, but I had let her down, the way my parents had let her down. What I had done really wasn't fair to her or her memory.

In the end, I had to let her die in order to survive myself, in order to be the woman I was meant to be.

Her end was my new beginning.

I finally did get to say goodbye. I took a plane to Thailand, using her passport. I spent a week on the island of Ko Tao. Swimming, frolicking in the sea, sunbathing. It was my way of saying adieu. And this time around I succeeded in giving Cece a sea burial. I wrapped some string around her passport, tightly, with indelible cord and tied it to a big rock. I took a boat way out to sea and dropped it in a deep part of the ocean, where it sank and plummeted its way down, down, down.

I finally said goodbye.

I wrote a message on her Instagram page with a real photograph of myself in a bikini, bronzed and happy.

> *It's with a heavy heart but also great happiness that I am saying goodbye to all you guys. Thank you for taking this incredible journey with me for the past six years… it has been so amazing to share myself with you. But I'm finally saying goodbye and moving on.*
>
> *In one month this Instagram page will be deleted for good. Goodbye my lovelies, thanks again for being so awesome!*

There were thousands of comments and tearful emojis and hearts.

When everybody had had a chance to say goodbye to her, I deleted the page and all the data that went with it.

I never told the detectives what I'd done. Luckily, nobody asked me any questions. Before I left for Thailand, I closed down all her bank accounts too. I returned to the US, using my passport, Sara Keller. I was no longer my sister's keeper. She and I were free. No more conversations in the mirror, no more late-night phone chats.

As for Bradley, it turned out he wasn't a serial killer after all. His mother had taken her own life. His only crime had been telling fibs. All the disappearances of the various women in his life could be explained. Jenny called me one day with news about Jacinda, the yoga teacher, the one Bradley had been dating.

"Oh, by the way, I totally forgot to tell you," Jenny said. "I'm so sorry, honey, it slipped my mind. Remember how I thought that Jacinda had disappeared? She's been teaching in the Village all along. I went to her class the other day. She had some trouble with the IRS so, you know, she's doing very small private classes now from a friend's apartment. I managed to grab a spot because one of the students has a bad knee—Jacinda can't have more than five of us at a time. So glad to be back doing her classes again."

Jenny met a man at her new yoga class, and Robbie, amazingly, cleaned up his act. Got a job working for a video design company. All those thousands of hours playing videos had given him a skill. He's actually a kind of nice person these days. Now that he's not so unhappy with himself.

That's what it all boils down to, doesn't it? When you're happier with yourself, you're kinder to others.

As I walked through Central Park with Poppy I thought about this simple truth and my new state of mind: my acceptance of who I now was and how I had gotten here. Cherry blossom falling from the trees and beads of jeweled raindrops dripping from the leaves made me remember the Japanese word Sakura, and Bradley, and everything he had brought into my life over the last year, for better and for worse, but definitely, in retrospect, for better. He had helped me, albeit unwittingly, learn to be myself. I hadn't contacted him in a while, but who knew? Maybe one day he'd reach out.

Poppy was no longer using her wheels and was trotting along confidently beside me, her back legs a little shaky, but now there was plenty of muscle mass and I could tell she was getting stronger every day. Naturally she was now a lot slower without her wheels, so we ambled instead of dashed, sauntered instead of raced, both of us sniffing the sweet spring air, inhaling the blossom, while Poppy snapped at falling petals, trying to catch them in her mouth. I was focusing on her little hind legs, her paws like white booties, marveling at what a long way she had come and smiling to myself about her new life as an Instagram star: @poppy_delight, the New York wonder dog.

Poppy's Instagram page was Jack's idea, actually. We hang out quite a bit. He's a good, solid friend, Jack is. Someone I can rely on.

CHAPTER SIXTY-ONE

Jack

Revenge is a dish best served frozen.

The thing about committing a crime is you have to make damn sure nobody'll have any clue whatsoever it's you.

Any clue... and you're screwed.

And if you're really clever, you'll lay the blame on someone else. Subtly, without actually saying anything, just putting doubt into other people's minds. Laying those itsy-bitsy little seeds. Embedding them. Nice and deep.

I started laying the seeds of doubt in Sara's mind when I spoke about Bradley's ex-girlfriend Cassandra. It was all bullshit; my boss didn't know her boss, whatsoever. I cooked up some crap story. I knew she'd died of cancer. And although Sara was angry with me and didn't really want to hear what I had to say, I knew she was listening. That's the thing about seeds; you just plant them, water them, and wait to see what happens.

I knew Bradley had a bad relationship with his mother because of stuff my mom had told me. She and Charles Daniels, Bradley's dad, were still in communication. Just the odd email, no big deal, no romance, but he always kept in touch because he felt so damn guilty. And so he should have.

What a weak pathetic man Charles was, letting that bitch wife of his take over his life. It was her fault my mother ended up in a wheelchair. Linda and mom used to be friends, you see. And mom was dating Charles. But Linda had set her sights on Charles and when Linda wanted something there was no stopping her. Like Bradley, Charles was also a handsome man. Linda was working at a sports activity center in Florida and took mom parasailing in tandem with her. What a coincidence that mom's harness broke and she plummeted into the ocean. Parasailing was virtually unregulated by federal Florida state laws in those days. It was a miracle my mother lived although she was in a coma for several months. Enough time for Linda to get her claws into Charles. Mom was partially paralyzed, so, of course, despite Charles's apparent pang of consciousness, he went on to marry Linda. Nothing was proven and even the harness went uninspected, because the only requirements for parasailing at that time was the U.S. Coast Guard's approval of the boat used to winch the parasail up, and a boating license. The sports equipment: the harness, towline and the parasail chutes were not regulated, not even inspected immediately after the accident. And by the time there was an investigation, several days later, nobody could verify which harness had been used in the first place, or even if the particular harness for the excursion had gone missing or not.

Mom sued the company and was awarded some money. But that bitch Linda had ruined her life. But because my mother is such a forgiving, spiritual and kind human being, she has never wanted to get revenge, even though she always had her suspicions.

Me? I'm not so forgiving. Unlike my beautiful mother, I'm no angel. It took me three years to woo that bitch Linda. Not me, Jack… obviously, but the character I made up online. It's famous, isn't it… creating a fake, online profile? Usually it's pedophiles grooming innocent girls, not some young guy grooming some lady in her sixties. Pen pals, that was what they used to call people like us. Ironically, it was Sara who gave me the idea. Not literally, but figuratively speaking. I thought, *If she can get away with creating a whole Instagram profile in another name, why not me too?* I did it with Facebook. Found a stock photo of a very attractive elderly gentleman and started gathering friends… very easy to do… you can even buy them. Yup. Facebook, with all its policing rules of what you're allowed to do or not allowed to do, offer a service where you can actually *buy* friends to boost your online credibility with a "genuine" social media following. Linda believed I was a widower and lived in New Jersey. I even showed her photos of "my" beautiful house and grandkids. My fabulous trips to Europe. Sara had showed me a thing or two about how useful Photoshop could be. How easy it is to slip a gorgeous shot of Notre Dame in Paris or the Trevi Fountain in Rome into the background!

Finally, after three years of chit-chat, Linda and I moved onto texting by phone. That's when I deactivated my Facebook account, deleted every scrap of my character's online data. Since those privacy violation laws, you can do that now. I erased any online trail that could be connected back to me via my IP address. I had gained Linda's trust by this point. My texts were always sent from a burner phone. I asked her to come to New York, invited her to a Broadway show. Even told her she could bring her husband if she felt "uncomfortable." Of course she said no, told me "he couldn't make it." But I knew she was angling for an affair with me, because I really was such a handsome, debonair gentleman. And very wealthy. I told her I had arranged to put her up in a five-star hotel for two nights. Her own room, of course. And arranged a chauffeur for her, who would wait, with her name on a placard, to collect her from the airport. So when I picked her up, she was smiling and delighted, thinking she was on her way to the Westin in Times Square. She assumed I was the chauffeur, of course. I won't tell you where I drove her, or what I did… it's all a bit unpleasant. Let's just say she fell from a great height. Of course, I made sure her phone was wiped clean of all text messages. Used her thumbprint to gain access. Even scheduled a post from her Facebook page that would appear two days later, that read:

If you're reading this, please don't be sad, but I'm gone. Be happy to know I am no longer in pain, that I am leaving for the Other Side. Goodbye, my friends and beautiful family. It's not your fault, you did all you could. I love you.

I swiped that idea from a real suicide, a poor young girl I read about in the paper… she had a scheduled post on her Instagram that her followers would see after she'd jumped.

I gleaned a lot about Bradley and his family via my mother, because Mom had kept in touch with Charles Daniels over the years. But I never let on. Hated the lot of them. It wasn't Bradley's fault, but the minute he started dating Sara, well, that didn't go down too well with me. I knew all about his contentious relationship with his mother. So when Linda disappeared, I knew probably the first person they would look at would be Bradley, and that was fine by me.

Just to be extra careful I gave Mom a great alibi. Bought her a ticket to Jamaica. She's always told me what a great son I am to her. And it's true. There are no limits when it comes to Mom.

I would kill for her all over again if that's what I had to do.

And I have to be honest, there's something so satisfying about getting away with murder.

A LETTER FROM ARIANNE

Dear Reader,

Thank you so much for reading *The Guilty Sister*. There is such a plethora of fabulous books to choose from, I am so grateful you picked mine. If this is your first time reading my work, I really hope you enjoyed it and will check out my other books. If you have come back for more of my stories, that's wonderful! I can't tell you how much I appreciate your time and trust in me as a writer.

I have more books in the making, so if you'd like to be the first to hear about my new releases, you can sign up using the link below:

www.bookouture.com/arianne-richmonde

As you may know, I love setting my books in beautiful places that inspire me. I came to New York City when I was nineteen years old to study at Parsons School of Design and lived with a loving family on the Upper East Side in Manhattan and walked their beautiful, black standard poodle, Nancy, who could outrun all the dogs in the Central Park! We went to the park every day, come rain, slush, snow, or sun. New York feels like home, and I try to come back every year to visit. Central Park is very dear to my heart, and I have met dogs like Poppy there, so I hope you too felt inspired by her joie de vivre!

New York, New York, so great they named it twice! Yes, I am biased; I do feel that New York is the greatest city in the world, so if you haven't visited, you have something wonderful to look forward to, so put it on your bucket list! Although most of my descriptions are based on real places, I have taken a little bit of artistic license with some of the settings. Sadly, there are no motels left in the city, only hotels, but I do remember there being one, so I have gone back a little in time. Likewise, The Empire Diner is now far swankier in real life than it used to be (and although no longer serves diner food, it's still there and looks the same on the outside!) It now offers a very upmarket menu unlike the diner I describe.

I'd also like to add a small disclaimer about some of the charities and organizations I have mentioned in this book. I have nothing but the deepest respect and awe for humanitarian doctors and nurses who work tirelessly for others, putting their lives at risk. These organizations and workers are incredible.

I started writing *The Guilty Sister* when it struck me how wrapped up with identity we are, now more than ever with the internet invading every part of our lives, for better or worse, all day, every day. It can make us lose a sense of ourselves, forget who we are, and also how wary we need to be of others, sometimes to our own detriment. Perhaps we judge too soon, or, when we should be cautious, we trust when we shouldn't. This was the main theme in this novel: identity. You often never know who someone really is. There are so many false identities in our new modern world, especially those online. It's overwhelming, sometimes it's scary. I am sure I am not the only one who sometimes suffers from social media burnout!

However, I'm also pretty sure it is because of the internet that you have discovered my book, and I am so grateful. Perhaps an email from a friend recommending it or an "also bought" on

Amazon or one of the online retailers, or a picture or review on Instagram from a blogger that caught your eye.

Thank you for coming along on this wild ride, and I hope that little Poppy Delight has touched your heart. If I have offered some fun escapism in these difficult and traumatic times of Covid and its aftermath, then I have done my job. I wanted to write something a little bit more uplifting than my normal fayre, with a splash of dark humor. If I made you gasp, or made you smile, or even made you shout with fury, please do leave a quick, spoiler-free review, even just a couple of lines (I read every review so please go easy on me!), and thanks again for sticking with this book to the last page… I hope the twists entertained you.

Oh, and if you'd like to reach out to me on Facebook or Instagram or Twitter, please do! I love hearing from readers and having an online chat. Writing can be lonely and you can be so inspiring.

See you next time? I hope so.

Take care,
Arianne

@arianne_richmonde

AuthorArianneRichmonde

@a_richmonde

ariannerichmonde.com

ACKNOWLEDGEMENTS

Two talented authors have helped me get my facts right for this book. The first, Roberta Gately, fellow Bookouture author and nurse and humanitarian aid worker, who has served in war zones ranging from Africa to Afghanistan aiding refugees. Thank you, Roberta, for all your inside knowledge and for your insightful book, *Footprints in the Dust*.

And my new favorite pen pal, ex homicide detective, animal lover, and author, Suzie Ivy, who told me so much about working in the force, and police procedural, and interviews… thank you! You are one cool ex-cop, and your memoir in-the-making blew me away. A woman who starts a career in the police force at forty-five years old and goes on to make detective and solves serial killer cases has my attention! Bravo! Thank you for answering all my questions!

A big shout out to Walkin' Pets for giving aging, injured, and disabled animals another chance with mobility. Your sturdy wheelchairs are incredible. From forests and creeks to walks in Central Park, you have helped millions of dogs, cats, and even horses, cows, ducks, goats, and all manner of our four and two-legged friends live a full life. Thank you! What an amazing company you are. Please find @walkinpets on Instagram to see their inspiring stories.

Thank you, as always, to my editor Helen Jenner for "getting" me and for making my work the best it can be, and to everyone in the Bookouture team. Noelle, Kim, Carla, Sarah, how do you do it?… superwomen, the lot of you. It is so great to be able to write your heart out and know you all have my back. Thanks, Lisa Horton, for yet another amazing cover, and to Liz and Jane for catching any typos and embarrassing mistakes.

And finally to all the bloggers who spread the word, you work so hard and nothing but pure passion for books drives you to do so much for authors, we love you! Stu Cummins, you are the best of the best, and more thanks to all you readers and friends for making my job possible, you are amazing.

Last but never least, my animal muses, my fur children, my family, who make me laugh and give me so much love. This book is for you. And Nancy, one of the true loves of my life, I will never forget your beautiful doggy spirit and the joy you brought me.

Made in the USA
Las Vegas, NV
31 August 2023

76913571R00177